A Spell of Midlife Mayhem

Witchy Ways After Forty, Volume 1

Raven Raine

Published by Raven Raine Publishing, 2023.

A SPELL OF MIDLIFE MAYHEM

First edition. September 18, 2023.

ISBN: 978-0473676902

Written by Raven Raine.

Chapter 1

I ENTERED THE CLASSROOM, trying to ignore the gnawing pain in my abdomen. The students evidently hadn't missed me. The rowdy bunch of teenagers stared out the rain-swept windows or messaged on their phones. Some of them only ever read words on a screen.

'Before my time away from school, class, I set you reading to do. A short book on the early Roman emperors. Who completed the assignment?'

Four kids put up their hands. My mouth tightened. They were the same kids who always did the homework. No one else read it.

'Why should we have to read about dead people?' Chantelle called, making a derisory face. 'It's not relevant to us, is it? The world's different now.'

'Human behaviour hasn't changed much over time,' I said, but the cacophony of kids hooting and agreeing with the protesting girl, and the cascade of high-fives, drowned me out. They were playing up more than normal on my first day teaching after my hysterectomy.

Bryan—one of my smartest and most troublesome students—stood. 'I wanna make history, not read about people who died two thousand years ago.' He laughed and held out his phone. 'I'm writing an AI app to predict social trends.'

The other students became more raucous, laughing and shouting encouragement.

Control of the class slipped away from me like dropping the reins on a runaway horse. The usual anxiety lines creased my forehead. Soon, the familiar headache, never far away, would stab behind my eyes.

This couldn't go on. I'd taught in schools for twenty years, and in my mid-forties, I should be right on top of a bunch of misfits like this, stuffing ancient history into their minds like beans into a beanbag. And for much of those twenty years, that's exactly what I'd done. But in the past few months, my customary self-assuredness with teaching had evaporated.

Why? I shook my head. Stress from the hysterectomy? Or accumulated overwork or tension at home? Maybe a change or a break would help.

The time recovering from the operation didn't count as a break.

Bryan swaggered to the front of the class, uninvited. He had two rings in his left ear and jerked his jaw in my direction. 'Have a look, Heather,' he said, shoving the phone at me. 'My AI app predicts a rise in the popularity of AI apps. It's cooler than that old history.' He flipped his fingers at the *Early Roman Emperors* sitting on my desk.

Giving them their way today might mean they'd be more settled next time. They were too far gone today for me to settle them into any routine lesson. None of them would listen if I tried to give a lesson—they'd use their phones or talk. History lessons weren't any use on social media, they'd say.

I gritted my teeth.

'You know what? Why don't you talk about your app to the class? Explain how it's going to predict historical trends.'

Bryan stared at me as if I was kidding. I wasn't. 'Are you serious?'

'Yep. Go for it.' It might even get them interested in studying actual history.

'Sick.' He grinned and turned to face the class. 'Who wants a copy of the app?'

The class cheered as I made my way out of the room, leaving them to their discussion. They'd made it clear AI apps were more relevant to them than the lessons of ancient history.

In the hallway, I took a few deep breaths to quell my anxiety. Sweat dripped down my neck, my heart raced, and my forehead tightened with the strain.

Something had to change. Fast. The operation had taken so much out of me, leaving me self-conscious, moody, irritable and fatigued. And I'd returned to work before I'd recovered. The problem with my handling of the class was I had post-op brain fog. and everything was more difficult as a result.

A hand settled on my shoulder. I cringed. Graham, the other history teacher in the school, stepped in front of me. At least ten years younger and twenty kilograms lighter than me, he tended to sneak up on me before I could avoid him.

'You're back! So soon.' He smirked, his eyes gleaming.

'Can't keep away, that's all.' *What does he want?*

'Nice hairstyle.'

'It's a French twist.' I crossed my arms. *Get to the point!*

He released my shoulder. 'Great to see you. I guess you're not getting out much, what with your...' He gestured to my nether regions. 'You know.'

'Yeah, it's quiet nights in for me at the moment.' I grimaced. He had me trapped.

'Well, look... you could really help me out here, Heather. I have a lot of assignments to mark, and things are a bit busy for me at the moment, so I wondered...'

'If I would mark them for you,' I said. *Why did I say that? My big mouth let me down again.*

He chortled and clapped me on the shoulder. 'I knew I could rely on you. I'll put them in your cubbyhole. They're due tomorrow. Thanks so much. I'll pay you back, of course.'

'Of course.' *Like never.*

'You're so kind. Well, I'll be seeing you.' He sauntered off.

Kind. That's how most people describe me. I'm altogether too helpful for my own good, even when I'm not tired. And two weeks after a major operation, I was exhausted. My eyes strained to stay open as if they were stitched together with catgut.

I trudged towards the staffroom. I needed a coffee. It might eliminate some of the lethargy hanging around after the hysterectomy. But even if it didn't, a coffee would help with *something*.

I entered the staffroom and grimaced at the worn furniture and shadowy corners. Even the florescent tubes had given up on life. Rather than a place to rest and recharge, our teacher's lounge had the appeal of a vat of lumpy porridge with décor to match.

The peace lily that I looked after stood out as the only beautiful thing in the room. Someone had kept it alive while I'd been away. *Thank you, whoever you were.*

The filter coffee machine was empty. I'd have to make an instant coffee. Why didn't other people refill it? I always did when I found it empty.

My watch read eleven o'clock. How was the class going? They might be playing on their phones by now. But they had to take individual responsibility for that. I wasn't going to sit their exams for them. I couldn't be in thirty places at once, even if I wanted to do it—which I didn't. If only they would try... they could do it. Oh well, they could have their fun today. Tomorrow, I'd get them back on track. Hopefully, by then I'd be more like my old self.

Eleven in the morning. Terry might have gotten out of bed. He would be in for a surprise when he sees I hadn't prepared his lunch today. I ran out of time. The lazy sod could damn well make his own sandwich.

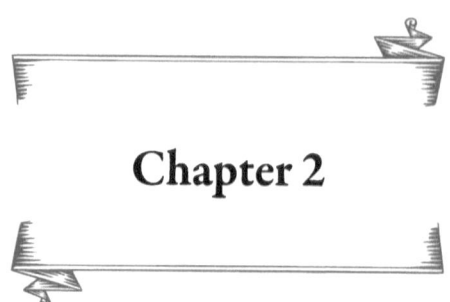

Chapter 2

I STRUGGLED OUT OF my 2012 Toyota with a pile of assignments tucked under one arm and my handbag hanging from my other shoulder. My abdomen twinged in pain at the effort.

It had been a typical winter's day in Christchurch—chilly but sunny—and the sun lay low in the sky, a real pain when driving home, thanks to the glare off the windscreen. Not to mention the other drivers on the road. Christchurch had the worst drivers in New Zealand, and most of them seemed to be on my side of town.

A moment after I closed the front door, Terry called out, 'You didn't make me any lunch today.'

'You could get it yourself, couldn't you?' He had had nothing to do ever since being made redundant from his middle management job at the airport.

'Not like you can, love,' he grumbled. 'You know I'm too depressed after losing my job. So, what's for dinner, then?'

'Can't you wait until I've had a rest? I've been working all day. And see these?' I showed him the bunch of assignments under my arms. Several fell out onto the carpet.

'I've got to mark these tonight, and they're not even for my students.' I slumped into an armchair. 'I don't have the energy to cook tonight, Terry. Can't you do it for once?'

'You know I'd only ruin it. Hey, why don't you nip out and get us some fish 'n' chips? That'll save you some time. I would go, but I'm still in my PJs.'

I bit back a retort. As usual, he'd come up with an excuse for why he couldn't get off the sofa and go himself. Instead, he expected me to go. Me, who'd worked all day and still recovering from a major operation that had removed some of my feminine parts.

'It'll take you five minutes,' Terry added, switching on the television. *The Chase* filled the screen.

'All right,' I grumbled, too exhausted to argue with him.

He gave a smug grin. 'It's so nice of you, love.'

So nice. That was me. Too damned nice.

I went back out into the cold and returned home with the fish 'n' chips twenty minutes later. Rain pelted down, drenching the paper wrapping when I scurried from the car to the house. The changeable weather in Christchurch makes the forecasters appear to be geniuses whenever they get it right.

I plonked the hot paper-wrapped bundle of greasy food on the table.

Terry started unwrapping it. 'Bring the tomato sauce, will you?'

I shuffled into the kitchen and leaned against the wall, wiping my forehead. Water from rain and sweat dripped off me. My legs wobbled. The fridge was too far away.

I'll be fine in a few weeks. I'll have my energy back. Then things will change around here.

My vision blurred. I blinked several times to bring everything back into focus.

It didn't work. On the other side of the kitchen, the door to the back yard fogged up. It swirled. Or it may have been me having another dizzy spell. Ever since my op, they'd been coming and going like the tides on fast forward.

The inside fogginess coalesced into a vague cylindrical shape, like a fuzzy cloud the height of a person. The mistiness dissipated, and an apparition emerged.

I gasped. 'Mother!'

There was no doubt it was her, the perfect image of her appearance before her sudden death a year ago. Diminutive. Fine white hair. Fit and well. Except, in real life, she hadn't been well at all. Her body been concocting a lethal heart attack.

Now I allowed myself to slide to the floor, my back against the wall. A chill ran down my spine and into both of my arms. My fingers tingled with static electricity from the shock of my dead mother, or more accurately her ghost, standing before me.

Was I seeing things? Was this part of the post-op brain fog?

I blinked several times, rubbed my eyes with the heels of my hands, and looked again.

Nope. The apparition was still there. Was it truly the ghost of my mother?

Unless I'd gone crazy from exhaustion, it was the only logical explanation.

Her mouth opened in a round shape as if she were about to speak, but no sound came forth.

Could ghosts speak? What a question. A minute ago, the idea that ghosts existed seemed preposterous. Now the ghost of my mother was visiting, ready to chatter on like old times.

'Mother, what is it?' I croaked. In real life, she'd talked incessantly. Why was she so quiet in ghostly form? I took the initiative. 'Why are you here?'

She gestured, the loose sleeves of her wispy top wafting as if in a soft breeze, then shook her head, frowning.

'Um... do you have a message for me?' Isn't that what you're supposed to ask a spirit? Did she know what was going on in my life? Could she even hear me?

My ghostly mother nodded. She tried to speak again, but once more no words came forth.

'Mime it.' From the floor, I mimed the action of miming so she would get the idea. It was ridiculous, but she seemed to hear and understand me, no problem. Yet she couldn't speak herself.

The ghost pointed at me, and my heart almost stopped.

'Are... are you here to tell me I'm about to die?' I choked out the words.

She shook her head, and I exhaled with relief. She spread her arms wide and glanced up.

That stumped me. I'd always been useless at charades. I preferred written words to mimed actions. But I could make a wild guess.

'You're going away somewhere?'

She shook her head.

9

'You're moving on to a better place?' *But aren't you already there? Wherever* there *is*.

She took a deep breath and huffed it out like she had done when she was frustrated in life. She planted her feet and pointed at me with both index fingers.

'You mean I'm going to a better place?'

She clapped her hands soundlessly. I grinned at my unexpected success. I was clever at this ghost charade stuff after all. 'Don't worry, Mum,' I whispered, glancing at the doorway to the living room. 'I know what you mean. When I'm recovered, I'll move on. My marriage is dead.' I winced. Bad choice of words. 'Sorry. I meant it's over.'

She shrugged, then shook her head.

A frown creased my forehead. Maybe I didn't have the right answer after all.

'What's going on?' Terry leaned around the doorway. 'I thought you were getting the tomato sauce.'

Ghost Mother vanished and I almost jumped at my husband's sudden intrusion, which would have been quite a gymnastic feat considering I was sitting spread-legged against the wall.

'You look like you've just seen a ghost.' He flipped the light switch on.

'You gave me a scare, that's all.'

'Why are you sitting on the floor, anyway?' he said, while opening the fridge and retrieving the sauce bottle.

'I was tired, Terry, that's all. Forget about it.'

'Sure.' He closed the fridge and ambled away, tomato sauce in hand, leaving me alone.

The ghost of my mother didn't return. Why had she indicated I would go to a better place? She must have come for one of two purposes: either to warn me or to wish me well.

But which was it?

Chapter 3

THE NEXT MORNING WAS still and crisp. A thin coating of frost clung to the street and sidewalks, reflecting the weak winter sun into my eyes. The low, pale sun cast shadows across the road as I drove to school.

My abdomen ached as I carried the pile of marked assignments inside and dumped them on Graham's desk with a loud thunk. He wasn't in yet. His cluttered desk was disorganised. A coffee cup with the words 'World's Greatest Teacher' was half-full of yesterday's coffee. Two empty cups with grimy rings inside kept it company. He also appeared to have the world's largest collection of teaspoons. No wonder there were never any in the staffroom.

I'd be lucky if he showed any appreciation for my heroic effort. What had been keeping him so busy he couldn't mark them himself? It better have been something important.

I had a free period first, and the principal, Bruce Cross, waylaid me on the way to the staffroom before I could get my first coffee. He wore his usual dark suit with patches on the sleeves. His pale, pasty skin tone highlighted his black mono brow. 'Ah, Heather, I need a word with you.'

'Sure,' I said, edging past him towards the staffroom. 'Can I get a drink first?'

He jerked his thumb behind him. 'In my office.'

I abandoned the idea of a coffee and followed him down the corridor, my shoes clomping on the hard floor in time with the beating of my heart. What was this about? Perhaps leaving the class to discuss AI apps had come back to haunt me via a complaint from a parent.

He sat in his oversized leather chair and leaned back, gesturing for me to take a seat in front of his desk. I did as he asked, like a student about to be disciplined for a minor misdeed.

'What is it, Bruce?'

'It's about the vacant deputy principal's job. You expressed an interest in it a while back.'

I brightened and the air of dread lifted. Had they chosen me for the role? My long hours had paid off, as they should. I was the hardest-working teacher in the entire school, and Bruce knew that.

'The school board and I have made our decision,' he continued with no inflection in his voice. He wasn't giving anything away.

'I'm ready to step up and take on this new challenge, Bruce. You can rely on me.' My smile could have fronted a dentist's advertisement.

He scratched his nose before replying. 'We have always been able to rely on you, Heather. You're an exemplary teacher. Everything that has to be done gets done. Your work has always impressed me. In fact, I'd hate to lose you as a front-line teacher.'

My smile cracked a little. 'So, you want me to transition to the new role over time? Help train my replacement? Is that what you're saying?'

Bruce leaned forward, folding his arms on the desk, and scrutinised me carefully. 'You misunderstand me. We're giving the deputy principal role to Graham.'

I gasped. 'Graham? You can't be serious!'

He nodded, as if this ridiculous decision was the wisest and most considered conclusion ever. 'He's a go-getter. The confidence oozes from him. The students love him.'

'That's not true. He's hopeless. The kids hate him because he doesn't explain anything properly.' *The only go-getting he does is to go and get me to do his work for him.*

'I don't expect you to see the big picture here, Heather. It's the balance of the overall team that concerns me. You're an excellent teacher. I can't afford to lose you to an administrative position.'

I stared at him, speechless.

'Great. I knew you'd understand.' He sat back and picked up a report on his desk and began skimming it, as if I had already gone.

There was nothing for me to do but get up and leave.

Now I needed that coffee. After all the hard work I'd put in, it appeared I was stuck in my role with no chance of advancement.

In the staffroom, I texted my best friend, Rachel. *I didn't get the DP job.*

Rachel texted back almost immediately. *Shit. You deserved it for all the work you did. How do you feel?*

Me: *Completely bummed!*

Rachel: *You should look for a new job, gf.*

THAT AFTERNOON AFTER school, Terry went out. He didn't say where he was going, only that he would be awhile. He'd better not spend too much of the money I'd been earning. We had only my salary now, and money was getting tighter than a python's skin after swallowing a goat. We were down to the last drops in our money well, apart from some modest savings we'd set aside for a rainy day. And it wasn't raining yet.

I video called Rose. It had been a week since our last talk. It was her first year away at Victoria University in Wellington where she was doing a psychology degree.

She picked up and smiled. A weight lifted off me. Though she was grown up now, I still worried about my only daughter, even though she was less than an hour's flight away. She'd only left home a few months ago, but I worried about all the typical things a mother is nervous about when her daughter had flown the nest. Was she coping with the workload? Did she have enough money? Was she eating properly?

'Hey, Mum,' she said, flicking her auburn hair back over her shoulder to reveal the three studs in her right ear. A busy café bustled with activity around her. Rose raised a steaming cup. 'I'm working on an assignment.'

'How's it going?' I asked.

She wobbled her head from side to side as if undecided. 'It's due on Friday, but I'm starting it today. It should be okay.'

Friday was three days away. A dart of anxiety rushed through me. Deadlines. Rose always left things to the last minute.

'That's good, Rose. I hope it goes well for you.' I kept my voice measured and calm. 'Have you got enough money? Are you eating properly?'

'It's all good. My part-time café job pays enough, and I usually eat at home or at Uni because it's cheap there. Don't worry. I've got everything under control.'

'I knew you would have. I just need to make sure you're okay because I'm your mother.'

'Thanks, Mum. You're looking good. Better than when I saw you after your operation. And that green top you're wearing suits your hazel eyes. Anyway, what are you up to?' She lowered her voice and moved closer to the screen. 'How are things with you and Dad?'

'The same. No, not the same. Worse. He does less and less now. I think he's given up looking for another job.'

'Did he ever look, Mum?'

I thought about it before answering. 'Probably not.'

'He won't have, Mum. I guarantee it. Once his cosy desk job disappeared, he couldn't be bothered. It would mean doing some actual work if he got something else.'

'You shouldn't talk about your dad like that, Rose.'

Rose shook her head. 'No, he's lazy. Did you get the deputy principal's job?'

My silence must have spoken volumes. Or maybe my expression gave it away.

'I know you're not happy about your job, Mum, so why don't you do something about it? So, you didn't get the job?'

'I didn't. Graham got it, that lazy, manipulating piece of shit.'

Rose scowled. 'The bastard. He used you.'

'I know. And there I was, doing his work for him. I'm too nice. That's what it is.'

'What it is, Mum, is that you let people walk all over you. You need to stand up for yourself. You need to learn to say "no" sometimes. You need to believe in yourself rather than seek validation from others.'

'Yes, love.' She was right. I had a brainy daughter, and I'd made sure not to bring her up like I had been—a childhood of duty, of following orders, of not speaking unless spoken to first. And it had worked. Rose was confident and independent—everything I wasn't, thank goodness.

'There's something I need to tell you,' I said. 'Brace yourself.'

Rose scanned around the room. 'I'm sitting in a café. How am I meant to brace myself?'

'Put your coffee down so you don't spill it.'

'Sure.' She obliged and regarded me with a serious expression.

'You might find this hard to hear—'

'You're going to leave Dad, aren't you?'

I gasped. 'How did you know? Does he suspect? Did he say something?'

'No, he didn't say anything. It's obvious that's what you're going to do, Mum. I've been telling you to leave him for years. He takes you for granted.'

'I know, love. I know.' I sighed. 'I guess I should let you get back to your assignment. Love you.'

'Love you too, Mum.'

I WENT FOR A TWENTY-minute stroll after my conversation with Rose. The surgeon had said it would take weeks, even months, for me to get back to my full strength. The winter sun warmed my face, and when I passed into the shadows of trees, the temperature dropped. A few people were out walking their dogs.

I took it slowly. My abdomen ached, even though I'd taken Panadeine. I would tire before I'd gone far. The doctor had told me to increase my level of exercise a bit at a time.

Personal concerns swamped my thoughts. I'd been trying to define the problems in my life more clearly and figure out how to fix them. They'd been piling up. Health issues leading to the hysterectomy from which I was now recovering. Stress from overwork and my dying marriage. Grief at my mother's passing a year ago, which still hurt, even though my mother and I never got on. Empty nest syndrome since my daughter Rose had moved to Wellington in the summer to start university there.

Life was a challenge.

A mistiness like the one that had appeared in my kitchen formed in the shade of a weeping willow a few metres ahead, and I stopped short. I squinted into it, trying to make out anything within. Was my dead mother returning for another silent conversation?

I moved closer. The amorphous misty shape became more human-like, but still unidentifiable.

Was it my mother? Had she put on weight in the afterlife? Or was it a different ghost? I shivered as the brisk breeze gusted. It had no effect on the misty shape under the tree.

In a flash, the mist coalesced into my mother's form. I wasn't frightened this time. In a way, although she was dead, she seemed alive. As a child, I'd never gotten on well with her, but now that she was gone, I missed her. It was kind of comforting that she could pay a visit. The fact she couldn't talk was a bonus.

She frowned at me. Was she annoyed? Was I supposed to have done something? How could I know what to do when I couldn't understand her?

She opened her mouth again. This time, a low moan emerged.

I moved closer. 'Are you in pain, Mum?' Do ghosts feel pain? If so, I wasn't in any hurry to get to the afterlife.

She shook her head. 'Ruuuu...'

What was that she said? 'Rue'? French for 'street'? No, it surely wasn't that.

'You rue something? Is there something you regret, Mum?' I'd read that people on their deathbeds always had regrets. That was sad, but it was worse if they carried their regrets into the afterlife with them. It wasn't resting in peace if thoughts of things you hadn't done, or that you had done but shouldn't have, burdened your spirit after death.

She put her head in her hands in frustration. Not literally. As much as I liked to see my mother again, even as an apparition, I didn't want to see her take her head off. She had raised her hands to her head as if to ward off an impending headache.

'Do the charades again.'

She nodded, stretched her arms wide like last time and started flapping them like a bird.

'Fly? You wish you'd flown somewhere, Mum? But you travelled a lot in your younger days, and you visited your sister in England a few times when you—'

I caught myself. Her sister Ruth. She means Aunt Ruth in England. 'You wanted to see Aunt Ruth before you passed, Mum? Is that it?'

She shook her head and blew her cheeks out, frustration mounting.

'I call her every month, Mum. I keep in touch with her. She's doing fine.'

My mother's ghost raised an arm, then vanished. A little white dog burst through where she had been a moment before and landed on my feet. The cute thing swivelled round to stare at the spot Mum's ghost had been, but nothing was there now.

A man ran up. 'Sorry about that. Bella's a little frisky. I hope she didn't give you a fright.'

'No. No problem. You have a lovely dog.'

He walked ahead. The dog barked at the now-vacant space, then hurried off after her owner.

I continued in the other direction. In the next few days, I'd phone Aunt Ruth and find out how she was.

Chapter 4

THURSDAY ARRIVED. I hauled myself out of bed as if I hadn't slept at all. I'd done too much too soon. Even having a walk earlier in the week had stretched my minimal reserves of energy. Teaching history classes and doing the paperwork and assignment marking and planning the next set of classwork had worn me down, and it was only my first week back at school.

I dragged myself to the school despite my nauseous exhaustion. Graham avoided me as if I was going to call in one of the many favours he owed me for stepping in to cover for him so often. At the sight of me, he turned on his heels and sped off down the corridor like a startled gazelle.

I managed an hour. A single class. My students were subdued. Having my head on the desk for half of the lesson may have given them the impression I was below par. I was done, and I plodded to the principal's office.

'I've got to go home,' I told Bruce. 'I wasn't ready to return to work, and now I'm paying the price.'

The principal didn't argue. I obviously needed rest more than anything. 'Why don't you take the rest of the week off, Heather, and see how you are on Monday?'

'Thanks. I will.'

'Do you need anyone to drive you home?'

'No, I can manage.'

I took my time getting to my car. It was raining, but I didn't mind. The coolness was refreshing. Maybe it helped prevent me from falling asleep on my feet. I'd drive home with the windows open so the chilly wind would keep me awake.

Terry might not even be up yet. His lethargy wasn't caused by exhaustion or depression, though. Rose was right about that. He would not hunt for another job. In his mind, I would work and look after him. Well, today he could look after me while I rested and recovered a little.

I turned into the driveway and braked sharply. Someone had parked a little blue Suzuki there, right in front of the garage. It wasn't familiar. Whose was it? A friend of Terry's, I guessed, but it was early in the day for him to have visitors.

I backed out of the driveway and parked on the side of the road and got out. I had a box of assignments in the back of my old Toyota. Grunting with the effort, I fetched them and headed for the front door. I let myself in and dumped the box on the kitchen table.

Terry wasn't downstairs. No surprise there. He hadn't made the effort yet to drag himself down to the sofa and switch on the television.

I trudged upstairs. I needed to lie down. My lady bits—what remained of them, at any rate—were sore as hell and my energy was sapped like an over-used battery long past its best-before date.

'Can you make me a cup of white hot chocolate, please, Terry?' I said as I opened the bedroom door and stepped in.

I stopped dead in my tracks.

Terry was up, all right. Up to no good. He and a lady friend stared back at me in shock from the bed. They were both stark naked.

I stuck my hands on my hips and asked the obvious question. 'What the hell is going on?'

'Um... Heather, love, this is Stacey. From work. The company made her redundant at the same time as me.' Terry had the temerity to introduce her like this was a dinner party.

At least Stacey had the grace to blush in embarrassment. She was a little younger than me, a little slimmer—okay, a lot slimmer—and appeared to have the same poor taste in men that I did.

I fumed. 'How long has this been going on? Is this what you do all day while I'm slaving away at school teaching those unappreciative kids? You spend the day banging one of your old work colleagues?'

Terry stood and moved to put on a dressing gown. 'Be reasonable, dear. Remember, you're not allowed to have sex for six weeks. The surgeon told us that.'

'So, is that it? Stacey is your six-week fill-in?' I glared at Stacey, who had edged over to the end of the bed to fish her clothes off the floor. 'You need to leave and not come back. Both of you!'

I remained in the doorway until she had covered herself, but moved aside when she made her way out, not daring to meet my steely gaze.

'What are you doing home at this time of day, Heather?' Terry asked, pulling up his trousers. 'You're never home in the morning unless you're sick.' His eyebrows rose in shock. 'Have you lost your job too? How will we manage?'

'I'm sick, Terry. I'm sick of the school politics, I'm sick of being tired, and I'm sick of you.'

'Come on, love, be reasonable.'

There he was with the 'be reasonable' again. The nerve!

Rose was right. My marriage had been over for ages. I simply hadn't wanted to admit it.

'Get out of here,' I growled. 'Go stay at one of your mate's houses. Don't come back.'

I pulled a suitcase out of the back of the wardrobe, wincing at the pain in my abdomen, and threw it onto the bed. 'Pack some of your things and get out.'

He stared at me for a full half minute. I glared back. With obvious reluctance, he gathered some clothes and other things and put them into the suitcase.

I waited until he'd finished packing and gotten fully dressed, then I marched him to the door. He drove away in the only car we had.

My anger and disappointment threatened to overwhelm me. In the living room, I phoned Rachel. She'd be working, but if she wasn't in a meeting, she would answer.

She picked up the call. 'Hey, Heather. What's up? Aren't you teaching today?'

'Hey, Rachel. I went home sick. You won't believe this. I caught Terry having sex with some old work colleague of his.'

'Fuck! What did you do?'

I took a deep breath. 'I told him to get out and not come back.'

'Good on you, girl. I'm proud of you. You should have left him long ago, you know. Your marriage has been on the skids for years.'

'Yes. I needed a catalyst, something to make me take action. I'd been hoping things would change, that it would go back to the way it was when we were first married.'

'Oh, Heather. You can't live in the past. Let's catch up for drinks at the weekend and talk about it. Sunday night?'

'That'll be great.'

'I have to go. I have a client appointment in five. Call me tonight if you need to talk more. Or shall I come over with wine and chocolate after work?'

'Yes, that.'

'Great. See you then.' She hung up.

Now I had to video call Rose to tell her what had happened.

DESPITE BEING FATIGUED, I pulled all the sheets off the bed and remade it before lying down. Only then did I start to cry.

Quiet tears coursed down the sides of my face onto the new quilt. I hadn't wanted my marriage to end this way. It ought to have finished with a proper adult discussion in which I held my dignity, not when I walked in on my husband screwing a former colleague of his when I was supposed to be at work.

Damn him to hell.

Sleep came. When I woke, the afternoon sun was kissing the horizon, leaving most of the bedroom in shadow. I lay there for a while, unwilling to move. What would my future hold now?

It would change. I would change.

But was I ready for that?

I had friends who had separated from their partners, but I'd been so busy with work and home responsibilities that I'd neglected my friendships apart from my good friend Rachel from my days at university. She was divorced. We often shared our family dramas over a glass or two of wine. Like we would tonight.

I should have done more of that. Met up with friends for an evening out. I needed to do things for myself now. Not only for others.

Especially when one of those others was Terry, the lazy cheater. I wouldn't do anything for him ever again.

My thoughts returned to my mum. She'd had one marriage and had outlived my dad. If she were alive, she'd say, 'Good riddance to bad rubbish,' about my husband. She'd never liked Terry and called him 'a minor bureaucrat' to annoy him.

Her ghost. I sat upright. As if summoned by my thoughts of her, a sudden chilliness made me shiver. Was she here again? Something was different. That sudden drop in temperature.

'Mum?' I whispered.

Nothing.

I got to my feet, shuffled into a pair of slip-ons, and went downstairs. I switched on all the lights and made sure I'd locked the door. I couldn't remember if I'd locked it earlier when I'd shown Terry out, but I had.

Nothing was out of place. It was the normal level of messy in my house, where I was the only one to do any housework, and I'd been too damn tired to do any.

I tiptoed into the kitchen. 'Mum?' I whispered again and waited for a response.

She wasn't there. My brows drew together in disappointment.

I turned to go back into the living room and almost jumped out of my skin. A strangled scream emerged from my throat. She'd been right behind me. What's more, this time she wasn't a fuzzy humanoid shape—her form was almost solid.

'Don't sneak up on me.' I panted, out of breath with the shock.

'Sorrrrrrryyyyy, Heeeaaathhhaa.'

I stared at her. 'I understood that. Your speech is coming through.'

She shook her head. Maybe ghosts did that a lot. Or perhaps it was only her. She pointed at me.

'You mean I'm understanding you better now? Yes, I am.'

Her bright, dead eyes bored into me, demanding me to try again.

'I'm getting better at seeing you?' I guessed.

She clapped her hands. Again, there was no sound, though they did appear to collide.

'Can I touch you, Mum?'

She didn't respond. I reached out for her top anyway. It was one of her favourite cotton ones. Instead of cotton over cold flesh, my fingers poked icy air. Startled, I stepped back.

'You seem real, but my hand went right through you.'

'I... am... real. Just... dead.' Her voice resonated as if it came from far away, but it was definitely hers and had a better definition than before. 'I have a chance to depart, Heather, but first I must give you a message. I've been trying to tell you since I died, but you couldn't see me until recently.'

Her voice was clear now. It was almost like she were a television or radio that hadn't been tuned to the frequency, and now she had it spot on. Was that why I hadn't been able to see her before?

'What's the message?' I breathed the words and gritted my teeth. A message from my dead mother. It must be something serious.

'The art is in you, Heather. It didn't take to me as it did with Ruth. That was why she reinvented herself in her forties, and our family emigrated to New Zealand. Talk to her. She can mentor you in how to develop your gift.'

What is she talking about? 'Mentor me with what gift, Mum?'

It was too late. She was gone, like a bulb switching off. Grief stabbed me anew as I processed her message that her ghost might never return.

A frown creased my forehead as I wracked my mind, trying to figure out her meaning. Something about art. What kind of art? Surely, my mother hadn't returned from the dead to suggest I take up watercolours?

No, I'd never been good at anything like that. I could do a bit of handiwork, like putting up shelves, but I didn't have the patience or aptitude for detailed artwork. What could she have meant?

She said Aunt Ruth would know. A pang of guilt hit me. I hadn't called Aunt Ruth after Mum's ghost mentioned her name last time. It had slipped my post-op fogged mind.

I would phone, but later. England was eleven hours behind, and it was still too early in the morning there. I didn't want to wake her.

IT WAS LATE. I'D SLEPT most of the afternoon, and then Rachel came over with pizza, chocolate and wine. She'd gone home an hour before, but now it was almost midnight, I still didn't want to go to bed. I switched on the light by the door, took a book off the shelf and sat in my armchair. I'd read the book before, but I didn't care. I read the same paragraph over and over, but I couldn't focus on the words.

My landline rang. I moved to pick it up before it went to answerphone. It might be one of those scam credit card calls telling me I'd bought a pile of stuff in America. A few more of those and I would pull out the phone cable altogether. I'd have gotten rid of the wretched thing if it wasn't for Aunt Ruth. She hated cell phones, and video calls were completely beyond her.

The number was a UK number, but unfamiliar. I answered anyway. 'Heather Nicholls here.'

'Mrs Nicholls. Sorry for calling you at what must be a late hour for you,' the caller said by way of introduction. 'I'm a registered nurse at Kingston Hospital in Surrey in England.'

My breath caught in my throat. 'Yes?' I croaked. Light-headed, I sat in the armchair again.

'I'm sorry to say that your Aunt Ruth has been in a serious accident. She asked me to let you know. She said you are her closest remaining relative.'

'Shit!' I raised one hand to my mouth as if to stifle a cry of horror.

'Sorry to call you with bad news.'

'No. Thank you for calling. Yes, I am her niece. What happened? How badly is she hurt?'

'She slipped down a bank when out walking this morning. Unfortunately, she fell onto a stone wall and suffered severe back injuries. She is in a stable condition, but we are still assessing the extent of the damage.'

I gasped. *Aunt Ruth! How terrible.* I struggled to take in what the nurse had told me. 'Is she—is she going to survive?'

'As I said, her condition is stable. Her injuries are not life-threatening, but she will need a lot of physical therapy to recover. I don't want to alarm you, but it's possible she may not walk again.'

'Oh no!' I slumped forward in my seat, my head in my hands, the phone clutched so tight my knuckles whitened.

'It's too early to be sure. She insisted I tell you the worst possible outcome so you are prepared for that eventuality.'

My head spun, trying to process everything.

'Mrs Nicholls, from what your aunt has said, she has no relatives in the UK. Is that your understanding?'

I struggled to speak. 'Yes, that's right. Our family was small, and I'm the only one remaining apart from her.'

The nurse continued. 'Your aunt will be in hospital for a few weeks before she can return home, but she will most likely require help there. We will conduct assessments at a later time to determine what is needed.'

'Yes. Of course.' The knot in my stomach tightened. This day was too much. First Terry, then my mother's ghost turning up with a vague message, and now this...

'Our medical team will keep you updated. I'm sure your aunt will want to speak with you when she can. We sedated her because of her degree of pain and to let her rest.'

'Thank you for calling to let me know.'

I held the phone tight for ten minutes after the nurse rang off, trying to comprehend what had happened and how that would affect Aunt Ruth's life. How dreadful! She'd always been a bit of a recluse, but now that might become worse if she lost her mobility.

An unbidden idea crept into my mind like a prowling panther. My mother's ghost telling me that Aunt Ruth would teach me 'the art', whatever that was. And now Aunt Ruth was terribly injured and would require home help after leaving hospital.

A SPELL OF MIDLIFE MAYHEM

And I was half a world away.
I shuddered at the thought.

Chapter 5

I PLACED THE PHONE back on its receiver and headed for the kitchen, reeling from the news about Aunt Ruth. Her medical team could tell her what care arrangements her aunt would need, but how could she help from the other side of the world? Maybe she would require adjustments to her house for easy access. Modifications to her car—if she had a car. Did she even drive? She might need daily home help or a live-in carer.

There was too much I didn't understand about the situation and about Aunt Ruth's life. Whenever we talked over the phone, she asked me about my life, and in the past year, how I felt about my mother's death.

My mother had never talked much about Aunt Ruth, and Aunt Ruth had never talked much about her sister either. She'd grown apart from her since my mother emigrated to New Zealand as a young woman.

She hadn't shared much about her own life. Or was it that I hadn't asked her to share a lot?

A pang of guilt swept through me. I had always been so busy that whenever I sat down to talk to someone—and especially Aunt Ruth, it seemed—I would dump my problems and frustrations on them rather than listen to theirs. I wasn't a good niece.

Or a good friend. Perhaps that was why I didn't see my friends often. Not only was I too busy to meet up with them, but I wasn't there for them in a deeper sense when we did catch up. Now that I came to think about it, I only remained close to Rachel, my oldest friend.

Friendships enrich lives. I'd been so busy with work and family that I'd never stopped to appreciate the people around me. I'd lost sight of the value of close friendships, and a deeper connection with Aunt Ruth.

I made a white hot chocolate and carried it through to the living room, too rattled by the awful news about Aunt Ruth to go to bed. How long had Aunt Ruth waited until someone found her? Who found her? A dog walker? A local farmer? Whoever it was, I owed them a debt of gratitude.

If someone hadn't come along, she might still be lying where she'd fallen. I grimaced. She could still be lying in a field in unbearable pain, unable to move, with no one knowing she was missing.

I sipped my drink. I needed to help Aunt Ruth, but could I do that from little old New Zealand, nearly twenty thousand kilometres away? I'd have to make phone calls at night because of the time difference. Or, if I wrote an email, I wouldn't get a reply for hours.

That would make everything harder, wouldn't it?

It would be a lot easier if I was there in the UK for a couple of weeks to help Aunt Ruth settle back into her home, while I called around and found appropriate help for her before I returned to New Zealand.

Yes, that would be best. But I hadn't travelled much myself before, and never on my own. I'd been as far as Australia with Terry and Rose. England was a long, long way from here. Though putting it more accurately, New Zealand was a long, long way from anywhere.

I finished my drink, which had cooled somewhat because I'd forgotten about it as my concerns mounted. How could I afford the flights to the UK and back? We barely had enough to cover our weekly bills and food on my teacher's salary.

It hit me with a jolt that there was no 'we' anymore. I'd split up from my husband. Now, I was on my own. He had to support himself somehow, or sponge off a friend, until we'd sorted out the house and other assets.

Shit. I hadn't even given that much thought until now. If I was serious about this—about separating from him—we would have to sell the house and divide everything up fifty-fifty.

As soon as possible.

I'd never done this before. It was a giant step into the unknown. Neither was I familiar with legal and financial matters.

I chewed my lip. I could handle a class of teenagers—not always, but most of the time. Financial and domestic upheaval wouldn't be as hazardous as that—would they?

But where would I live? I couldn't stay here—I didn't have enough money to buy Terry out, and besides, I didn't want to live in this house after he had cheated on me here. But after selling the house, paying off the mortgage and splitting the assets, I wouldn't have anywhere near enough money for a place of my own.

Other women must find a way out of this situation somehow. Or maybe they don't. If they only have a choice between a terrible marriage and a poverty trap, what do they go for?

I fetched my tablet. Rose was still online, despite it being well past midnight now. Why was that?

Oh, that's right. She has an assignment due tomorrow. Today, rather. Should I bother her when she's busy, this close to a deadline?

She'd be pissed off if I didn't tell her what happened.

I video called her, and she answered in seconds.

'Mum, why are you calling so late? Is something wrong?' Worry creased Rose's forehead as she gazed out of the screen.

I took a deep breath. 'I'm sure you're busy with your assignment, but I've got two pieces of important news. The first is that your great-aunt Ruth has had a serious fall. She's in hospital in the UK, and she might not walk again.'

'Oh no! Poor Great-aunt Ruth! That's terrible. How are you, Mum?'

I sighed. 'I'm struggling to take it in.'

'Are you going to call her? Or fly over and see her?'

'I'll call as soon as I can, and I'm thinking about going over for a visit.'

'And what does Dad think of that?'

'That's the other piece of news. I've split up from your father.'

Rose was silent for a few seconds as she absorbed this. 'Good on you, Mum. I'm sorry for Dad, but you've done the right thing. Good on you.'

'Thanks, love.' I paused. 'I know you were expecting it, but now that it's happened, are you... upset?'

She shook her head. 'It's the best thing for both of you. Especially you, Mum. Dad will be fine, but he'll need to reconsider how he treats other people. He'd never do that if you stayed and put up with all of his shit.'

'I think you're right.' She was a clever young woman, my daughter, and she would breeze through her psychology degree.

'What made you finally decide?' Rose reached for a glass of water and took a big drink. *Is that only water? It's not vodka, is it?*

'He was cheating on me.'

'What? No way!' She set her glass down with a clunk.

'Yes, way. I caught them at it when I came home from work early.'

Rose shook her head. 'That's so awful, Mum. I'm shocked he did that to you. So, you kicked him out, then?'

'Yes. I don't know where he's gone. I'll tell you this—I'm not taking him back. Not after this bullshit.'

'I'm proud of you, Mum. I'll support you however I can.'

I used to say the same thing to Rose. Now, she's a young, independent woman. A warm sensation passed through me. I *had* done well raising her. 'I better let you get back to finishing your assignment. Bye, love.'

'Thanks for letting me know. Remember, stay positive. Talk soon, Mum.'

The screen faded to black. The warm glow inside me increased. Pride for Rose blossomed in my heart.

I WOKE LATE ON FRIDAY morning, got up, got dressed and headed downstairs. Would I find Terry sleeping on the sofa? No, he wasn't there. Nor did it appear that he'd been in the house at all.

Good. At least he felt some level of shame.

The house was quiet. I stood still in the kitchen for a minute, enjoying it. No football blaring from the living room television. No shouting orders for drinks or food. Nothing.

I allowed myself a smile until a pang of pain in my abdomen hit me, and I reached for the drawer with the Panadeine. I'd been taking those painkillers twice daily since my operation. They worked well enough without making me drowsy.

I made a bowl of hot porridge and took it into the living room. A pile of class assignments lay on the dining table. They weren't mine. I'd already marked mine. The principal had called and 'suggested' I mark Graham's class's assignments now he was doing deputy principal duties. I'd seethed at this, but he'd couriered them over to me.

What would Rose have done if she were me?

Halfway through my breakfast, a familiar shimmer appeared on the other side of the table. I let my spoon slip into the bowl and stared as the amorphous shape coalesced into the sharp image of my dead mother.

Her eyes held a sorrowful expression.

'You said you weren't coming back,' I said, surprised to see her again. 'It's not that I don't want to see you, of course. I thought you'd gone forever.' *Will my mother remain endlessly earthbound?*

'I have more to do before I can depart—like give you two more messages.'

'Two?'

She nodded and pursed her lips. 'I think something has happened to Ruth. I sense it in my bones.'

'You're right, Mum. Wait a sec—you don't have bones!'

She shrugged. 'It's a figure of speech. I just sense that something has happened. I don't know what it was.'

'She had a serious fall. She's in the hospital.'

'Oh no! I hope she's not too badly hurt.'

'I think she is, Mum.' I paused. 'Can you visit your sister the same as you visit me?'

'I can't get there. It's too distant. One thing I've learned since dying is that ghosts can't travel too far from where they died.'

'Really?' I scratched my head. 'Is it a rule? Or some unknown law of paranormal physics?'

'Probably the latter. I call it spirit stickiness. All I know is that I start fading if I venture into the outer suburbs. Tell me about Ruth. I'm worried.'

I filled her in with what I knew, which wasn't a lot. Then I went on to say I'd kicked Terry out of the house for cheating on me.

'Good riddance to bad rubbish,' she said, 'but you were too gentle. I'd kick him in the balls, if I could. Sadly, an ethereal kick won't do anything.'

'I appreciate the sentiment.'

My mother's ghost sighed. 'I hope Ruth's going to be fine, that's it not as bad as the doctors warned.'

'It's too early to know for sure. I'm sorry you can't visit her yourself.' Mum was still here, albeit in ghost form, but there was no way she could visit her sister because she was tethered in some ethereal fashion to the local area. That seemed cruel.

There was a silence, which became awkward. What could I say to help my mother feel better? A strange thought struck me. 'Um... Mum... as a ghost, do you still feel things?'

'Feel things? Like what? Touching things, you mean? No.'

'No, I meant, do you have emotions? Do you get sad? Happy? Anything?'

'Yes, Heather, I do. It alleviates some of the boredom of being dead, but the unfortunate thing is that I can't do a lot about the feelings I have. Like I can't go and see Ruth.'

'If you could, would she see you?'

'Yes, and that brings me on to the second message.'

'Okay. Go ahead.' I listened with anticipation.

'You're going to enter a new stage of life. There's a lot for you to learn. Ruth can mentor you—if she recovers enough to do it.'

'You mean menopause. Yeah, I'm having that full on since my operation. Headaches, hot flashes, irritability—'

'Yes, you'll get all that, Heather. But that isn't what I meant.'

'What am I going to learn, Mum?' I had no idea what she was talking about, unless it was about me learning to be single.

Her ghostly mother's lips tightened. 'I don't have time to tell you everything, even if I knew, which I don't. You see, I never developed the special abilities that run in our family, and so I never talked about them with you. I assumed you wouldn't inherit them from your grandmother, but you have.' She shrugged. 'I was unlucky, I guess. They skipped me.'

'You're not making sense, Mum.'

The ghostly image of my mother dimmed, and her voice quietened. 'I would like to escape the mortal world and move on if I can. I think I can do that when I know you are on your true path.'

Then she was gone.

I paced back and forth in the dining room, wearing myself out. Whenever I passed through the spot where my mother's ghost had been, a shiver ran through me. I smiled. I hadn't been dreaming and my mind hadn't gone on a wild insane trip through la-la land. My mother's ghost really had been there, talking to me. She'd visited several times.

I made a strong coffee and threw myself down on an armchair in the living room, tired. I would need weeks more to recover from the operation—perhaps months. The leather sofa opposite stood in front of me, and I regarded it with distaste now, though I'd always liked it. Since he lost his job, I would find Terry lying on it, claiming he's spent the day crippled by depression, whenever I got home from work. Instead, he'd been happily romping with his redundant colleague. No wonder he claimed to feel tired. She'd worn him out.

I didn't want that sofa any more. And the bed was another thing that had to go. I'd slept in it last night because I'd been so exhausted, but the idea that Terry and his mistress had been banging each other on it made me sick to the stomach.

He could take both of those items of furniture.

A rush of stress rose through me. If I was going to go through with it, where would I go? On my meagre teacher's salary, I wouldn't get a mortgage on another decent-sized house. I'd have to downsize to a granny flat. Or share with other dispossessed women.

No, that wouldn't do. I needed my own space, at least until all my swirling emotions and stresses had died down.

There was so much to arrange, and I didn't have the slightest clue as to how to start doing it.

Chapter 6

ON SUNDAY EVENING, Rachel and I went out for drinks. I'd suggested someplace close. I would walk there and back.

Rachel was an extrovert and had a great deal more life experience than I had, which she didn't mind sharing with anyone who would listen. The same applied with her opinions. We'd known each other for so long that we were comfortable talking to each other about anything and everything. And she was a lawyer. My lawyer.

But I wasn't ready to talk about the ghost of my dead mother. Not even after a couple of drinks.

The evening was chilly, and the wind gusted and swirled around me like the thoughts in my head, making it colder.

We met at the Atomic bar at eight o'clock, where we ordered cocktails and sat in a shadowed booth. It was an upmarket contemporary sports bar, but the TVs were never turned up too loud and there was plenty of space. Most patrons sat in groups watching rugby. We paid it no attention. I'd never seen the point in those ball sports other than keeping an eye on the guys bending over during the game and exchanging their shirts afterwards.

Rachel's outfit was smart that evening, as always: a black blazer with silver buttons worn over a white top with the sleeves of both rolled up. She had excellent fashion sense. I wore one of my casual outfits, a black long-sleeved tee above a pair of faded jeans, similar to what I often wore to school. We appeared to be from two separate worlds.

After the usual pleasantries, I told Rachel all the gritty details about how I'd found Terry naked with his work colleague in our bedroom and then thrown him out of the house.

She grimaced. 'Good work, girlfriend. I hope you gave him a good kick up the ass as he went out the door.'

'I was too fraught to think of that,' I said.

'Remember for next time, then.'

'Oh, I'm not taking him back. No way. This is it for the marriage. Would you please write up a separation agreement for me? Will it be expensive?'

Rachel waved a long finger in the air. 'Forget the cost. I'll do it pro bono first thing on Monday. The sooner that's completed, the sooner you can move on. And, if you haven't already, take half the money from your joint account and any joint savings and investments and put it all into an account in your own name in case Terry tries to swipe it. You may as well have it now rather than wait until later. You'll need money.'

'Good idea. Thanks.'

'Do you have any idea what you're going to do with the house?'

I grimaced. 'That's the issue. You know we're not well off. Neither of us can afford to buy the other out. We'll have to sell it and split the proceeds. I don't know where I'll go after that.'

'Maybe you could share with a friend until you get back on your feet.'

'Perhaps.' Was she offering to share her place with me? Or only making a suggestion in general? There wasn't anyone else I could move in with.

Rachel continued, trying to ease my worry. 'Getting separated and divorced isn't a big deal nowadays. After my third divorce, I couldn't be bothered with marriage any more. At our stage of life'—she lowered her voice—'why should we give a fuck? Your daughter has moved away and your husband is out of the picture. Why not have some fun? Take time out to enjoy yourself.' She slugged back her drink, then gestured to a waiter for another.

My friend was affluent from her successful career and didn't see that things were different for me. I sighed. 'There's something else. My aunt in England is injured, and I've got to see if I can do anything to help her. It might be expensive if the NHS there doesn't cover it all. I'm probably going to have to get a second job so I can pay my own bills and pay for her care too.'

Rachel shook her head. 'That's not your responsibility, you know. Maybe the government there will pay for everything.'

'I've no idea if it will, but the hospital called me and said Aunt Ruth will need help, and I'm her only relative.'

'Did she ask you herself?'

'No... but I don't think she would. She's proud and independent. But the nurse I spoke to strongly suggested she'll need family support at first.'

'Well, then, what about this: you could go and live with your aunt in England.' She sat back in her seat with a self-satisfied smile.

'I've been thinking of going over for a couple of weeks, but I hadn't considered *living* there for good. I've never been to England before. What if I hate it? And what about my job? How would I survive financially?'

Rachel leaned forward. She spoke with deliberation and the effect of alcohol. 'Things have a way of working out for the best if you have a positive attitude and a little bit of luck.'

I sipped my cocktail. It would be a big step for me. And luck was never guaranteed. If anything, I wasn't a lucky sort of person, unless you were talking about bad luck.

Rachel continued. 'You're reluctant to discuss the idea? Damn. It's crap I'm too busy with work. I wish *I* could go with you for a week or two and have a holiday. That would be fun.'

Except Rachel would have money and time to enjoy herself if she did that. I would have to look after Aunt Ruth and find a job, so it wouldn't be much of a holiday for me.

I GOT HOME ABOUT TEN o'clock, light-headed from the two or three (or four) cocktails I'd had. We'd had a bowl of crunchy kumara chips to mitigate the alcohol, which must have helped somewhat. What condition would I have been in if I hadn't had any food?

In the kitchen, I made a white hot chocolate and sat at the table to drink it. What was I going to do? My life had fallen apart in mere days. What would my future hold, and how could I turn it in my favour? The whole situation was overwhelming.

Rachel hadn't understood how complex everything was for me. Anything to do with money was a breeze for her because she didn't have to manage on a pittance salary like mine. She lived debt-free and had a somewhat Marie Antoinette view about people with mortgages and not enough to get by.

At quarter past ten, when my head had slumped onto my arms on the table, a video call from Rose came through on my tablet and stirred me from my drowsy state. I'd been too tired to drag myself upstairs to bed.

I answered it.

'Hi, Mum.' Rose was looking in a mirror, applying mascara. Her phone was angled against the side of the mirror, catching her at an angle that skewed her face. 'I'm about to go out on the town, and I thought I'd call you first to see how you're holding up.'

I grinned wryly. My late night out had ended before my daughter's night out typically started. A sign of aging? 'I've just come in from an outing myself,' I said.

She stopped applying her makeup and studied me for a short time. 'Not a date already?' She beamed. 'You look really nice with your hair done.'

'Not a date. I met Rachel to chat about my domestic issues.'

Rose went back to what she'd been doing, less interested now that there wasn't gossip-worthy news. 'I'm going to a club with a few friends.'

'Be careful, love. Mind your drinks.'

'I'm always careful, Mum, but thanks for thinking of me. How's Dad?'

'He may have gone to his girlfriend's place,' I said. 'He hasn't even come back for anything. It wouldn't surprise me if he'd set himself up there a while ago.'

'Bastard. He might be my dad, but he's still a bastard.'

'Sure is.'

Rose put her mascara down and stared at me. 'What are you going to do now, Mum? Have you decided?'

Everyone wanted to know what I was going to do. I still hadn't got my head around it all. Aunt Ruth, my husband's cheating... and my mother's ghost. I dared not tell anyone about her. They'd call the mental health hotline to have me assessed.

'I'm still considering my options.'

'That's sensible, Mum, but you have a habit of saying that and not following through. Sometimes, you need to have a bit of faith and just go for it.'

'And what is it you think I should go for?' I braced myself. Would my psychology student daughter suggest something insightful or something crazy?

Rose turned at a rapping on the door. 'My friends are here to pick me up. I've got to go, Mum. Let's talk again soon.'

She disconnected.

I exhaled, staring at the screen as it went dark. The promised advice wasn't forthcoming.

Rose was right about something, though. I had to decide what I was going to do. Soon. Otherwise, the decisions might be taken out of my hands.

I debated back and forth with myself at the kitchen table while I finished my drink. Would my Mum's ghost make another appearance? If so, I could grill her for more information.

She didn't. Had she found her way to the 'beyond' or whatever she called it after all?

There was a lot I didn't know about ghosts, but when she'd appeared before me at first, I hadn't been shocked. Instead, communicating with her as an apparition was natural and effortless. It was like you'd never painted a watercolour before, and then you discovered that you have an innate talent for it.

I shook off those crazy thoughts. Maybe I'd even imagined the whole thing, simply conjured the image of my dead mother because I was stressed and exhausted and lonely and needed someone to talk to. Even my mother. Yes, maybe that was it.

But more than once?

Unlikely.

Chapter 7

I WOKE UP IN THE EARLY dawn with a cricked neck, pins and needles in my arms and (for some unknown reason) in my butt, and a spilled half cup of chocolate. Dammit. I'd fallen asleep with my head on my arms on the kitchen table again soon after Rose had called. Perhaps Panadeine and alcohol don't mix. I hadn't checked.

Gingerly, I got up and stretched. That was better. My body had been through considerable trauma in the past couple of weeks with the hysterectomy, but I was recovering and regaining energy daily. Sleeping at the table wasn't sensible, but at least I could still move. That had to be positive for a Monday morning.

I cleaned up the spillage, had my blood pressure medications and got myself some coffee and breakfast. The buttered toast crunched as I ate. Would my mother's ghost come back? I finished eating. When she hadn't appeared, I tried again to convince myself she had been a hallucination. It didn't work.

I had a shower and changed into something that didn't look like I'd slept in it. Jeans, a white top and a grey merino wool sweater. Thanks to my waking early, I wasn't rushed.

Another cup of coffee would be helpful in easing me towards moderate alertness. Monday mornings weren't my favourite times of the week.

After making my drink, I went into the living room. The pile of unmarked assignments appeared before me like a tower of guilt. I hadn't even started on them.

For a few moments, my heart rate increased and butterflies swarmed in my stomach. The assignments had to be returned today. I had no desire to mark them, but Graham would be upset and the principal would be angry if I didn't.

Screw them.

I was tired of doing the work of others and not be acknowledged for it. I'd worked for more than a decade at that school and been passed over for promotion at least twice for more junior and less capable colleagues. I'd always been expected to do extra work for those who didn't want to do it themselves.

And, at home, I'd spent twenty years looking after my lazy, unappreciative husband who'd thanked me by cheating on me because I couldn't provide him with sex for six weeks after my hysterectomy. Or maybe even since he'd lost his job months before.

Not anymore.

A newfound confidence welled within me after this epiphany. I was a capable, and now independent, woman. Maybe I was hesitant about trying new things, but right now, I had no choice. Best make the most of it. View the situation as an opportunity, not as an obstacle.

What had been in those cocktails last night to give me this new self-belief? Or had it been whatever Rachel or Rose had said? Which was what, exactly? I was hazy on the details because of the aforementioned cocktails and the fact that it was early on a Monday morning.

I gathered the dreaded assignments and headed out to the car. The driveway was empty. I huffed, exasperated. I didn't have a car anymore. Terry had it. *Shit*. I still wasn't used to being without the reliable old Toyota. Why had I let him take it?

There was no way I could walk to school with that pile of papers under my arm, especially so recently after my hysterectomy, so I had no choice but to call for a taxi if I wanted to get there.

But why should I have to do that? I changed my mind. I wouldn't go to school. Graham and Bruce were part of the problems in my life. They took advantage of me in a professional sense. Going back to teaching there would put me right back in the same situation. I could do without this stress right now.

Back inside, I put the assignments on a chair. From a drawer in the kitchen, I pulled out a pad of paper and a pen. I drew a line down the centre and wrote 'Pros' and 'Cons' on both sides.

I didn't need my ghostly mother popping in to give her advice. For the first time in my life, I'd work out the best thing for me by myself.

IT WAS MY CONVERSATION with Rose the previous night that pushed me over the line with my decision.

Once I'd made it, everything seemed clearer. All my problems were in Christchurch: Terry, Bruce and Graham, the dead-end job at school, pressing financial issues.

I needed to leave it all behind.

A little after nine, I phoned the bank and moved half of our joint funds and investments into a new account of my own.

At ten o'clock, I phoned Rachel to confirm she would sort out a separation document. After arranging that, I'd need to talk to Terry and put the house on the market. I had enough funds to last me a few weeks and to buy a one-way airfare to the UK. Aunt Ruth needed help, and I'd sort something out for her. I may even stay there for a few weeks. Or even months. Maybe a year. It would give me time to clear my head and plan my new post-bullshit life.

I'd already phoned the school to say I couldn't come in for personal reasons. Bruce pressed me on the issue, trying to sticky-beak into my business, but I wouldn't elaborate. I told him Graham would have to drive over to pick up the unmarked assignments. I hadn't had time to do them.

With my life imploding with Terry's affair and our separation, I didn't want to go on in any semblance of my old life. I wouldn't return to teaching.

I needed something different, yet meaningful. Going to spend time with Aunt Ruth would be it.

A pang of regret hit me whenever my thoughts returned to Rose. I'd be on the other side of the world from her if she needed me. But I told myself she didn't need me much anymore. She was an adult living her own life in a different city. I'd probably only see her a couple of times a year anyway if I stayed. And we could video call as often as we wanted wherever in the world I was.

What about my mother's ghost? Would she find her way to where she needed to go now that she'd delivered her messages to me? I might never know.

Midlife crises. Funny how everything happens at once. When you thought everything was fine and settled, you get battered by a life storm like a hurricane on steroids.

Chapter 8

SIX WEEKS LATER

BREAKFAST IN AUCKLAND. Dinner in Singapore. Breakfast again in London.

Luggage in Los Angeles or San Francisco. The airline wasn't sure.

When I lined up at the airline help desk in Heathrow Airport, I wished I'd bought the travel insurance the agent had recommended. Now I had nothing except my handbag and a small carry-on with one change of clothes, toiletries, my various medications and Aunt Ruth's contact details. At least those weren't sitting on a luggage carousal somewhere in a different country.

'We apologise profusely,' the help desk clerk explained. 'Luggage rarely goes astray. Of course, we will reunite you with it at the earliest convenience.'

Yeah, right. Your earliest convenience, you mean.

I wandered from the help desk and found a bustling airport café, where I bought a coffee and sat with my bag on my knees. Hordes of people rushed past in endless streams in all directions. How many millions of people live in London? A lot of them seemed to be in Heathrow Airport at the moment. And this was only one of the five terminals.

The humdrum of hundreds of people talking at once mixed with announcements over the loudspeaker. Dozens of scents wafted by in a kaleidoscope of smells, making my nose wrinkle as one replaced another.

My eyelids drooped. Thirty hours of travel with only snatches of light sleep on the plane wasn't good for me. How on earth did the aircrew manage? I shrugged. Maybe they were used to it.

I sipped my coffee. With luck, it would help to keep me awake until I got to Aunt Ruth's house. She was still in the hospital, but she had arranged for someone to be there to let me in. I appreciated that. Now I just had to get there.

This was the start of the next phase of my life. As tired as I was, my optimism hadn't dimmed now that I'd left all my problems behind. Terry. A manipulating colleague. A crappy job. Money woes.

The nervous apprehension both scared and excited me.

Before all that, I needed rest. But first I had to get to Aunt Ruth's house in Kingston upon Thames, in Surrey.

I pored over a colourful map I'd picked up of the subway—which they call the tube in London—but I couldn't make sense of it. Kingston didn't appear to be on it, anyway. I pulled out my phone. The charge was almost gone. It wasn't any help. I'd forgotten to download offline maps before I left.

After finishing my drink, I made my way back to the airline help desk.

The clerk eyed me over his rimless glasses and fiddled with his dark red tie. 'Your luggage hasn't been located yet, madam, but we are working very hard to find it, I assure you.'

'Okay. Can you tell me how to get to Kingston upon Thames by train, please? I can't afford a taxi.' I pointed to my aunt's address on a piece of paper. 'This is where I need to go.'

'First time in London, is it?'

'Yes.'

He looked up something on his computer and wrote a series of instructions for me before handing it over. 'If you go by train, you'll need to change. Lucky that you aren't encumbered with bulky luggage.' One corner of his lip curled upwards slightly. 'Take the Piccadilly Line underground to Earl's Court, change there and take the District Line south to Wimbledon, and change there for a mainline train to Kingston. You can buy a single ticket for the entire journey.'

That matched the instructions he'd written, but there was more. 'What's the "X26" written here?'

'If you want to go by bus, that one goes directly to Kingston from here and takes an hour.' He tilted his head. 'You asked me about the trains, but this is the quicker route. About an hour.'

I thanked him and trudged off.

AUNT RUTH'S HOUSE WAS a ten-minute walk from where the bus stopped in Kingston. It wasn't hard to find, but I gasped when I walked through the gate in the tall hedge and it came into view.

The house had to be the oldest dwelling I'd ever seen. It must have been around for centuries, at least two or three. The wood was weathered and grey. Large bay windows upstairs and downstairs decorated the front of the house, but the shutters had long ago lost their colour. The roof was a patchwork of crooked and cracked slate tiles. It wore the pattern of a thousand storms, yet suggested that the next gale might blow them off.

The lawn and garden were well kept. Who was maintaining them since Aunt Ruth had her accident? A small pond lay at one edge of the garden with a sprinkling of pottery gnomes on its outer edge.

Something about the property, and not only the sloping roof, made it appear crooked. Yes! The far side was bent or warped several degrees from bottom to top. I guessed the floors wouldn't be level inside. I'd read that was common in old English houses. Yet they somehow remained standing.

Of course, they didn't have to deal with the terrible earthquakes we'd had in Christchurch. One of those would have turned this house into matchsticks.

I strode up the path and knocked on the front door.

A man in his late thirties or early forties opened it and grinned. He had a neat appearance, with tidy, light brown hair and a short, trim beard. He wore a loose buttoned shirt, tan trousers and slip-on shoes that could have been mistaken for slippers. But his casual appearance did nothing to hide his athletic body.

'You must be Heather Nicholls, right?' he asked.

I snapped my eyes up from his exposed muscled chest. 'That's me. And you are?'

'I'm Raven. I'm a boarder with your aunt Ruth. Come on in and put your feet up. Do you want anything to eat or drink? Or do you want me to show you straight to your room so you can freshen up?'

Raven? An unusual name, most often female, but he gave no sign of being self-conscious about it. I followed him in as if I was a guest at a country hotel. He was a lot more considerate than Terry had ever been.

'Tea?' he prompted.

My eyes must have been weary because my gaze had dropped again to the part of his broad chest exposed by his loose shirt. I lifted it upwards with effort. 'I have to rest. It's been a long journey.'

'Sure. Let me help you with your luggage.' Puzzlement swept across his face. 'Where are your bags?'

'The airline's best guess is they are somewhere in California, which is amazing, considering that I flew through Asia.'

'Crap. Sorry to hear that.'

I followed him up the wonky stairs. My stomach tingled with a strange anticipation. The muscles of Raven's butt clenched and relaxed as he took each step. A warmness came over me as I neared the top, and my breath caught in my throat. Why was I physically attracted to this man? It was an odd and unfamiliar feeling, one I had almost forgotten.

I'm single now. A strange mixture of sensations washed over me: excitement, light-headedness, desire to move away because of his proximity... and desire to laugh at the absurdity of life because of the whole crazy situation. But it was life. This happened in life. You meet an attractive person and you are attracted to them. Yet, at this moment, it was unexpected.

Raven paused on the landing. 'Are you okay?'

'Just tired.'

'Of course. Careful on the landing. It slopes a little down towards the far corner. This is your room here. It is—was—your aunt Ruth's.' He gestured to the second door along. 'I have this one.' He motioned to the one nearest. 'They each have private bathrooms, so no worries on that score.'

I feared the worst when he said my room *was* Aunt Ruth's, as in the past tense. The horror must have shown on my face because Raven added, 'Don't worry. Your aunt is fine. She's due to leave the hospital in three or four days, actually. She wants to have the bedroom downstairs now that...' His voice tapered off.

'If she wants her room up here, I'll investigate how to get a stairlift installed,' I said. After thirty hours of travel with minimal sleep, the room was spinning, and my eyelids were drooping. 'I don't mean to be rude, Raven, but I have to rest, otherwise I'll fall asleep on my feet.'

'Right.' He moved aside so I could get past him. 'I might see you later, then. I'll be downstairs most of the day if you need me. I left a key for you on the table next to the coat stand.'

'Thanks.' I entered my room. It was spacious and well-lit thanks to the large bay windows. I went to the bathroom and breathed a sigh of relief to find modern fittings instead of eighteenth-century ones.

I'd remembered to pack an adaptor for the UK with my phone charger and plugged it in. I quickly sent a text to Rachel and another to Rose to say, *I've arrived, but sans luggage, talk soon.* Then I closed the curtains and lay on the bed, fully dressed, and kicked the shoes off my aching feet. I was asleep in seconds.

Chapter 9

I UNDERSTOOD THE CONCEPT of jetlag, but I hadn't experienced it before. Neither had I bothered to ask anyone how to avoid it. I soon discovered I'd done the wrong thing by lying down in the late morning, because I didn't wake until evening. I'd slept nine hours straight, and now I was famished and wanted breakfast. My medications cycle was all out of sync too. No wonder my blood pressure had spiked.

Damn these time zone flips. Now I'd probably be awake all night.

I went downstairs, irritated with myself. How could I reset my body clock? I found the kitchen. A note on the counter caught my attention:

I made pasta. Help yourself. Raven.

That was thoughtful of him. For a boarder, he was helpful. He hadn't needed to do that, and I appreciated it.

The pasta was in the fridge. I reheated it in the microwave. When had my husband last made anything for me other than a piece of toast? I couldn't remember.

After eating, I explored the house. It was much larger than it appeared from the outside, stretching backwards at least three times as far as it was wide. Downstairs, besides the kitchen, was a large, comfortable and surprisingly modern living room, a spacious dining room with one end converted into a study area, a bedroom with en suite that would be Aunt Ruth's when she returned home, and a separate bathroom. There was also a guest bedroom. I exclaimed in delight when I opened another door off the hall. Instead of opening into a closet, a library with bookshelves on all walls and comfy armchairs in the centre of the room spread out before me.

A warm glow pulsed through me. *I would love living here.*

Upstairs was another separate bathroom, plus the rooms Raven and I had. The other doors were closed. I guessed they were bedrooms or other private rooms. I wouldn't intrude, though I was curious.

Back in my room, I video called Rose.

'Hello?' Rose answered in a drowsy voice. Bleary eyes topped with last night's mascara stared out at me.

'You should see this place, Rose. Aunt Ruth has the most amazing house. It's got a library!'

'Mum, it's only seven in the morning on a Saturday. I was out late. Did you have to call this early?'

Oops. 'I only wanted to let you know I got here safely, love.'

'That's great, Mum, but you did text me. Next time, remember, there's a huge time difference.'

'I will. Is everything all right with you?'

'Yes, everything's good. Don't worry.' Rose yawned. 'Is Great-aunt Ruth out of hospital yet?'

'No. I'll see her tomorrow before I start job hunting.'

'Sounds great, Mum.'

We talked for a while. I could almost convince myself it was like being at home on the phone to my daughter, where she wasn't far away, less than an hour's flight. Almost. The call's sound quality was crystal clear, and there wasn't even a noticeable lag, but that was deceiving. She was no longer a short flight away.

When our conversation was over, anxiety swept through me. I was literally on the other side of the world from Rose. It wasn't possible to be any farther away while being on the same planet.

Had I done the right thing by upending my entire life and moving to the UK?

I STAYED UP HALF THE night and slept the second half, anticipating this trick might reset my circadian rhythm, or at least give it a shove in the right direction. Now it was my Saturday morning. In Wellington, Rose would head out with her friends in a couple of hours for a Saturday night out.

After a quick breakfast, I checked the map to determine the way to Kingston Hospital. As luck would have it (or not), it was on the far side of town, too far for me to walk. My downstairs bits had recovered from the operation, but I hadn't got back to my usual self energy-wise yet. Maybe I never would.

What were my options? Taxi? Bus? Eventually, I'd need a more permanent solution. Especially after I landed a job.

Raven strode into the kitchen. Once again, he wore an open-neck shirt that drew my attention. His deep brown eyes regarded me as he smiled shyly at me. 'Morning, Heather. Sleep well?'

'Morning, Raven. I didn't sleep well at all. I didn't realise jetlag was a real thing. It's really got its grip on me. Do you have that problem when you've been flying?'

He stopped in his tracks and cocked his head as if he was considering his answer. 'No. Can't say I ever have.'

I fanned my face with my hand, as I was hot. 'I'm going to visit Aunt Ruth. Can you tell me the easiest way to get to the hospital?'

'You can drive. Ruth has a car you can use. The keys are on the sideboard in the hall.' Raven sauntered towards the toaster and stuck two slices of rye bread inside.

'Great, thanks.' That was one minor problem solved. Now, why was it so hot in here? Was the toaster faulty?

I hung around and chatted with Raven while he ate his breakfast. Afterwards, we each had a cup of tea.

'Are you going to do some sightseeing in London, Heather?' Raven asked.

'I sure will. There are lots of landmarks I've seen on TV that I'd love to visit for real, like the Tower of London and the Millennium Wheel.'

'Yeah, they're popular with tourists. Anything else?'

'I've always wanted to see the big art galleries of Europe. In London, there are two of the best, the National Gallery and the National Portrait Gallery.'

Raven's face lit up. 'You appreciate art?'

'I do. I always went to the art exhibitions back home, especially those of famous European artists.' I caught Raven's sudden interest. 'Are you an art lover too?'

'Yes. I've been to most of the main European galleries several times. I have an art history degree.'

'Wow. Fascinating.'

'I'd be happy to go with you to the main London galleries if you'd like.'

I beamed at him and shivered with excitement. A whole day with Raven showing me around the top London art galleries. Was he asking me on a date? 'I'd really like that. You can share your knowledge with me.'

'Of course. Shall we go some weekend soon?'

'That'll be great.' I drained the rest of my cup of tea. 'What do you do for a living, Raven?' I asked.

He eased back in his seat and took his time to answer. 'Historical research in specialist areas, plus my own study.'

'Sounds interesting.'

'It can be. At times...' He shrugged. 'Dead ends are all I find.'

'I found teaching history to thirty teenagers was a dead end when all they wanted to do was message each other on their phones. I tried, but few of them really cared for lessons from the past.'

'As someone once said, "Wisdom is not a product of schooling but of the lifelong attempt to acquire it." They might get there in time.'

'Who said that? Dr Suess?' I laughed.

Raven grinned. 'Albert Einstein.'

MY FIRST MISSION OF the day was to call the home care service the hospital had emailed me about. Besides the frequent visits by her physiotherapist, Aunt Ruth was eligible for a substantial package of home care. A nurse or an aide would come to the house three times a day to help her with personal cares and other tasks she could no longer do by herself. I'd already made some of the arrangements by phone from New Zealand, calling at all hours of the night because of the time zone difference. Now, I only needed to notify the nursing agency that Aunt Ruth would be discharged in three days.

Once I'd done that, I left for the hospital, as visiting hours were about to start. Ten minutes later, I parked in the hospital car park and gasped when I discovered how exorbitant the fees for parking were. Could I leave the car here without paying? Yes, but it wasn't mine, and it might get towed if I did that. I couldn't risk it, so I drove out and parked on the street a few minutes' walk away.

The walk may have done me good, but I regretted it. I was huffing and perspiring once I'd got to the main entrance of the hospital. I caught my breath, then asked at reception for directions to the ward where I would find Aunt Ruth. I took the elevator.

Aunt Ruth had a room to herself. She was dressed and sitting in a wheelchair. Her skin was weathered and tanned from years spent outdoors. I was relieved to discover she wasn't covered in bruises or arm slings or eye patches. Indeed, her cobalt eyes were bright and her hair was snow white, giving the impression of an aged Disney princess.

Her face lit up with joy when I walked in the door, holding out a bunch of flowers I'd cut from her garden and made into a bouquet.

'Heather! I'm so glad you're here. And you brought lilacs. You're always so thoughtful. Are you settled at the house?'

'Yes, I am, thanks to Raven. How are you doing, Aunt Ruth?' I put the flowers down on a side table and gave her a long hug. I hadn't seen her in person for a long time, not since she'd visited us in New Zealand years before.

I took a seat in a visitor's chair. We talked for half an hour while she filled me in on the operations and the physical therapy she'd had and how she may be wheelchair bound forever. That news hit me like a blow to the stomach, but Aunt Ruth appeared to have accepted it and seemed at peace.

I told Aunt Ruth about my missing luggage, and she kindly said I could borrow any clothes of hers until my bags turned up or I replaced my things. Inwardly, I breathed a sigh of relief.

We chatted for ages. We didn't mention my mother, Ruth's sister, but my thoughts drifted to her from time to time—or more precisely, to her ghost. Should I tell Aunt Ruth about seeing her or not? Aunt Ruth had always been an open-minded and esoteric thinker. She might be more likely to believe me than anyone else. Would she want to know that her sister was still earthbound?

If I kept quiet, I'd be withholding a secret that would gnaw at me every day.

I made my mind up. In a lull in the conversation, I said, 'I want to tell you something about Mum.'

'Oh, yes. Go on.' Aunt Ruth leaned forward.

'I don't know how to say this, Aunt Ruth... but Mum came to visit me. After she was dead. As a ghost, I mean.'

'Froggy farts. I feared this might happen.' Aunt Ruth scratched her head.

I jerked back in my seat. 'You what?'

'She's tethered here because she's got unfinished business.'

'Um... are you sure? How do you know this?'

Her sharp, intelligent blue eyes fixed on me. Despite being in her late sixties and having recently had a serious accident, my aunt had lost none of her smarts. 'It's uncommon knowledge. That is to say, it's common knowledge for uncommon people.'

She was losing me. 'I don't understand.'

'I'll explain it all, Heather. Don't fret. I told your mother she needed to tell you about all this, but it doesn't surprise me she never did. She didn't have the abilities herself, you see. For some unknown reason, she missed out on witchy genes.'

'What are you talking about?' Heat rose in my cheeks.

'And she wouldn't allow me to talk to you about it, either. She had some idea it would interfere with your life, corrupt you somehow. Maybe she hoped you wouldn't inherit the abilities and you could live a normal life.'

'Aunt Ruth, I have no idea what you mean.'

'In our family, Heather, when women reach their mid or late forties, they undergo a change.'

Ah, now it all made sense. 'I know, Aunt Ruth. Damned headaches, irritability, hot flashes, sweats, all at unpredictable times. The menopause. Mine came early because of my hysterectomy.'

She chuckled. 'Yes, I remember those days. But I wasn't talking about all that stuff.'

'What, then?'

'We grow into our witchy powers. It's slow at first. Seeing your mother in ghost form is probably the first sign that you can perceive the supernatural world. Almost all witches can detect ghosts and other supernatural or paranormal creatures. Did your mother speak to you?'

My jaw dropped wide open. Was my aunt for real, or was she having me on? Not only did she believe me when I'd confessed that I'd seen the ghost of my mother, but she even seemed to expect it, and now she's telling me it's only the beginning!

'She spoke to me, but at first, I couldn't make out what she was saying. Her words didn't become clear until later.'

Aunt Ruth nodded. 'Yes, your emerging witchy radar needed time to zone in to the paranormal.'

'You're saying I'm a witch?' I still couldn't quite grasp this concept. 'And you're a witch too? But Mum wasn't a witch? Is that right?'

'Exactly.'

I got to my feet and paced up and down the room. 'This is a lot to take in.'

'Of course it is. When I first learned this would happen to me, I ran down to the pond in the paddock and hid in the rushes for an hour, bawling. But I was only six.' She frowned. 'Sadly, your mother didn't tell you all this when you were younger, and that must be the reason she can't move on. She needs to be sure that you're going to learn what you need to learn.'

'And then she won't be tethered anymore? She'll be able to go—where?'

Aunt Ruth shrugged. 'I don't know where. No one does. Possibly ethereal witches and their family members have a get-together in the afterlife. Can't say I'm looking forward to it myself if that's where I'm going. I never enjoyed family get-togethers in this life. Having them for eternity would be torture.'

I agreed. My head spun with a hundred questions about all this. It sounded bizarre, but it explained a lot. How Aunt Ruth had reinvented herself in her forties—which would have been when she came into her own witchy powers—and maybe why my mother had emigrated to New Zealand with her family at that time. She wanted to get me away from her sister's influence.

A burst of anger rose from my gut. My mother had cheated me out of this family knowledge. She might have thought she was protecting me, but in the end, all she did was leave me oblivious to our family's special traits.

And now I was finding out in unexpected ways. It was a midlife crisis with witchy phenomena thrown in, and I wasn't ready to deal with this.

Thank the stars that I had Aunt Ruth for advice. Without her guidance, where would I be?

'Heather? Are you all right?'

I swallowed and took a deep breath before exhaling slowly, giving myself time to return to equilibrium. 'Yes, Aunt Ruth. It's... it's just such a shock.'

'It's come to most women in our family. Your mother was one of the few exceptions.'

'What if I don't want it? Do I have a choice?'

She inclined her head and pursed her lips. 'No. It's clear the witchy powers will come to you. You need to learn about them so you can control them. When and whether or not you use them is up to you. But I'll help you, Heather. You can ask me anything. And you can stop calling me "Aunt Ruth". You're forty-four. Just "Ruth" is fine.'

'You'll always be Aunt Ruth to me.' Just 'Ruth' would take some getting used to. I guess it was another reminder that change was hard for me. But here I was, in a new country, starting a new life. Change would be the only constant in my life for a while, so I had better learn to embrace it. But dropping the 'Aunt' prefix was perhaps a bit too soon.

'Tell me more about these witchy powers, Aunt Ruth. What am I in for?'

She laughed. 'That's the spirit, Heather. And do you know something? I sense your mother is free now that you've accepted this truth.'

Chapter 10

THERE WAS PLENTY FOR me to do rather than have a holiday. Back at Aunt Ruth's house, I phoned a bathroom modifications company and organised them to carry out the work Aunt Ruth's occupational therapist had told me was required. They would come first thing on Monday. I checked the internal doorways to ensure they were wide enough for her wheelchair, and they were.

Also, I needed to get a job before my money ran out. Given that the cost of everything in the UK was way more than I'd expected, my funds would run dry sooner than I would have liked.

Though it was summer here, the day was overcast, and the grey pallor it cast over everything around me reflected my worry about Aunt Ruth and concern about finding employment.

After lunch, I went to the town, found a local job centre and went inside. In the small room, the stench of stale sweat and desperation assailed my nostrils. Job cards and encouragement posters lined the walls and stand-up panels. One panel had a fist-sized hole in it.

The place was almost empty. Only a couple of other people browsed the postings. Maybe that was a good sign. There mightn't be much competition for job vacancies.

I was willing to do almost anything. Teaching didn't appeal any longer, but I might return to it in the future. At the moment, doing something different would help me with my fresh start.

Most of the jobs advertised sounded tedious or the level of pay wasn't stated or was abysmal. I groaned. This was no use. I was half way through the listings, and nothing appealed at all.

A woman rose from a desk at the back of the centre and approached me. She was about my age, smartly dressed, and appraised me with a thoughtful gaze.

'I'm Pamela. Can I help you with your job search?'

'I'm Heather. I hope you can help me. I'm looking for an interesting job, something unusual or extraordinary. I've been teaching history for the past twenty years, and I could do with a change.'

Her eyes lit up. 'I've got the perfect thing for you. You obviously have people skills. But there's been some difficulty filling the position. I've never understood why. Most people only last a day or two.'

I raised my eyebrows. I'd asked for something out of the ordinary. Perhaps this was it.

'The role is as a house guide at a local manor owned and managed by a public trust. It's open to the public. You would join a small team of people who manage the house and talk to tourists. Full training is included. The pay is reasonable.' She went into more details of the position. My interest intensified.

'That seems ideal. I'd love that. Why do you think people leave the job? Is it particularly stressful? It doesn't sound like it is.'

'Word is that the house is haunted.'

'Haunted? By ghosts?' I laughed quietly. 'You mean ghosts are frightening the staff away?'

'Look, I know it sounds ridiculous, but this is England. Ridiculous is part of our national culture. And so are haunted houses. Chirtlewood House is hundreds of years old. Of course, it has ghost stories. Parts of the house probably creak with changes in the weather or gusts of wind. It simply doesn't take much to scare some people away.'

'I guess it doesn't. I taught teenagers for years, and I could tell you a few horror stories. Ghosts won't scare me away, I promise you.' Especially since I was already well acquainted with one. Surely any apparitions in the manor couldn't be worse than my dead mother, who'd been scary enough in real life.

'Yes, you strike me as someone who will give this opportunity a good go and not run for the hills at the first creaky floorboard or rattle of tiles. Shall I call them and let them know you'll take the job?'

'Won't they want to interview me first?'

Pamela lowered her voice so no one could overhear. 'They're desperate for anyone. Word has got around about the place. No one has wanted to apply since...' she trailed off. 'Never mind. You'll be fine.'

'Honestly, it'll be great. Surely, it can't be harder or more dangerous than trying to teach a bunch of sixteen-year-olds political history.'

Pamela laughed. 'Come over to the desk, and I'll call them. We'll arrange a time for you to go in. They'll give you a week of training, and then you'll be part of the team.'

I grinned. This ought to be fun.

I RETURNED TO AUNT Ruth's house later that afternoon in a state of excitement. Landing a job so soon—and one that sounded so interesting, at that—gave me a boost of energy. I parked the car and would have skipped to the front door if I could. Instead, I made do with a purposeful walk.

Inside, I found Raven poring over a bunch of notes at the desk in the dining room. He looked up. 'Hi, Heather. Good day?'

'Fantastic. I visited Aunt Ruth, and then I got a job. I'm going to be a guide at Chirtlewood House.'

His eyes widened. 'That old place. It has a varied history.'

'So I've been told. Do you know a lot about it?'

'I knew someone who was there for a while, but it was some time ago. I'll tell you about it another time. I need to get back to this work.' He turned back at the piles of notes and books on the desk.

Oops. Not a good time. I'd interrupted his research. 'I didn't mean to disturb you. Sorry.' I turned away.

'Forgive me. That was rude of me. It's just that I don't have good memories of that place.'

'Okay. Well, I'll leave you to your study.'

I made myself a white hot chocolate. What should I do for the rest of the day? I didn't know anyone in Kingston except for Aunt Ruth, and I'd already visited her. Was there something useful I could do in the house?

Of course there was. Aunt Ruth had told me she didn't want a stairlift, as it would ruin the house's character. As she couldn't use the stairs, she would move to the downstairs bedroom. I could prepare it for her. Change the linen, bring down all her clothes and photos and jewellery and so on from her old room upstairs. The room she'd given me.

I was uneasy about displacing Aunt Ruth from her room, but it made perfect sense. She would live downstairs from now on. I was able enough to manage a flight of stairs a few times a day.

But Raven... with his leg muscles, he could walk up and down all day without tiring.

A long breath left me. Yesterday, he'd climbed the stairs right in front of me, providing me with the perfect view. I'd never even glanced at another man in all the years I'd been married to Terry until then. Maybe it was a sign that I was moving on from that tired relationship, from the cheater who took advantage of me in so many ways.

I entered the downstairs bedroom. It was stuffy, so I opened the window. The sheets appeared fresh, so I left the bed untouched and opened the drawers of the dresser and examined the wardrobe. Those were empty. Good.

Returning upstairs, I paused at the top to catch my breath. While I'd recovered from the operation, I wasn't as fit as I had been prior to that. Though I could never have called myself fit. Maybe a three out of ten. Now I was over the operation, it was more like a two out of ten. Or one. Oh well, going up and down the stairs would help.

I made several trips with armfuls of clothes from Aunt Ruth's old room—now my room—apart from a few things I'd borrowed until my luggage turned up or I bought something to replace it. It took the best part of an hour before I'd finished putting them into the dresser and wardrobe downstairs. Photos and other personal items took another fifteen minutes, and I was getting exhausted by then, but being on a roll, I didn't intend to stop until I was done.

A tall wooden-framed mirror leaned against the wall in the bedroom. While I wanted to keep it for my own use, it would be fair to swap it with the much smaller one in the downstairs bedroom. Aunt Ruth would surely want her own mirror rather than one of the guest ones.

I slid it along the bedroom carpet and out onto the landing. It was heavy. There was no way I could carry it downstairs without risking life and limb. I might overbalance or trip over it. There had to be an easier way.

Raven was busy, and I didn't want to bother him again. I lay the mirror on its back so I could slide it down the stairs. But now what? Should I go first and ease the mirror down after me, or lower it from above? Both were tricky manoeuvres. If I went first, the mirror would crash down on me if I lost control of it. That was too dangerous, so I slid it down the top steps from the landing above.

And it slipped from my grasp.

'Shit!' I snatched at it with one hand, the other hanging onto the top balustrade for safety, but I was too slow. The mirror slid down the carpeted stairs, accelerating towards the bottom. The leading edge caught on one of the lower steps. The mirror somersaulted and smashed onto the wooden floor of the entrance hall with a rattle of wood and an explosion of glass. Shards flew out in all directions.

I facepalmed.

Raven came through the dining-room door in a flash. 'What happened?' he cried out before taking in the mess at his feet.

I unpalmed my face and gestured at the damage. 'I dropped the mirror. That's seven years' bad luck, I suppose.'

He frowned. 'It's a big mirror. I'd say you're looking at fourteen, maybe twenty-one years' bad luck there.'

Yeah, maybe. A small puddle of blood forming by Raven's bare left foot caught my gaze. 'You're bleeding!'

He looked down. 'Damn. I must have stepped on some of the glass.'

'Wait there. Don't move. I'll get a bandage.'

I fetched first-aid stuff from the main bathroom upstairs and made my way down to Raven, who was leaning against the doorframe of the dining room.

'Take a seat somewhere. I'll clean and bind the wound.'

He hopped to the nearest chair in the kitchen, apparently to avoid getting blood on the wooden floorboards.

I pulled a triangular shard of glass out of his foot, and it began bleeding more heavily. I wiped it clean, sprayed it with antiseptic and bound it with a bandage, leaving his foot wrapped like an Egyptian mummy's.

Raven eyed my handiwork with a bemused expression. 'Looks like I won't be going out for a run today.'

'Best not.'

'Do you think you might have overdone the wound care a little? It had almost stopped bleeding.'

My cheeks heated. Maybe I had. 'I wanted to be sure you wouldn't bleed out.'

He chuckled. 'No danger of that from this slight scratch, Heather, but thank you for the attention.'

I left him to return to his study and went in search of a dustpan and shovel. It took a few minutes to sweep up all the glass fragments after I'd put the mirror frame away in the cupboard under the stairs. I'd have to get it repaired as soon as I had my first pay from Chirtlewood House. Hopefully, it wasn't a family heirloom. Might Aunt Ruth be upset?

Clearing up involved dumping several dustpans of shattered glass into the rubbish bin before I could put away the brush and pan. Tiredness swept over me. I'd started out with good intentions, but it hadn't ended well. Should I move any more furniture? What if I broke something else?

I shook my head. I'd ask Raven for help some other time.

Chapter 11

THE NEXT MORNING, DURING breakfast, I texted Rachel. It would be her evening in New Zealand.

Me: *Hey, Rach, I got a job. I'm going to work at an old manor house as a guide for visitors.*

Her reply came back a couple of minutes later. *Wow. That was quick. It sounds like something you'll enjoy.*

Me: *Yep. How are you doing? Any news?*

Rachel: *I'm on a date right now. He's a hot lawyer from a rival firm. Tall, dark and rich.*

Me: *Is that a conflict of interest?*

Rachel: *Lol. No.*

Me: *Enjoy your date. TTYL.*

Shortly afterwards, I drove out to Chirtlewood House. The nearest village was Richmond upon Thames. Chirtlewood House sat on exquisitely manicured lawns with precise gardens stretching to the edge of the river Thames. The morning was much brighter than the previous day, without a cloud in the sky. It seemed the weather around here was almost as changeable as back home in Christchurch.

When I first caught sight of the manor house as I turned off the road, I almost went off the driveway. My eyes boggled at the size of it. Nothing that size existed in New Zealand. As I drove around the back to the staff car park, the manor house loomed above me, putting the car park in shadow.

The manor was a giant brick three-storey building with an uncountable number of chimneys. Two wings extended forwards from the front of the building, both with vast bay windows on every floor. Around the back, floor to ceiling windows opened out upon even more extensive gardens that included a small lake, a hedge maze, a tennis court and outbuildings dotted among mature wooded areas and expanses of lawn as fine as a billiards table.

I stood admiring it for a few minutes, not even closing the car door. Ducks splashed on the lake in the distance. A sign nearby directed tourists to the maze and to the Orangery, which had been converted into a café. Several 'Keep off the grass' signs lined the immaculate lawn edges.

'It's quite something, isn't it?'

I spun at the voice. A woman of a similar age to me stood by a car, smiling. Her dark red-streaked hair was tied in a bun. Her clothes, though fashionable, appeared a size too big, and her handbag screamed chain-store value.

'It sure is. I can't believe I'll work in this fascinating historical house.'

'You must be Heather. I thought so. Welcome to Chirtlewood. I'm Melissa Hawkins, one of the guides here.'

'Nice to meet you. I love your hair.'

'Thanks.' She grinned. 'Come on inside and meet the others. We open to the public in half an hour, and we must get the house ready first.'

I followed her through the staff entrance at the back of the house into a pokey office. What function would this have had when people lived in the manor? A butler's office?

Two other women sat inside at a small table. I introduced myself, and they both welcomed me.

Lydia Barksworth was the senior house guide. She was about ten years older than me and was wearing a dark green jacket and a white top. She had a self- assured manner, and she greeted me warmly.

Penny Bishop was a similar age to Lydia. She didn't smile and presented a standoffish manner. Perhaps she was slow to warm to other people, in which case she might be hard work to befriend. Or maybe she simply hadn't had enough coffee this morning—or tea, I corrected myself. This was England, after all. I wouldn't pass judgement. I could be crabby and sour too.

As we completed the introductions, I relaxed. Working in this amazing place with these people would be awesome.

Pastries in a box sat on the table. We shared them for a work breakfast. I could certainly get used to that.

'This is a great way to start the day. Thank you,' I said.

'It's a ritual of ours,' Melissa said, taking a dainty bite from a Danish.

Penny added, 'We all take turns at buying them on the way here. There's a roster pinned to the wall.' She pointed with the tip of a half-eaten croissant.

'Where should I buy them from when it's my turn? Is there a place you recommend?'

'The best place we know is a bakery on the fringe of Richmond. I'll give you the directions later,' Lydia said. 'I hope you're happy to join in?'

'Of course. I don't mind at all.' Perhaps I'd better reconsider joining the gym after all to counteract the extra calories.

When we'd finished the pastries, Lydia drew me aside while the others went to set up the house for visitors. 'Penny and Melissa are going to put out the signs and the guide ropes so eager tourists don't smear sticky hands on our valuable paintings and furniture,' she said. 'I'll give you a quick walk-through of the house. What we normally do is spread ourselves around, trying to keep an eye on as many tourists as possible at any one time, and tell them interesting things about the house.'

'But this place is huge! It must be impossible to check on everyone!'

Lydia nodded. 'It is. Chirtlewood is simply too big for that. We'd all have to be in five places at once. All we can do is monitor the house and any tourists as best as we can. One of us must always be at the front entrance to sell tickets and to ensure no one walks off with an oil painting or a Louis thirteenth chair. A few rogues have tried it before.'

'Really? Has anyone gotten away with it?'

'Nothing that large and valuable has been taken, but some items of value have gone missing. That's why we put in this security system.' She indicated the cameras and alarms placed in the upper corners. 'But it doesn't always help.'

Lydia motioned for me to follow her. We left the small office and entered a dim passageway running the width of the ground floor.

'This is a seventeenth-century house,' Lydia said with the practised ease of someone who had spent years educating tourists. 'Most of the furniture is from that time. This hallway would have been lit by candles in those days, and servants would have to replace them several times a day. Now, of course, we have electric candles to give a sense of what it would have been like to walk along here in those times.' She smiled brightly at me.

'Any secret doors here? I've heard that old English homes sometimes have them.'

'Sure. There's at least one that we know of upstairs. The door at the end of this corridor opens onto the servants' staircase. There's a sign on it to prevent people from going that way. The staircase is narrow and too dangerous for the public. The treads are quite slippery in places, worn smooth by centuries of servants' feet. We don't want anyone falling.'

We took a doorway that led to the entrance hall, where Melissa was setting up the ticket sales desk. The front double doors were open, leading to wide stone steps down to a pathway bisecting the front garden. The floor of the entranceway itself was marble tiles. Massive portraits hung on the wooden walls, their subjects appearing to glare down their noses from up high, an army of ancestral faces.

'On this floor is a ballroom, a morning room, a drawing room and a formal dining room, among others. There is also the kitchen and pantry. You can see all those later. Let's go upstairs.'

We mounted a wide wooden staircase that turned back on itself as it rose to the next floor. The thick balustrades bore carvings of hunters and mythological creatures.

Some stairs creaked as we went up, but it wasn't the boards beneath our feet. It was the steps below us, where we'd already passed.

A chill ran up my spine, and I gritted my teeth to prevent myself from flinching.

'Old floorboards,' Lydia said. 'Don't mind them.'

I wouldn't have minded, but someone was following us, and it wasn't Melissa. She was knocking information signs about in the entrance hall. And Penny was upstairs somewhere. So... who was it? One of the infamous manor ghosts?

Don't turn around. I want to keep this job. Being a scaredy-cat before the house even opens on my first morning wouldn't be a good sign.

Lydia stopped and glanced back. 'Everything okay?'

I'd paused on the stairs. 'Yes, fine. Just not used to so many stairs, that's all.' That was certainly true.

'Don't worry. You'll get fit soon enough.'

We continued up and came to a landing, from which another long passageway stretched into the distance, lit like the one downstairs. The stairs continued upwards, but a rope blocked the way.

'The servants' rooms are upstairs,' Lydia said. 'They're all pokey and dark. In the summer, they're blisteringly hot, and in the winter, they're cold as ice. We close them to the public. Most visitors wouldn't be interested, anyway. You can check them out sometime if you want to.'

'Sure. I'd love to.' I was drinking in this history like it was sweet white hot chocolate on a winter's day.

Lydia moved along the passage. Doors opened off on both sides. 'These are mostly bedrooms, dressing rooms and bathrooms. There's also an incredible library here with thousands of books, most of them between one hundred and three hundred years old, some even older. As you might expect, we keep a close eye on that room in case anyone tries to take a book. It's not a lending library.'

'Which room is it?' I asked. I couldn't see from my position in the passageway, but with my next step, it came into view, and I gasped.

I stepped inside. Floor-to-ceiling bookcases crammed with volumes of all kinds lined the walls, except for a wide window. A sunshade blind was pulled down to prevent too much light entering and damaging the old books. A solid silver candlestick sat on one large shelf, acting as a bookend. Two old lounge chairs sat in the centre of the room, askance to each other. A massive wooden desk with a blotter and an inkwell on it sat at one side of the room, leaving enough space to pass between it and the bookcases behind.

'This is amazing!' I spun, trying to take in everything at once, but it was too much for my overwhelmed mind to process.

Lydia poked her head in the door. 'It's something special. We have a guest researcher who comes in most days. He's investigating seventeenth century witchcraft. Apparently, he's writing a master's thesis.'

The breath caught in my throat, and I froze. 'On witchcraft?'

Lydia grinned. 'We have all sorts of books here. It's a veritable treasure trove. Come on. I'll show you the earl's and countess's bedrooms. We'll have to be quick. The house opens shortly.'

I could have stayed in the library all day, but I followed Lydia further down the passage. 'They had a bedroom each? Or have the rooms been made up that way?'

'I'm talking about the original owners, the earl and countess of Chirtlewood. No one knows now what area Chirtlewood covered, but we believe it's now part of some other noble's estate. Anyway, their real names were Thomas and Charlotte Deaville, and yes, they had separate bedrooms. That was common for nobility in those days.' Lydia stopped before a door and leaned towards me. 'Sometimes, I wish I had a bedroom to myself. My husband snores loud enough to rattle the windows.'

Lydia rapped on the door before entering. I followed her into the room, puzzled. Was it occupied? If so, why hadn't Lydia waited for a response? But no one was there. So why had she knocked?

A massive four-poster canopied bed dominated the room. Several pillows lay at the head end. Despite its sumptuous linen and the wooden bedposts, it looked uncomfortable. The distinct sag in the middle would give me terrible back spasms if I slept in it.

'This is the countess's bedroom,' Lydia said. 'What do you think of it?'

'Wow. It's grand.' An old wooden dresser that might also be of seventeenth century French origin sat on one side of the room. On the other stood a table with a jug and a large bowl for water. I guessed it passed for en suite back in the countess's day.

A tall mirror stood on a stand near the dresser. I glanced away, remembering how I'd smashed Aunt Ruth's mirror yesterday.

'I wouldn't look into the mirror too closely if I were you,' Lydia murmured.

I turned and regarded her with a curious glance, but she wasn't paying attention. She was hovering near the doorway. I took the hint and went over.

'Why? Is the house haunted?' I asked, trying to make a joke of it, but something about the room—and what the person from the recruitment office had said—spooked me.

Lydia glanced at me as we strode towards the stairs. 'This is England, and the house is four hundred years old. There's bound to be stories of ghosts in any property this age. That doesn't mean they exist.'

'Um... I was told—'

Lydia laughed. 'I'm kidding you. Of course it's haunted. We have several ghosts here. Usually, we only hear them walking about.' She paused at the top of the stairs and regarded me. 'I hope that won't be a problem.'

I shook my head. 'I'll be fine.'

She grinned. 'Glad to hear it. Let's go downstairs. I've got a roster for duties—yes, one for chores as well as one for pastries. I love my lists and charts. We can move around the house to watch tourists as we see fit. But they will ask you a lot of questions, so you should stick with us for a few days and learn as much as you can. You can take a guidebook as well and read it in quiet moments. The recruitment centre said you used to be a teacher, so I'm sure you've got an excellent memory. You'll learn everything in next to no time.'

'Thank you. I can't wait to learn more from you and Penny and Melissa. I'm sure there's an incredible amount to know about Chirtlewood and its history.'

Lydia smiled.

Excitement pulsed through me. I wanted to inhale the house's secrets.

When the ghostly inhabitants made an appearance, I'd be ready. I wouldn't let them drive me away.

Chapter 12

BY FIRST THING ON MONDAY morning, my luggage still hadn't arrived. When I called the airline, they didn't know where it was or even seem to care much. They advised me to claim on insurance—which was a great idea in theory, but I hadn't arranged any.

I'd been to visit Aunt Ruth in hospital yesterday morning, and I hadn't told her about the broken mirror—I'd save that piece of bad news until she was out of hospital. I was also keen for her to start mentoring me in witchy things, as she put it, but I didn't want to bug her about it until she was settled at home. There'd be plenty of time later.

Unfortunately, I couldn't visit today. The bathroom modifications company turned up while I was still eating breakfast. I showed them the downstairs bathroom and left them to it. They could call me at Chirtlewood if they needed anything, or ask Raven, if he was at home. I could always nip back and lock the door if they finished and were ready to leave.

The second day in my new job was exciting. The environment was spellbinding. I spent time with Lydia, Penny and Melissa as they talked to tourists in the house, fascinated by everything they said about the history, the architecture, the furnishings and the people who had lived in Chirtlewood House over the centuries. They'd been a colourful bunch.

The day passed quickly. I learned heaps and was a little sad to leave when closing time arrived at Chirtlewood. But I did have things to do.

I parked in central Kingston and went shopping. I needed at least the basics of a new wardrobe. I only had two outfits of my own. I'd been raiding Aunt Ruth's wardrobe for things to wear, but her mostly black clothes were not quite my size. I needed my own things. And this was the perfect opportunity to create a new style for myself—a new image for a new me.

As long as it was cheap. My funds were evaporating, and payday was almost two weeks away.

I found the market square. It wasn't hard; all I had to do was follow the smell of fish. The buildings surrounding the square were old. Older than Chirtlewood House? They all contained modern shops now. I turned and faced one building squeezed between others. It was white with thick, dark wooden beams diagonally across it. The year it was constructed stood out boldly on the front.

A gasp left my lips. It was six hundred years old!

They obviously didn't have earthquakes here. The entire row of shops would tumble like a house of unglued matchsticks if they did.

I gave up on the market square. Most of the clothes shops were boutiques, and I couldn't afford their stuff at the moment. I needed to find a decent middle-of-the-range department store. Even better would be thrift stores or op shops, where I might pick up a few things for a fraction of the price of something new.

There were a couple not far away, but I had only an hour before they closed. I'd have to hurry. Though I wasn't normally one for whirlwind shopping, starting this late in the afternoon left me no choice.

I spent twenty-five minutes in the first shop, rifling through the racks with gusto before leaving with a couple of bags containing two skirts of varying lengths, two pairs of trousers of different colours, a pair of trainers, a pair of loafers and three tops. I'd only had time to try on the shoes. Everything else I bought on faith.

But I wasn't finished. I entered the second op shop to do it all again. I needed more shoes (because who doesn't?), more tops and a couple of jackets. As in the first shop, things that I would never have worn when I was with Terry caught my eye. Brighter colours. More adventurous designs.

Reinventing my image was fun!

I was browsing through a rack of smart casual wear when a familiar voice drew my attention.

Melissa. A pair of sunglasses sat atop her hair. She was at the counter, talking to a sales assistant. 'Excuse me, but do you have any label clothing in today?'

Second-hand boutique clothing? That would be a bargain. *Should I go over and say hello to Melissa? Maybe not. I've only just met her. She might consider it an intrusion. But if I don't, would she consider it rude of me? What's the British convention in this situation?*

'Sorry, there's nothing like that at the moment,' the attendant said. 'It all goes so quickly when it comes in.'

'Okay. Thank you. I'll try again in a few days.' She left without browsing around the shop before I could pick up the courage to speak to her.

I found and bought several things and emerged ten minutes before closing with shopping bags clasped in both hands. Now I had enough to throw together a few outfits until my luggage arrived or I got paid and could afford a few more things.

Paying for the broken mirror might have to wait. Hopefully, Aunt Ruth would understand.

I headed for the car. The bags were heavy. Maybe I'd been too enthusiastic about buying clothes... no, wait! That's impossible.

I had only bought enough to last a fortnight. Maybe three weeks.

A figure stepped into my path, interrupting my thoughts. I looked up. Raven stood there. A tiny unexpected frisson of excitement shot through me.

'Need a hand with those bags, Heather?'

'I can manage, but if you're offering, thank you.' I let him take half of the bags from me.

Raven walked with me. 'So, do you like Kingston town centre?'

'It's cool. I love the old buildings.'

'Did you see the coronation stone?'

'No. What's that?'

'It's a big square rock over by the Guildhall. Some of the early Anglo-Saxon kings were crowned on it, apparently. Guys like Æthelstan, Eadred and Æthelred the Unready.'

'There's a pattern there with those names. And what's the "unready" bit about? Was he always late?' The image of Rose starting her assignment when it was almost due came to my mind. 'Rose the Unready' might fit.

Raven came to a stop outside a small café. 'I don't think it means he was always late. Who knows? It was almost a thousand years ago.'

A thousand years. A whole millennium. Coming from a country like New Zealand with only recent recorded history, I couldn't get my head around that span of time.

Raven inclined his head towards the café entrance. 'How about we take a breather and get a coffee?'

'Absolutely.' I bustled past him and went inside before he could change his mind. A tingle went through me. *It's not a date, it's not a date...* but coffee out with a man for the first time since my marriage ended was *almost* a date.

We ordered and sat at an outside table with rickety wooden chairs. Rather than being annoying, they added to the character of the place.

Raven contemplated me with sharp brown eyes. His gaze was intense. I couldn't take my eyes off him, either. My palms became sweaty. I took a deep breath and tried not to let my mind wander too far, too fast.

Why would he be interested in me? Raven was handsome, thoughtful, smart, empathetic and as fit as an Olympic athlete. I was... sort of attractive, thoughtful in a muddled kind of way, smart and empathetic, but as far as fitness goes... yeah. Not been there yet. I considered having a relationship with the gym once, but I didn't think it'd work out.

'Your aunt told me you're married, Heather. What does your husband think of you coming over here on a one-way ticket?'

I laughed, and he frowned.

'I split up with my husband because I caught him and an ex-colleague of his having sex in our bed. I threw him out of the house. And he doesn't know I'm in England, because I didn't tell him.'

Raven raised his eyebrows. 'Sorry to hear that, but it sounds like you did well to get rid of him. So, you're divorced, then?'

'No, only separated. Under New Zealand law, it's not possible to divorce until there have been two years of separation, and then it's only a matter of filing forms.'

He nodded. 'Convenient.'

I fixed him with the sultriest look I could muster. 'I'm effectively single.'

Our drinks arrived. I sipped at mine. Raven seemed a little fidgety. He shuffled several sugar packets around on the tabletop.

'You don't get out much, do you?' The words were out of my mouth before I could stop them. No filter. Big mouth, too quick.

He inclined his head. 'No, you're right, I don't. I'm... I guess you could say I'm a bit of a recluse. I get out to the gym, to exercise, to specialist libraries for my studies, but that's all. The social life doesn't suit me much.'

My heart thumped in my chest. 'Girlfriend?'

He shook his head.

I raised an eyebrow.

'I've had other priorities for a while. Since my last relationship ended, I mean.'

I didn't press further. It was none of my business. That said, I was as curious as hell.

He swallowed, then reached up to rub a hand through his long, black hair. 'Your aunt told me a lot about you. And now that I've met you, I can see she wasn't exaggerating about your qualities.' A blush spread over his face. It was cute. He was working hard to be nice and complementary. Maybe he thought he was going too far.

I didn't mind. It had been a long time since anyone had shown an interest in me. But was that his intention?

My mind raced. I wanted to know. 'How about you and I go to the National Gallery to view the artworks like you mentioned? We could make that a date?' I smiled while my stomach turned somersaults.

His eyes widened. I'd caught him by surprise. Oh no. This would be awkward when he turns me down, with us sharing the same house.

'I'd like that,' he said, returning my smile. He was fidgeting again, tapping his fingertips on the tabletop.

'Great.' I beamed at him. 'I think this could be the start of a—'

A flash of light blinded me. People at neighbouring tables turned in alarm. Was it an electrical fault? Something set alight in the kitchen?

When the bright spots in my eyes finally cleared, I opened them.

Raven was gone.

I WAS MORTIFIED AT his abrupt disappearance. What was going on? What did he mean by that? How did he vanish so suddenly?

I waited half an hour, but Raven didn't return. Nor did he call. After a while, my patience ran out. I ordered another cup of tea and pulled my phone from my pocket.

It was six thirty here. That meant, in the New Zealand winter, it would be five thirty in the morning. Could I call Rachel at that time? I winced. She got up early for work, but that was *too* early to call.

I sipped my tea and fiddled with my phone for fifteen minutes before I video called her. It *was* an emergency, after all.

She answered. Eyes like slits peered out at me from under saggy lids. Her hair was all mussed up, and she wore a long-sleeved nightie. Not the image of the successful professional lawyer at the moment.

'What's happening, girlfriend?' she said, a quiver of concern in her voice. 'Is something wrong?'

'Sorry to call so early, Rach, but it's an emergency.'

'What? Is it the house? Is Terry being an arsehole? Couldn't you have called me later in the morning?'

'None of those things. It's a *date* emergency.'

'Did you say a date? You've only been there a few days. A job *and* a date. Go, girl.' Rachel whistled. 'What's he like?'

'At the moment, he's MIA. That's why I'm calling you. I want your advice. You're much more in touch with the dating scene than I am.' I hadn't dated for two decades.

'MIA? You mean he never showed up?'

'It's not that. We went to a café together, and things were going well—I'm sure they were—but then poof! He disappeared.'

Rachel rubbed one sleepy eye. 'You're not making sense. What do you mean, he disappeared? You mean he went to the toilet and didn't come back?'

'No. It was weird. There was a flash of light and... when I opened my eyes, he was gone.'

Rachel's gaze fixed on me and hardened. 'Is this a joke? If it is, it would be funnier later in the morning.'

'It's not a joke. That's how it happened.'

'Okay. Maybe there was an electrical fault, and he's gone to help fix it. Or he got spooked. Just wait a while.'

'I've waited over forty-five minutes already. What do I do now?'

'The bastard. He's not coming back.'

'You think so?' My face fell.

'Yeah. Maybe he's not into you as much as you thought. Sorry to give you the bad news, girlfriend, but some guys can be rude. Forget him. Don't see him again.'

'But I'm living with him.'

Rachel's eyes widened. 'You're living with him? But you only just met—'

'I meant he's a boarder at my aunt's house.'

'That might be awkward, then. I suggest you pretend the whole thing didn't happen. Hopefully, he'll do the same.'

'Okay.' I frowned. 'But that doesn't feel right.' Especially as I did like him.

'It's the best thing, girlfriend. I've been in similar situations before.'

I sighed. 'Thanks, Rach. How was your date with the hot lawyer, by the way?'

She groaned. 'He talked about himself the whole damn time. It was the most boring date I've been on for ages.'

'Sorry to hear that. At least he didn't disappear on you.'

'Honestly, it would have been better if he had!'

I chuckled. 'Better luck next time.'

'Look after yourself.'

I gathered my shopping bags and trudged back to the car. Had Raven gone home? Maybe the flash of light had startled him, like Rachel suggested. Or perhaps he'd used that as an excuse to get away because he didn't want to go on a date with me.

Whatever. The situation was awkward. What would I say when I encountered him at home?

I drove home and parked in the driveway. It was still light. That took some getting used to. I'd flown from winter, where it was dark before five. Here it was summer and light until nine. It was topsy-turvy, but I much preferred summer over winter.

As I pulled my bags from the car, movement in a silver birch tree caught my attention. A grey squirrel crept along a branch and leaped to a neighbouring tree. I put the bags down and hurried over, trying to follow it. We didn't have squirrels in New Zealand. This was the first time I'd seen one, and it was the cutest thing ever.

It gathered a nut or something and skittered up the tree, out of view. I looked everywhere for the squirrel, but it stayed out of sight.

I was about to turn back when two sharp brown eyes peered at me from amongst the leafage—a large bird, dark, almost hidden in the shadows of the tree leaves. Bigger than a blackbird. A crow, maybe? It edged backward until it was out of sight in the gloom.

I inhaled sharply and stared into the trees. That bird...

It was a raven.

Chapter 13

THE NEXT DAY I HAD the day off, as I was due to collect Aunt Ruth from the hospital. Before I went downstairs, I hovered outside Raven's room for a few seconds, listening. It was silent. No light seeped under the door. I went downstairs to eat breakfast. Would Raven appear?

He didn't. Maybe he was avoiding me.

I put that out of my mind. What I needed to do was figure out how to get Aunt Ruth home from the hospital. Her car might do, if a nurse could show me how to transfer her from the wheelchair into the passenger seat.

At ten o'clock, I set off for the hospital, then remembered about the exorbitant parking fees. For Aunt Ruth's sake, I'd park there anyway. I wouldn't be long.

I strolled into the hospital and went to Aunt Ruth's room.

'You're here! Wonderful!' She beamed, reaching out of her wheelchair for a hug with such enthusiasm that I burst out with, 'Don't fall out, Aunt Ruth!'

She chuckled. 'No chance. I'm so happy you're here.'

'I'm so glad you're ready to leave this place,' I said, returning her hug with equal passion. I checked around the room. Her packed bag was sitting on the bed.

I found a nurse and received the discharge forms. Aunt Ruth was almost bouncing in her wheelchair, unable to contain her excitement about going home. That wasn't surprising. She'd been in the hospital for several weeks.

We didn't talk about whether she could ever walk again. The medical consensus was that she might be wheelchair bound for the rest of her life, but it wasn't certain.

Anyway, it was time to go home.

Getting Aunt Ruth in the car was awkward, but between us, we managed it without me dropping her into the gutter. On the ten-minute drive home, she brought up the topic that had been burning my curiosity ever since my ghost mother introduced it weeks before.

'I need to teach you what I know about witchy things. There's a lot for you to pick up. You told me your mother's ghost appeared to you. Anything else supernatural happening for you yet?' She stared at me with a curious expression. 'If you're like I was, it'll happen quickly now the process has started.'

Thank goodness she's mentioned this. 'Nothing like that comes to mind at home, but I'm uneasy at work. There's a presence there.'

'I should hope so. You're not working in that big house on your own, are you?' Aunt Ruth cackled.

'No. I didn't mean the other guides. I meant... they've all told me the place is haunted. At the moment, it's only a vague sensitivity, but—'

'Trust your instincts and open yourself up to it, girl. That's one of the first witchy things you need to know. If your gut tells you something, it's almost always right.'

I risked a glance sideways, not wanting to take my eyes off the traffic for too long. 'Why do you say "witchy things", Aunt Ruth? Don't you mean "witchcraft"?'

'Witchcraft, witchy things, same thing. There was a lot of crafting in the old days when people had to collect their own toads and herbs and stuff. Nowadays, we get most of it by internet shopping.'

'Right.' Of course you do. But toads? You could buy toads over the internet? Is that alive or dead? And what on earth did you do with them?

'Anyway, I only call it "witchy things" because that's what your grandma called it. Also, sometimes I forget words. You've got that to look forward to, my girl, as you get older.'

'It's probably not age. Your brain is still adjusting after the accident.' I took a right turn, then cursed quietly. I should have gone left.

Aunt Ruth didn't seem to care or even notice. 'And we'll enrol you in the witchy correspondence course straightaway. That will cover the basics.'

'There's a correspondence course?' I took a left turn. *Where the hell are we?*

'You'll learn a few basic spells and the importance of nature communion, moon phases and so on. You'll breeze through it. The harder stuff you have to learn by yourself afterwards, or with a mentor.'

'But you can help me with that, right? The mentoring? At least, that's what Mum said.' I'd found the river and had a vague idea where we were now, which was nowhere near where we needed to be. But at least the direction I had to go was clear.

Aunt Ruth pursed her lips for a while. I glanced sideways again. What was she waiting for?

'I hope to be around to help you when you get to that stage, Heather.'

'What do you mean by that? You're fine. Except for your paralysis. I mean, you're not ill, are you?'

'Are you taking the scenic route around Kingston for any particular reason?'

My cheeks burned. 'Only because I still don't know my way around. But look, we're back on track.'

A few minutes later, I pulled into the driveway and parked. As I tugged the folded-up wheelchair from the back of the car, Raven rushed outside to help.

I opened my mouth wide in shock. Raven! Where had he been?

He gently scooped Aunt Ruth up in his massive muscled arms and deposited her in the wheelchair. Then he turned to me with a sheepish expression.

'Um, I'm sorry about yesterday. It's... ah...'

I jutted my chin forward. 'There's no need to explain. We only had a coffee, that's all. If you had something better to do, I understand. It would have been polite if you'd told me instead of simply vanishing.' My eyes narrowed. 'How did you leave so quickly, anyway?'

'It's not what you think,' he protested.

'Is anyone going to wheel me inside?' Aunt Ruth said. 'Oh, upside-down thunderstorms! I forgot about the porch steps. How are we going to manage those?'

The steps! Oh no! I'd forgotten about them. Obviously, I had to sort that problem out. I'd arrange for a ramp to be built.

Meanwhile, Raven had lifted Aunt Ruth, wheelchair and all, up the steps and into the house.

'Thanks, Raven,' she said. 'What would I do without you?'

I fetched the bags from the car. How useful am I going to be if Raven is around to do everything? And why is he almost always here? I frowned. He had avoided directly answering my question.

I followed them inside. Aunt Ruth was wheeling herself now, manoeuvring from the hall to the living room, followed by Raven. She swivelled around the corner with a quick dexterity. She seemed to be coping extremely well with her new condition. Had she accepted it and adjusted to it already, or was she simply hiding her emotions?

'Would you like a cup of tea?' I asked Aunt Ruth.

She grinned. 'I'll make it.'

'Oh, I can do it. You rest, Aunt Ruth.'

She ignored me and gestured towards the kitchen area. Her fingertips sparkled. My hair lifted and my top rustled as a warm breeze swept past me.

In the kitchen, the kettle lifted from its stand and glided to the sink. The tap ran, filling it with water. A cupboard door opened and three cups and a serving plate floated out to rest on the bench top as the kettle returned to its stand and switched itself on. Tea bags flew from a box to the cups. A drawer opened, and teaspoons popped out one by one. As the first cupboard door closed, another opened, and a tin dragged itself to the edge before the lid lifted. A selection of biscuits emerged. They flew to the plate and arranged themselves in a circle. The tin closed, dragged itself back inside, and the cupboard door closed behind it. The kettle turned itself off.

I stood shock still, eyes wide. The process continued until the tea was made, my jaw almost to the floor. How was she doing this? *Oh, I need to learn how to do it!*

Aunt Ruth's voice broke me out of my stupor. 'Sugar, anyone?'

Chapter 14

AT CHIRTLEWOOD HOUSE the next morning, we ate pastries again. This time Melissa had brought them. Once again, she was smartly dressed with black trousers, a white cotton top, black loafers and a grey wool cardigan, accompanied by a pearl necklace and a flashy handbag. I was pretty sure the necklace was fake and the handbag was a knock-off.

Melissa raised a finger as if she'd remembered something and she wanted to hold a place in the conversation while she finished chewing. 'You missed some excitement yesterday, Heather. A couple of tourists ran downstairs, their faces white as chalk, claiming that someone or something had touched the wife's shoulder with an icy hand. When they turned around to see who it was, there was no one there.'

My eyes widened. A ghostly encounter in my first week! And I'd missed it. 'Where did it happen?'

'In the countess's bedchamber.'

'It's not infrequent,' Penny said tonelessly. 'We used to record these events in journals that we set aside for the purpose, but we stopped because we ran out of time.'

'And journals!' Lydia added, giggling.

I laughed with them. 'What did you say to the tourists? Did they ask for their money back or want to make a complaint?'

'No. They went to the Orangery for a drink and then came back asking if they could have a selfie with the resident ghost.'

Melissa sniggered. 'And we asked, "Which one?"'

'Has anyone caught anything on camera?' I asked, intrigued.

Lydia shook her head. 'No. They're camera-shy.'

Penny inclined her head. 'Maybe they don't show up on film. Remember that film crew who were here for half a night?'

I frowned. 'Why did they stay only half a night?'

'They intended to stay all night, but most of them ran off after eleven. We found the last two clinging together in our office in the morning.'

'You know, I'm so glad I found this job. It's such an incredible place, and you're all such amazing colleagues.'

'We're more than just colleagues,' Melissa corrected.

'Yes,' Lydia added. 'We sometimes get together for movies at home with wine, chocolate, snacks, whatever. Book club once a month. Are you interested?'

What could be better? 'Wine, movies, chocolate, snacks, books... count me in! But not horror movies.'

'We don't watch those. That's too much like work.' Melissa giggled.

AFTER EATING OUR PASTRIES, I made my way upstairs to the library. The first visitors would arrive soon. I'd do some dusting and check out the intriguing volumes on the shelves at the same time.

Ten minutes later, a lean retired gentleman with metal-rimmed glasses came into the library. 'Hello,' he said with a smile. 'I haven't met you before. You must be new. I'm Ronald Morris. I'm often here doing research.'

I introduced myself. 'What research are you doing, Mr Morris? If you don't mind me asking, I mean.' *Is he the one Lydia told me about?*

'Not at all. I'm researching witchcraft in the seventeenth century. There're a few old tomes in here with relevant history. I'm, ah, I'm writing a book, you see.'

'Wonderful. How long have you been working on it?'

'Oh, twelve years now.'

'Twelve years? It must be... detailed.'

He nodded. 'I am thorough, if nothing else. But I am keeping you from your duties. Lovely meeting you.'

He selected an old volume from a high shelf and carried it to the desk. From his bag, he brought out a vellum-covered notebook and a pen. A laptop would have seemed incongruous in this beautiful old library.

I continued dusting along the shelves, checking every so often for anyone else on the upper floor. We were alone. Being more curious than seven cats, I edged around the room with my duster so I could get a better look at what Ronald was up to. He'd donned a pair of cotton gloves and opened the volume to a page on which several arcane-looking symbols decorated the fine-printed text.

I was almost at the point where I could peer over his shoulder to get a closer look at the symbols and read the text when Melissa entered the room.

'Mr Morris, how are you today?'

'Very good, thank you. And you?'

'I'm well. I thought I'd pop up for a minute to see how your research is going. Have you found that spell book you said you were looking for?'

His eyes glinted with glee. 'Possibly. This might be it. If it is, it's extraordinarily valuable, but I'm not sure yet. I need more time. As you know, with these things it's important to be—'

'—thorough,' Melissa finished for him.

'Exactly.'

I put down the duster, left them to their discussion and headed into the passageway, listening for tourists.

A couple emerged from the earl's bedchamber and stopped when they saw I was a guide.

The woman addressed me. 'Oh, may we ask you about the earl? Any interesting snippets of information you can tell us? His room seemed so... dreary. Was he an old bore?'

I recalled all that Lydia, Penny and Melissa had told me when I had accompanied them around the house on my first three days. 'Thomas Deaville, or Earl Chirtle, was seventy-two when he died in 1648. He was a quiet, melancholy sort of man who apparently liked only his wife, the countess. Because of that, few people liked him. His chief joys in life were reading, hunting, racing his horses and spending time with his dog, whose name was...' Snuffles? Scuffles? 'Scruffles.'

'Oh, thank you. Is there a portrait of him somewhere in the house?'

There was, but at the moment I couldn't for the life of me remember where it hung. 'Yes, there is. Watch out for a portrait of an elderly gentleman sitting by a fire with his dog smoking a pipe.'

The woman's husband gasped. 'He gave his dog a pipe! Well, I suppose there was no SPCA in those days, was there?'

They continued on their way. I swallowed the correction I was about to make. Let them think the dog smoked a pipe if they want.

I patrolled the corridor for a few minutes. The couple moved in and out of various rooms. No one else was about until Melissa came out of the library.

'How's it going, Heather? Any problems?'

'Only that I convinced a couple that Scruffles was a pipe smoker.'

Melissa laughed. 'Good one. The things people—'

A shriek came from the countess's bedchamber. A moment later, the couple I'd been speaking with minutes earlier scampered from the room, eyes wide and faces white. The woman whimpered, and her husband gasped in his effort to keep up with her. They dashed past us and headed for the grand staircase.

I glanced at Melissa. 'Should we go after them?'

She shook her head. 'Lydia's down there. She's good at calming down any visitors who experience a shock.'

'Okay.' I turned and advanced towards the countess's bedroom.

Melissa grabbed my arm. 'Don't. Best to let things settle for a while.'

I pulled my arm free. Melissa had experience of this situation. I didn't. But I needed it.

'It's fine,' I breathed. 'I'll only peek in the door in case someone is still in there.' I was damn well certain there wasn't, but I wanted to check inside for myself. Maybe I was wrong, and whoever—or whatever—had startled the couple was hanging around.

I opened the door and paused, aware that Melissa was a few paces behind me. She stopped. There was no one in sight, so I went inside.

A chill came over me, as if stepping outside into a frosty morning, despite the sunlight streaming through the windows. Something was there; a presence, like when my mother's ghost had appeared before me. Nothing was visible, though. Yet.

The bed cover, always smoothly spread over the linen, was rumpled. An image of the old couple romping on the old bed and messing it up came unbidden to my mind, and I dismissed it.

I peered closer. The bed had a depression in it, like someone was lying in there.

But there wasn't anyone.

'Heather!' hissed Melissa. 'What are you doing? I thought you were only going to look from the doorway.'

'There's nothing in here.' I wasn't so sure, though.

'Let's go downstairs and get a cup of tea.'

'You go ahead. I'll catch up.'

Melissa waited a few moments before she headed for the stairs.

I edged towards the bed, hand outstretched.

The lump vanished.

I drew in a deep breath. What in the hell was going on?

Laughter came from behind me. Not Melissa's polite twittering. Or Penny's or Lydia's.

I turned, my chest tightening.

The mirror appeared odd, more like a window opening into a darkened space than a mirror, as there was no reflection. A tall woman came into view. Her face was attractive, yet pale. Her midnight-black hair flowed halfway down her back like a river of darkness. She wore an open high-necked chemise, dark green sleeves tied on with ribbons, and a broad-brimmed, plumed black hat. Round her neck, she wore a bejewelled heart pendant with a ruby in the centre.

She continued to cackle while I regarded her. The mysterious woman wasn't a reflection. She was in the mirror itself.

'What are you laughing at?' I demanded.

Her hilarity cut short. 'Art thou able to perceive my presence?'

I jutted my chin out. 'Yes. I know who you are. You're the countess, right?'

She grew curious. 'I am Lady Charlotte Deaville, Countess Chirtle. Pray tell, who might thee be?'

My history teacher experience came in useful. She was speaking Early Modern English, probably post-Shakespeare. I could understand that easily enough from my readings of the bard's plays. She wanted to know who I was.

'I'm Heather. I started work here a few days ago, showing visitors around your lovely home.' A bit of flattery mightn't hurt. 'It's great to meet you in the flesh, Charlotte. I mean, in ghost form.'

She sniffed. ''Tis "My Lady" to thee.'

'As you wish, My Lady.'

'Only those gifted with witchery may see mine apparition. What manner of enchantress art thou, Heather?'

'Currently, an inexperienced one,' I admitted. 'I didn't even know about witchy things until a few weeks ago.'

'"Witchy things"? Art thou referring to witchcraft?'

I bit my lip. 'Yes. Were you a witch yourself?'

The ghost of the countess glared at me.

'My Lady,' I added hastily. Was I really being deferential to a ghost almost four hundred years old?

She stepped out of the mirror into the room itself, the glass oozing around her white satin shoes like gloop before springing back into the frame. 'Nay. I was oft many things, but never hast I been a witch.'

Booted footsteps clattered on the wooden grand staircase. 'Heather?' Lydia's voice came from the landing. 'Are you okay?'

Swivelling toward the open door, I opened my mouth to call out that I was fine and not to worry. Before I could get the words out, Lydia shouted she was coming in to get me.

I spun back, but the countess's ghost was gone.

Chapter 15

I DROVE TO AUNT RUTH'S house straight from work. My feet ached and my legs were weary from a day's work at Chirtlewood. *That damned operation.* I'd lost all my fitness, and getting it back wasn't as easy as when I was younger.

Raven met me at the door and gestured me into the living room. 'Please forgive me about the coffee and the, um, disappearing. It's...'

'It's what?'

'It's complicated. May I make it up to you by taking you out to dinner tonight or tomorrow?'

I narrowed my eyes. 'You won't disappear and leave me to pay again?'

He hung his head. 'I'll try not to let that happen. Look, it's not always easy...'

'Yeah. You said it's complicated. What are you, some kind of undercover detective or spy pretending to be a student?'

He folded his arms over his massive chest. 'No.'

'Of course, you'd say that even if you were.'

Raven gave a wry smile. 'I guess I would. But you haven't answered my question. Will you go out to dinner with me?'

'I can try it. But let's be clear about this. Is it an apology-for-being-rude dinner, or is it a second-chance date dinner?'

'How about both?'

I beamed. 'That's what I hoped you'd say.'

Relief swept over his face. 'Great! When shall we go? Tomorrow? Tonight?'

'Why wait? Give me an hour to cook dinner for Aunt Ruth and spend some time with her first.'

'Sure thing.'

I brushed past him to get through the door, smiling, and went in search of Aunt Ruth.

I found her in her new bedroom downstairs, folding and rearranging clothes in the dresser. We exchanged pleasantries.

'Heather, I need your help with a couple of things, dear.' Her eyes were wide. She wasn't the type of woman to ask for help. Whatever she was going to ask was important to her.

'Of course, Aunt Ruth. What can I do?'

'In my old room upstairs, there's a large mirror. I would like it in this room, please. You can take the smaller mirror from here if you like.'

'The large mirror?' The breath caught in my throat.

'Yes. You must have noticed it. It's essential for me. Ask Raven to help you move it. I'm sure he won't mind.'

'Ah... can it wait a few days?' *Shit, I need to get it repaired pronto!*

Aunt Ruth fixed me with her notorious interrogation stare. 'Why the delay?'

I had to come clean. I couldn't lie to Aunt Ruth. 'I already tried to move it, but it smashed,' I blurted out. 'I'll get it fixed, I promise, as soon as I get paid.'

'It smashed?' Aunt Ruth's head went back, her eyes wide. She stared at me as if I'd confessed to writing off her car.

'I meant it disintegrated. I kept the frame, though. That solid thing didn't break, but the glass went everywhere.'

'Oh, Heather, you don't realise what you've done. You kept the glass, didn't you? Please tell me you did.'

'No, I put it out in the rubbish.' Which had been collected this morning.

'Witchy creepers. Stink and putrid blowholes!' Aunt Ruth's cursing was mild but descriptive.

'I'm really sorry. Was it a family heirloom?'

Aunt Ruth's lips tightened. 'You might say that. It's been passed down from witch to witch in our family. It's a conduit for magic.'

Shit, shit and damned shit. I swallowed. 'So, it was valuable, then?'

'Priceless. Oh, whirling dervishes!'

'But you were doing magic yesterday. Making the tea. So, maybe you don't actually need the mirror?' A thought occurred to me. 'Could you use magic to help your recovery?'

Aunt Ruth pursed her lips. 'Possibly. There are powerful healing spells, but I don't know them offhand. Minor spells like making tea and sweeping floors and so on are easy enough, but if I want to work on something special... I. Need. The. Mirror.' Her voice hardened.

Fuuuuck. 'There must be somewhere I can get you another mirror like that one, Aunt Ruth?'

She rolled over to me, so close the wheel of her wheelchair brushed the edge of my feet. She glared at me and jabbed me in the stomach with a bony finger. 'Yes, there is, and you will, because you'll need it yourself when I'm gone from this world.'

'You're still young and healthy. I'm sure you'll hit a hundred.'

'Don't count on it. By the way, getting a replacement mirror isn't easy.'

'What do I have to do? There must be something.' Where on earth would I buy a magical mirror, even if I had enough money?

'It's not the cost so much, as who can make one. Only the most powerful witches and warlocks can do it, and there aren't many of them.'

'What's a warlock? A male witch?' I asked.

'No. There are a few male witches, but not many. A warlock is what we call a witch—male or female—who has reached a certain level of magical power and mastered at least two witchy disciplines.'

'What do you mean?'

'I'll explain it when you start your correspondence course.'

'Okay. Do you know of any warlocks?'

'I know of one. He's up north. I've met him before. I don't know him particularly well. We can look up his contact details on the Witchnet.'

'The Witchnet? Is that the Internet for witches?'

'You got it. He won't do it for free, of course. We'll have to trade something.'

A creeping sensation rose from my stomach. 'What kind of something?'

Aunt Ruth shrugged. 'Whatever he wants.'

What could a powerful warlock actually want that he couldn't get for himself? 'Let's discuss that later. In the meantime, what would you like for dinner, Aunt Ruth? I can get it for you.'

'Oh, thanks, dear. Some scones and cream would be lovely. The meal delivery service brought me a roast beef dinner in the middle of the day, and the home carer baked some scones this afternoon.'

I grinned. 'Sure. I'll get them.'

'Heather?' Raven called out from the hall. 'Are we still going out?'

'Give me another ten minutes.'

I fetched the scones and cream for Aunt Ruth. She licked her lips. 'What about the warlock and the magic mirror?' I asked.

'Go on out, dear. We can sort that business out in a few days. I need a bit of time to settle back in at home first, and you have just started your job. We can't go gallivanting around the country in search of magical mirror repairs right now.'

I breathed a sigh of relief. Do one thing at a time...

'Go on out with Raven. I guess he's taking you to dinner? He asked me if I minded.' Her eye glinted with mischief. 'I think he likes you.'

'I like him too. Thanks, Aunt Ruth. See you later.'

I WALKED OUT OF THE living room and found Raven in the hall. 'I'm ready. Have you got a place in mind?'

'I do, but would you mind driving? I don't have a car.'

'No problem.'

He gave me directions to an elegant Italian restaurant on the riverfront.

Inside, the lighting was subdued, allowing for a clear view of the river itself because of the lack of glare from the windows. Kingston Bridge was lit up, and the lights reflected off the water in a colourful, ever-changing dance. We had a table by the window; the setting was more romantic than any time I'd ever been out with Terry. His kind of dinner out was the pub special on the two-for-one night.

I relaxed in Raven's company. He had the body of a UFC fighter, yet a gentle and considerate temperament. Though we had what might be the best view in town through the window, I had the best view of my life facing me across the table.

We ordered from a tantalising menu. I choose the cheapest option, wanting to conserve my dwindling funds. Raven asked me about my work day at Chirtlewood, and I told him about the visitors we had and about the library there. He made knowledgeable comments. He'd obviously visited there himself at least once. I left out the huge fact that I encountered the ghost of the countess—it could wait until I knew him better, as I hoped to do.

In return, I asked him what he was researching, and what he had done before that.

'Didn't I tell you I'm studying sixteenth century literature at the moment?'

'What aspect of sixteenth century literature exactly? As a former history teacher, I'm curious about these things.'

'I haven't narrowed down my area of study yet.' He gazed out the window for a few seconds too long and his lips twitched, as if he was trying to keep a straight face.

'And before your current research?' I pressed.

'Various things. Small business ventures, some time in the military, failed author... and many other things.'

'Go back a bit. You were in the military? Doing what?' He probably still did military-style workouts to maintain that great body.

'It was overseas, long ago,' he said. The evasiveness was back.

He had secrets. Well, I liked people with secrets. They piqued my curiosity.

Our dinner arrived, served with a flourish by an Italian waiter. An entree plate each and a shared plate of steaming vegetables. A heavenly aroma of meat cooked with garlic wafted under my nose, and my stomach rumbled.

We ate and chatted some more. When we'd finished our mains and were ready to peruse the dessert menu, something brushed my leg under the table for a moment. Raven's foot? Was that accidental, or on purpose?

Raven's gaze was fixed on the lights on the river.

'Raven?'

'Hmmm?' He turned to me, one side of his mouth curling up slightly.

'Were you trying to play footsies with me?'

He took a few moments to answer. 'Yes. I wanted to get your attention to see if you wanted dessert.'

'Oh no, you weren't. You were looking out of the window.'

'Yes, I was, wasn't I? Okay, you're right. It was my attempt at flirting. I'm not used to this. Where and when I grew up, flirting wasn't really a thing.'

'No? What did you do, then?'

'Well, usually, marriages were arranged. It's a long time ago.'

'We're about the same age, and I'm pretty sure I remember a little flirting in my younger days.' Though it had been only a little, and I'd been too flattered by Terry's insincere attentions that I'd accepted him before getting a proper look at the rest of the local talent.

'If I've offended you by inappropriate flirting, I apologise. My intention was to see if...' His voice trailed off.

'To see if...' I tried to encourage him to continue, but his only reply was tight-lipped silence, like a brick wall. 'To see if I'd play footsies with you too?' I tried to fill in the blanks.

He cringed and reddened. 'I wanted to indicate that I like you, but I'm making a mess of it, aren't I? Where the hell are the dessert menus?'

I chuckled. 'It's fine, Raven. It was funny, actually. You're a cool guy, smart and handsome, and I'm at ease with you. I've separated from my husband, as you know, and I'm ready to move on.'

'You are?'

'I moved on years ago, really. My marriage was on life support for at least the last five years. We were only going through the motions.' I leaned closer and lowered my voice. 'It might sound cruel, but I don't care if I don't see my husband again. We'd drifted apart so much. While I was angry when I found him banging his work colleague in our bed, it was a relief that at last I had a reason to call the whole deal off.'

Raven nodded slightly. 'I understand that perspective. I feel you.'

I hope so. I relaxed back in my seat. 'Great. So, we're officially dating, then?'

His broad smile broke out. 'Sounds excellent.'

Warmness embraced what was remaining of my feminine nether regions. 'There's something else I want to tell you.'

'Okay, what's that?'

'I had a hysterectomy a short time ago.'

He grimaced. 'That must have been painful. How are you recovering?'

'I've been very sore, you know, down there.' I pointed downwards for clarification, but he kept his eyes level with mine. 'The surgeon told me, "No sex for six weeks."'

'Oh, Heather, if that is worrying you, take it easy. We've only just met. Let's take things slow and not do anything before you are ready.'

But I'm ready now. I haven't had sex for months. Even the idea of staying for dessert was being relegated to second place by the prospect of imminent sex. 'It's not a problem. I had the hysterectomy ten weeks ago. I'm sure I'm fine now, and the good news is that when we have sex, I can't get pregnant.'

Couples at the neighbouring tables turned their heads to stare at me. I must have spoken up in my excitement. I frowned at them, and they hurriedly went back to their own conversations.

I turned back to face Raven with a coy smile, but a flash of light forced me to blink. I opened my eyes as the light faded, spots in my eyes. Once again, no one else had reacted to it.

Raven was gone.

On the back of his chair, a wide-eyed black bird stared at me. My mouth dropped open.

'How did that bird get in here?'

A waiter ran over, flapping a cloth at the bird, and it took flight. It circled once around me while the waiter tried to shoo it towards the open door.

With a look over its shoulder, the bird dashed for the door and outside. I turned and stared through the window while it circled outside for a few minutes, above the river, before it headed off into the night.

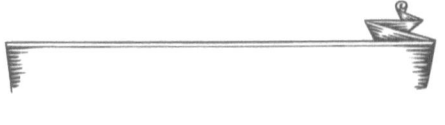

Chapter 16

I WAS EMBARRASSED BY the whole situation with Raven's sudden disappearance—again—but not so much that it put me off ordering a cheesecake and eating it.

Once again, Raven had left me to stump up the payment for everything. I paid on my credit card, which was racing towards its limit like a horse with the stables in sight. Then I drove home, my mind in a whirl that couldn't be explained by the single glass of prosecco I'd had with my meal.

Raven was... an actual raven? Like a werewolf, but much lower down the food chain? Was it even possible?

I'd have to ask Aunt Ruth. She'd know if were-beasts were real or not. But did she know Raven seemed to be one?

What did I mean, seemed to be one? I was almost sure he was one. A were-raven or a raven-shifter, or whatever they were called.

I hadn't seen it happen in front of me, but what other explanation could there be? One moment, the man himself was there, and the next, a surprised bird gawked at me in his place.

Even his name, Raven, was an unsubtle clue.

Did he have any control over changing form? Maybe not. If he did, why would he change to raven form in the middle of our date? Before dessert, even?

I needed answers, but Aunt Ruth had already gone to bed. I didn't want to knock on her door and wake her. I'd have to be patient and ask at the first opportunity tomorrow or the next day.

Raven wasn't home. Perhaps he was too ashamed to come back right now. Maybe he was stuck in bird form, out cruising the night sky, trying to avoid hawks. Whatever the problem, it was an obstacle to our budding relationship even getting off the ground.

I made a white hot chocolate, carried it upstairs to my room and sat in an armchair, thinking. I'd left everything behind in New Zealand to come over to England: a ruined marriage, a crappy job, a few friends I rarely saw due to overwork, my busy solicitor friend Rachel and my daughter who had already moved away from home to university in another city. Rachel and Rose were the only people in my old life whom I missed, and that gnawed at me.

Loneliness overcame me. A few tears rolled down my cheeks. When would I see Rose again in person? Twenty thousand kilometres was a long way.

I picked up my phone and video called her. It would be morning there. She may not have gone to classes yet.

Rose's don't-wake-me-up face filled the screen. 'Mum. Is there an emergency?'

'No, Rose. I only wanted to see you and hear your voice.'

'Okay. Can you do that a little later in the morning next time? I have a late start today.'

'I assumed you'd already be up and studying.' I wish. She'd probably had a late night out. That seemed to be the student way of life.

'Yeah, I was going to get up soon, anyway, I suppose. How are things with you? How's Great-aunt Ruth?'

'She's home now, and she's getting around with her wheelchair. I need to arrange for a few alterations to be done inside and outside the house. Otherwise, she's coping well.' *But I broke her damned magic mirror.*

'And what about you, Mum? How are you doing?'

I hesitated. How much should I tell my daughter about everything going on for me? 'I like living here. Aunt Ruth has a lovely, huge old house that's a pleasure to be in. There's even a big library upstairs!'

'Wow.'

'And Aunt Ruth has a boarder. His name's Raven, and he's a hottie.'

Rose grinned. 'Send me a picture.'

'I'll do that when I can get one.'

'What about a job? Found one yet?'

I beamed. 'I have. I'm a guide at a seventeenth century haunted manor house. It is so cool. There are fascinating stories about the people who lived there and wonderful old furniture and there's even a library there too.'

'That's great, Mum. I'm pleased for you. You won't want to come back home.'

A pang of sadness stabbed me in the chest. 'I miss you, though, darling daughter.'

'Maybe I can come over and visit during the holidays. Though it'll be winter then, won't it?'

'Yes. Anyway, apart from missing you as much as I do, getting away from Terry was the best thing for me. And changing my job. I've left all my problems behind me.'

Rose drew her lips tight and hesitated before commenting. 'That's just it, Mum. You've left them behind. You walked away from them.'

'That's right, I did.'

She didn't reply.

'That's a good thing, isn't it?' I asked, confused.

'I don't know about that, Mum. You're over there in Kingston, and you've taken the first job you found and you're seeing the first guy you've met and you're doing everything you can for Great-aunt Ruth. Have you learned to set any boundaries for yourself yet?'

She'd lost me. 'What do you mean, love?'

'Back here, with Dad and the school, you never said "no" to anything. You'd do whatever anyone wanted you to do, even if you were exhausted or you didn't have time. Has anything changed? It sounds like it's just the same to me.'

'I'm a lot happier with my daily life. Apart from missing you, of course, and my friend Rachel, but you'd already moved to Wellington.'

'Okay, Mum. I hope you know what you're doing. I've gotta get ready for classes.'

We said goodbye and disconnected. I sat with the phone in my hand for a while. What did Rose mean? Did she have a point? She seemed to say that I wasn't in control of my own life.

I am, I told myself determinedly. There hadn't been the need to say 'no' to anyone yet in my new life.

My white hot chocolate was now a white cold chocolate. I went to bed without drinking it.

MY PHONE WOKE ME IN the morning. It wasn't the alarm, so it was early. Was it Rose?

I rolled over and grabbed it from the side table to answer, glancing at the number. Terry.

'Where are you?' he demanded. 'I need to talk with you about the house. I asked Rose, and she wouldn't say where you are.'

Good.

'What exactly do you want, Terry?' I glanced at the clock. It was three fifteen in the morning. For Terry, though, it was early afternoon.

'We've got an offer on the house. We need to discuss if we're going to accept it or not. Can we meet over coffee somewhere?'

Fat chance. He thinks I'm still in Christchurch, or at least close to there. 'No, I can't do that. We can discuss it over the phone.' I yawned. Thankfully, this wasn't a video call. I wouldn't have connected if it had been. He'd see me sitting up in bed and wonder what the hell was going on.

'All right.' He went on about the offer on the house for a while. I didn't listen. The estate agent would send me an email about it, anyway. I'd check for that in the morning. The house was sitting empty, but still furnished, while our estate agent hunted for a buyer. Apparently, she'd found one.

Finally, Terry finished droning on. 'So, I think we should push for a higher offer. It's not enough.'

I was about to agree with him, which is something I would automatically have done in the past, but Rose's words from last night echoed in my head. I don't have to always agree if I don't want to.

'I'll think about it and let you know.' I fist-pumped silently. That was a win for me.

'I'm glad you agree—wait, what did you say? You'll think about it?'

'Yes, I'll let you know in a while. At the moment, I'd be happy to take the offer and get the whole thing over with.'

'Now, wait a second—'

I hung up. I'd listened to Terry for far too long. It was three thirty, and I wanted to go back to sleep.

Of course, he rang back straightaway. 'Why won't Rose tell me where you are? Are you living with some new man?'

'No, and even if I was, it wouldn't be any of your business. We're separated.' Another fist-pump. If I wasn't so tired, I might enjoy myself even more than this.

'Yeah, I wanted to talk to you about that too, but we got cut off. Look, Heather, I made a mistake. A terrible mistake, yes, but we all make mistakes like that, don't we?'

'I haven't.'

He coughed. 'Well, that's true, but I'm sorry. Is that what you want to hear? I shouldn't have done it, but please understand. I was depressed from having lost my job and being out of work. I had all that time on my hands, and my colleague was in the same position and we just, you know...'

'Fucked?' *A little thrill raced through me. I'd said the f-word, not just thought it.*

'If that's what you want to call it, sure. A few times. Maybe twenty or so. But it meant nothing. You know, affairs never mean anything. It's you who I married, and it's you who I love. I think we should call off the house sale, get back together and get back to our lives. I talked to the school this morning, and they're willing to give you your old job back. They miss you too.'

I bet they do. 'I'm not interested, Terry. It's over.'

'Where are you? Can I come over? Let's talk about it like sensible adults.'

'No, I'm in a much better place now, and I'm not going back to that old life. Goodbye, Terry.'

I hung up again and put the phone on silent, but when I tried to go to sleep, rest evaded me. My mind raced with a plethora of thoughts and concerns: Rose, Terry, Raven, Aunt Ruth, and even Countess Chirtle occupied my thoughts through the hours until dawn.

Chapter 17

I GOT UP EARLY BECAUSE I couldn't sleep and quietly made breakfast. Aunt Ruth was still asleep. Raven wasn't up yet, if he'd come back at all. His bedroom door was closed. Maybe he was like the early bird—off getting worms, or whatever ravens ate.

My shift at Chirtlewood House didn't start until 8.30 a.m., but I was ready an hour before that, so I went anyway, stopping to buy the pastries from our favourite bakery on the way, which opened at 7 a.m. I let myself into the house, left the pastries in the office and went upstairs to the library. I could browse the shelves for a while before my colleagues arrived and we got ready for the day.

A tall, elderly man sat in one of the leather chairs in the library, staring into space. He was dressed in a buff coat with scarlet doublet sleeves and a matching baldric and cape. A white linen shirt poked through his open-seamed sleeves. A short linen collar and leather boots with the cuffs rolled over finished his outfit. A pipe protruded from his mouth. It didn't seem to be lit, but the smell of burnt tobacco permeated the air.

I stopped inside the doorway. 'Who are you, and how did you get in here? The house doesn't open until nine. And there's no smoking allowed.'

The man gave me a derisory glance before resuming his blank stare. 'Begone, maid.'

I bristled. 'I'm not a maid. You need to leave. How did you get in, anyway?'

He ignored me.

I debated with myself about what to do. I couldn't grab him by the arm and drag him out. That would be assault, and there was a risk he would fall. An ancient walking cane leaned against the armchair, suggesting he had mobility issues. How had he made it up the stairs? I could call the police, but would they respond to a report of a septuagenarian burglar? Besides, he had taken nothing as far as I could see.

'At least put your pipe out,' I said lamely. Maybe it would be best to wait for Lydia so she could sort this out. She was the head guide, after all, and this old guy might be a regular visitor who had his own key.

''Tis already done,' grumbled the old man. 'Leave me in peace.'

I stepped closer and peered into it. He was telling the truth. It wasn't lit. I examined the unusual pipe closely. It had a thin stalk and was made of white clay with a small bowl. I'd never seen a pipe like it.

The elderly gentleman was vaguely familiar. Had I seen him around town when I was shopping?

No, that wasn't it.

I scurried through the house as fast as I could, hunting for the portrait in my mind. I couldn't remember where it was, but if I was right...

It hung on the wall on the stairway. A large oil painting of an elderly gentleman sitting by a fire, smoking a pipe. Thomas Deaville, Earl Chirtle. I stared at it for a minute, then climbed back upstairs, out of breath. *Damn that operation. Damn this lack of fitness.*

Back in the library, the figure was still there, staring into space.

'You're Earl Chirtle,' I said. 'You died in 1648 when you were seventy-two.'

'And not a moment too soon, I daresay. I hadst wearied of the toils of life. But, I welcome the respite that death tenders.' He looked up with a bewildered expression. 'Thee can perceive me. How queer! Thee wouldst be the fresh one that Mistress Chirtle spake on to me about.'

'I'm a new guide here, yes.' He seemed to have mellowed a little now that I wasn't demanding he leave. He was a house ghost; I wouldn't try to turf him out of his own property. 'So, you talked to the countess, did you?'

'Verily, I endeavour not to. After four hundred and twenty-three years of matrimony, 'tis tiring thoroughly.'

'Don't you get on with your wife?' I shivered at the disturbing thought of living with Terry for over four hundred years. If that was my fate after my death, I needed immortality.

'Nay, 'tis not that. I cherish my wife dearly. 'Tis only that the lady prattles overly much. As do thee, evidently. A sir needs his solitude from time to time.'

'Sorry.' Yet again, I was apologising to a ghost.

The spectral earl went back to his staring pose. I turned to see if he was looking at anything in particular—perhaps a certain book. It was hard to make out which one it could be. Several dusty old histories and a silver candlestick lined the shelf he was gazing at.

Should I offer to read to him?

Maybe another time.

I ABANDONED MY ATTEMPT to browse the library and went downstairs. I hadn't long to wait until Lydia, Penny and Melissa arrived. I studied the artwork while I waited for them.

Fifteen minutes later, Lydia came in first. 'Oh, Heather, you're here already. You're super keen.'

'I woke early,' I said. 'Besides, I love working here. It's the most beautiful and amazing house.'

'A house with its own ghosts.' Lydia scrutinised me.

Did she suspect that I'd seen them? I chose my words carefully. 'You said there were several stories. Do you know anyone who's seen ghosts here? I mean, someone you trust.'

Lydia nodded. As she opened her mouth to speak, Melissa arrived, and a half minute later, Penny came in. Lydia sent me a meaningful glance.

Yes, we'd have this conversation later.

We shared the morning's pastries and chatted.

'I had a date last night,' I said shyly.

'A date! What's he like?' Melissa asked. 'Tall, dark and handsome?'

'Intelligent and a gentleman?' Penny said.

'Cute and funny?' Lydia added.

I laughed. 'All of those things. He's a great guy. We had dinner at an Italian restaurant by the river. Le Amore.'

'Fancy. I wish I could afford to eat there,' Penny said dourly. 'I suppose the food was top notch?'

'It sure was. We had fun.'

'Is he rich?' Melissa asked.

'I have no idea.'

'And have you had sex with him yet?' Lydia's eyes gleamed with mischief.

My face burned, and I let out a breath. Why be embarrassed? I was in my mid-forties and single. This was my second chance at a good life, and I could do what I damn well liked. Even have sex on the first date, if I so wished. But I didn't get the chance.

'He had to leave early.' I sighed. 'From the restaurant.'

'What?' Lydia asked. 'He wined and dined you and then just... left you there?'

'Did he get an urgent phone call? Does he have a job where he must rush away sometimes, like... is he a doctor or a cop or a journalist or something?' Melissa's confusion showed on her face. It mirrored mine.

'No. It was weird.'

'Maybe he didn't like you,' Penny said.

'Penny!' Melissa and Lydia rounded on her.

'What? It could be that. Why else would he leave? Anyway, there are plenty more birds in the sky.'

I stared at her. Why did she use that turn of phrase instead of the usual 'fish in the sea'?

Lydia stood. 'We better get on with preparing the house for visitors. Heather, speak up if you want to chat more later. I know you're new to this country, but you're one of us now. You don't have to face your problems alone.'

'Thanks, Lydia.' Things between Raven and me were confused. Was he my boyfriend... or not?

At the moment, I guessed not.

RONALD MORRIS ENTERED the house five minutes after it opened. 'Morning,' he said, his eyes bright over his metal-rimmed glasses, before he made his way to the grand staircase.

He'd be on his way to the library, of course, to carry on with his research.

I gasped. The library! But the earl's ghost was there!

Ronald was already halfway up the first flight of stairs. He reached the middle landing by the time I had hurried over and planted a foot on the first stair.

'Wait, Mr Morris!' I cried out.

'I'm going to the library,' he called back without slowing. 'I must get on with my research.'

He was at least twenty years older than me, but he put on a surprising burst of speed, and I was not anywhere near top form, thanks to the operation. Though, to be honest, my best had never been much good anyway. My usual idea of exercise involved unwrapping a chocolate bar.

I turned the corner at the middle landing, my hands gripping the thick wooden balustrades for support. The exertion of scampering up the stairs left me puffing, and I stopped for a quick breather. Ronald nimbly climbed the remaining steps and set off for the library.

'Mr Morris, wait,' I tried to shout, but only a cough and a hoarse wheeze came out.

I hastened up the rest of the stairs, hauling myself along the banister as I went, and emerged onto the top landing.

Too late. Ronald turned into the library from the dim passage.

My teeth gritted. I waited for the scream, but it never came.

Melissa poked her head out of the countess's bedchamber, frowning. 'Are you okay, Heather?'

I waved an acknowledgement and nodded as I caught my breath. 'I'm fine. Just hurried too much.'

'It looks like you've been running. Don't do that in this house. People trip sometimes.'

'Thanks for the advice.'

Melissa turned back into the bedroom.

Breathing hard, I made my way to the library, entered and looked around. It was empty, apart from Ronald. The earl had vanished, or gone through a wall, or whatever ghosts do when they want to make their exit.

'Everything all right, Mr Morris?' I asked as the retired researcher set up his notes on the desk and fetched a book from the shelves. It was the same volume he'd studied on the previous occasion.

He lifted his head. 'Yes. Absolutely fine.' He held the bulky book up so I could see it more clearly. The cover was dark leather with silver etching in the title. 'This is a long-lost witch's spell book. I've been searching for it for months. Do you know what that means?' he asked, a thrill of excitement in his voice.

'Your search is over?' I was confused. 'Do you mean it's the spell book of a witch who's missing, or is it the book that was thought to be missing?'

He chuckled. 'The latter. And it was shelved in the library here all along. Now, I've verified this is the right one.'

'Congratulations. What's in it? Anything interesting?'

Ronald put the book down and stroked his chin. 'Unfortunately, I cannot read it. But I do know what it is supposed to contain from other academic texts.' He sat at the desk and reached for his pen.

I was far too curious to leave now. 'So, what's supposed to be in it, according to those academic texts?'

He looked up. 'Well, apparently, it contains many spells—some mundane, some powerful. It's written that there are love spells, healing spells, attack spells and more. If you believe in that sort of rubbish. I'm investigating only out of academic curiosity.'

'Of course.' I had to get a peek inside that book! Maybe I can take photos of several pages and show Aunt Ruth. Perhaps she can read them. Maybe one of the healing spells can help her recovery, perhaps even regain her mobility.

Ronald didn't reply. As he became more engrossed with his work, I left the library. I could examine the book and its contents closely myself later. Would Lydia let me borrow it if it might help Aunt Ruth?

I wandered along the hall, checking the rooms for other visitors.

An American couple were in the earl's bedchamber, chatting about how the furniture would suit their summer house. I hovered at the doorway in case they intended to steal something, but moved on when they chortled. They'd been joking.

I wandered back to the grand staircase. Down below, Penny's voice rang out as she welcomed someone to the house. Half a minute later, a young man bounded up the stairs. He was dressed in a heavily decorated white jumpsuit zipped open to his waist. White dancing shoes complemented his outfit. His hair was slicked back with an oily mixture.

I did a double-take. It was Elvis Presley.

I stopped him. 'I'm honoured to meet you,' I said. 'I've always loved your music.'

He gave me a sideways look for a few moments, then laughed. 'Gee, thanks. It's great to find a fan.'

'You're looking wonderful. But I don't understand. Aren't you earthbound in Memphis? How did you get here?'

'Memphis? No. I came by bicycle from Richmond. I'm staying in a boutique hotel there. It was easy.' He tried to move past me, but I blocked him.

'Ghosts ride bikes?'

His expression changed. 'Are you for real? Or are you making fun of me?'

A creeping wave of embarrassment came over me. I'd really blundered here. Elvis wasn't a ghost. He wasn't the real Elvis at all—only someone dressed like him for some reason of their own. 'No, I'd never do that. I'm sorry. I mistook you for another person.'

'Yeah, right. You sound a little crazy to me, lady. You're cute, though.' He eyed me appreciatively.

My heart thudded at those remarks, but I had to be polite in my role as a house guide. 'Have a pleasant visit.'

I went downstairs, my cheeks burning. I shouldn't leave visitors unattended, but Melissa was up there somewhere. She would monitor them. I went to the office and sat for five minutes to regain my composure. The office had a small kitchenette, and I made a cup of coffee. I needed it.

But before I could drink it, all hell broke loose.

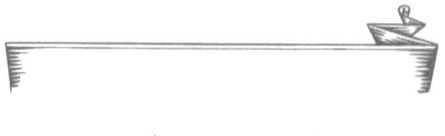

Chapter 18

I HURRIED BACK UPSTAIRS. In my mind, anyway. My hurrying was more of a slow trot across the entrance hall and a climbing expedition up the staircase. But at this rate, I would soon get fit, just like Lydia said.

A woman was screaming. It wouldn't be Melissa, and Penny and Lydia were behind me, bounding onto the lower stairs. It must be the American visitor screaming.

A man with an American accent called for help. Was it the couple from the earl's bedroom? Had the woman fallen and hurt herself?

I reached the landing and paused to catch my breath, but I wasn't given a chance. Penny and Lydia grabbed me as they went past on either side and swept me along with them.

Melissa stood ahead of us, staring through the door of the library. The couple stood next to her. The woman was crying and being comforted by her husband. She didn't appear hurt.

Whatever had happened had taken place in the library. Where Ronald Morris was working on his notes. Why hadn't he come out to see what the commotion was?

Melissa turned to us, her face grave. 'We have to call an ambulance. And the police. It's Mr Morris.' She groaned. 'I can't call. My phone's out of charge.'

Lydia glanced inside, gasped and raised a hand to cover her mouth. She tried to stop Penny and me from entering, but I slipped past and stepped inside, pulling my phone from my pocket.

Mr Morris lay on the floor, half hidden by the desk. Blood seeped from his head. A heavy silver candlestick lay on the floor next to him.

I moved closer, careful to avoid disturbing anything, and reached out. My fingertips pressed on his neck.

No pulse.

I dialled the emergency services. 'Hello? Police and ambulance, please. Chirtlewood House. A man is dead.' My voice shook. Poor Ronald's glassy eyes stared back at me. Lydia came up next to me and put her arm around my shoulder in support.

'I've dispatched those,' the operator said. 'Are you sure the man is dead?'

'Yes. There's no doubt.'

'Can you tell me the circumstances involved?'

'I don't know. It may be a terrible accident. Or it may be... murder.'

'The emergency services are on their way. Please remain calm and don't touch anything.'

I was calm. The experience of being a high school teacher served me well in most circumstances, even such a terrible one as this.

I stepped away from Ronald's body and studied the room. Everything appeared normal, but the desk where he had been working was almost clear. Only pens remained. The witch's spell book and Ronald's notes were gone.

Lydia spoke up, taking charge. 'Penny and Melissa, go downstairs. Make sure no one leaves the house. One of you check outside and call anyone inside. The police might want to talk to them. Heather and I will find any other visitors in the house and bring them to the entrance hall. We'll wait for the police there.'

The old couple had regained their composure, and Lydia guided them downstairs. I checked every room upstairs, twice, in case I missed someone. There was no one else, so I made my way to the entrance hall.

Lydia, Melissa, Penny and the elderly American couple were there, plus a family of four, who must have been wandering in the downstairs rooms.

But someone was missing.

'Where's Elvis?' I asked.

Chapter 19

THE POLICE AND AMBULANCE arrived five minutes later. Three police cars in all careened to a halt, mere metres from the front entrance, and the ambulance drew up next to them.

I'd undergone a lot of change lately. But dealing with a murder at my workplace topped all the rest combined. And I'd only been there a few days.

The ambulance crew raced upstairs.

'I'm Detective Inspector Pentecost.' A tall, smartly dressed black woman flashed a badge to Lydia. 'I'm in charge of this investigation. My officers will need to talk to everyone present. Until we know more, we will presume this is a crime scene. You'll have to close Chirtlewood House until our investigation here is finished.'

'Of course,' Lydia said, her voice almost breaking with strain. 'Anything to help. The gentleman who died—was killed—was often here. He was a—'

'Please lead the way.'

Lydia hesitated. Her pose was tense, her brows had drawn close together, and a grimace contorted her face. She'd told me Ronald had been a regular visitor to Chirtlewood House for several weeks.

She wouldn't want to see his body again.

'I'll take you,' I volunteered.

Lydia's relief was palpable. She sagged back, her hand pressed to her chest.

I led the inspector upstairs. Behind us, police officers asked questions of the others.

Inspector Pentecost asked me about what had happened, and I told her in as much detail as I could what I remembered as it had occurred.

'Thank you,' she replied.

The ambulance crew had stepped out into the passage. We went into the library.

'Here he is,' I said. 'Mr Morris.'

The inspector crouched down beside Ronald's body and examined the wound before she stood and scanned the bookshelves. 'Where is that candlestick, usually?'

'On that shelf.' I pointed to a spot two or three metres from the desk. 'There's no chance it could have fallen on him.'

'I agree. I will call for the pathologist. Please go downstairs and wait with the others.'

I cast one last look at Ronald, saying a silent goodbye to him. I hadn't known him for more than a few days, and only spoken to him twice, but he had seemed an amiable man. He didn't deserve a violent end like this.

I returned to the entrance hall and joined the others.

It was busy. Even more police had arrived, and everyone was being interviewed. A young officer approached me and asked for my statement. I repeated what I'd told the inspector, and then I recalled I hadn't mentioned Elvis.

'There was another guest upstairs about five minutes before the American lady screamed. A young man dressed like Elvis Presley.'

'Who's Elvis Presley?' the young policeman asked. 'A Youtuber?'

I inspected him. He looked like a kid. He still had acne, even.

'A singer from decades ago.'

'Right. Thanks for your statement. You'll need to wait until the guv'nor says you can leave.'

Now it was my turn to ask. 'Who's the governor?'

'The inspector. Please wait over there.' He gestured.

The interviews were winding up. I joined Melissa and Penny, who were commiserating together. Penny appeared pale. Lydia joined us a couple of minutes later, her eyes moist and trails of tears on her cheeks. The visitors stood in another group, silent.

I peered over Lydia's shoulder. In a far corner of the entrance hall, a freckled girl of about twelve stood, slouching, arms and head hanging, staring at us all. She hadn't been there earlier. She wore a tatty plain dress or a nightgown. In addition to her bedraggled appearance, her face was grubby. I squinted. Her freckles weren't freckles after all—they were spots. Measles spots.

Her gaze caught mine and she vanished. Another ghost?

I kept watch, but she didn't return.

Outside, a constable put crime scene tape around the entrance to the house. Specialists arrived and went upstairs with various types of equipment.

After a while, the inspector came downstairs and told us we could all leave. We'd all given our phone numbers so the police could contact us if they wanted to ask more questions. They told Lydia they would notify her when the house could be reopened to visitors.

We chatted in the car park for a few minutes before heading off. I sat in the car for a few minutes. Going home didn't seem right. I needed time alone to process everything, so I drove to Richmond Park, which I'd been told was wonderful for walking in, and went through the gate, looking for a car park.

It was still morning, and the temperature was rising. Broken clouds swept across the sky. It might be another beautiful day.

But not for Ronald Morris.

Signs in the park pointed to various landmarks, but I ignored them and set off in a random direction. The park was huge, and I hadn't appreciated how large it truly was. I ambled for half an hour before tiredness overcame me, and I sat on the grass beneath an old oak tree.

The loud squawking of birds drowned out the passenger jets that descended into Heathrow every couple of minutes. In the nearest tree, a green parrakeet with a coloured ring around its neck came into view. An escaped pet?

And then I saw the others. A dozen, twenty, thirty or more of them, all in the same tree. They were the ones making a racket.

Not one escaped pet, then. A colony. A breeding pair or a bunch of them must have gotten loose.

I stared at them. A park in Greater London with wild parrakeets? I would never have guessed.

My phone beeped with a text message. Rachel.

Rachel: *How's it going, gf?*

Me: *You wouldn't believe it. A man was murdered at my work this morning.*

I waited for a minute before the reply came.

Rachel: *Seriously?*

Me: *Yes. It's terrible. The police sent us home while they investigate.*

Rachel: *Fuck. Are you safe there?*

Me: *I think so. I'm pretty sure this was a one-off event. I've been thinking of poor Ronald, the man who was killed. He seemed a nice gentleman.*

Rachel: *Now I'm worried about you.*

Me: *Don't worry. I can look after myself. How are things with you? What are you up to?*

Rachel: *I just got home with a pile of legal documents to wade through with a couple of glasses of wine.*

Me: *How long will that take you?*

Rachel: *Four hours or so. I'll be up half the night.*

Me: *Good luck. I'll let you get onto it.*

After resting for a while, I walked back the way I had come. I'd only ventured through a tiny portion of the park, but I was far too tired to walk further. I could explore more of the park at other times. This could be something to do every couple of days to build up my strength and fitness.

Might Raven come with me on some of those outings?

My thoughts returned to Chirtlewood House and the untimely death of Ronald Morris. No way could it have been an accident. It was definitely murder. Someone killed him and stole the witch's spell book.

A pang of regret filled me. I wanted to see inside that book in case I could help Aunt Ruth, or so she could help herself with the healing magic it contained. Was it really a witch's spell book? The murderer likely thought so.

I'd neglected to tell the police about the stolen spell book. I hadn't meant to forget... but I didn't mind. To the police, that wouldn't be important. They wouldn't seriously consider following a line of inquiry about a stolen book purporting to contain witchy spells in a police investigation.

But I would consider it. I wasn't going to let that book disappear without trying to find it.

And if I found it, I was sure I'd find the murderer at the same time.

A stab of doubt hit me. Investigating a murder was beyond me, surely. How could I think I might pull this off?

I trudged along, worn out now. *Look at me after walking less than an hour. Exhausted.*

I was being too hard on myself. I'd come a long way since the operation—and not just in distance.

Yes, I got tired easily, but I was still recovering from the major surgery I'd had. The surgeon had told me it might be months before I was back to my old self.

Yes, I hadn't been assertive or confident in the past, but I'd been living with a bully who took me for granted.

Now that was all in the past. I'd chosen to change my life. I had a second chance now to create a new me. And I could craft that me to be whoever I chose.

While I hadn't been assertive in the past, that could change. I could stand on my own feet, take care of myself, accomplish whatever I set out to do. I'd always been capable. I'd taught a high school history class, dammit!

I would not be passive any more. I'd prove to everyone my worth by setting out to solve the murder and recover the witch's spell book. Finding the murderer would bring justice for Ronald. But the real prize was the spell book. There would surely be something in there to help cure Aunt Ruth.

Damn right. I might even get myself fit too.

Chapter 20

I DROVE HOME, A PECULIAR mixture of melancholy and self-confidence in my heart.

Ronald Morris hadn't deserved to die. Someone in the house had done it. Presumably, someone I'd seen that morning. But who?

I parked in the driveway and went inside. Would Raven be there? What would he say to explain his sudden disappearance last night?

He had gone out or, perhaps, hadn't returned from last night. So, I couldn't confront him and demand an explanation. But the silver lining was that I could ask Aunt Ruth what was going on with him. Assuming she knew, of course.

She was in the living room, reading a book on wheelchair yoga.

'If you do that, you'll soon be fitter than I am,' I said with a grin.

She looked sideways at me without raising her head. 'That wouldn't take much, Heather.'

Ouch. That barb hurt because it was so close to the truth. *No. It is the truth.*

'I've been for a walk,' I said. 'I have to start somewhere, but my recovery is taking longer than I hoped. How about I take you for walks in Richmond Park? Maybe every couple of days? That'll give you some fresh air, and I'll get fitter.'

Aunt Ruth smiled. 'I was only joking, dear. We all do the best we can. We're not spring chickens, you know. We're old birds now.'

'I'm only a middle-aged bird, and I'll have you know that forty-odd is the new thirty-odd, so I'm not really middle-aged either. I'm still young in heart and mind.'

My aunt eyed me with interest. 'Something's different about you. What's up? Have you had a few Proseccos?' She paused. 'Aren't you supposed to be at work?'

'Something terrible happened. A visitor to the house was murdered.'

'Blazing carbuncles!' Her expression changed to one of concern, and she put her book down. 'Are you all right, Heather?'

I took a deep breath and exhaled. 'I'm sad about it, but I coped. Someone killed the poor man in the library with a candlestick. The police are at the house now, investigating. They sent everyone home.'

'Farting familiars! Luckily, it wasn't you they got. Why was he killed?'

'No one knows for sure, but a witch's spell book he was studying at the time was stolen, along with his handwritten notes, so that's probably the reason.'

'What spell book?' Now Aunt Ruth's interest was piqued. Her eyes brightened and widened with curiosity.

'I only saw it for a few seconds. I intended to get photos of several of the interior pages, but it's too late now.'

'And someone killed the unfortunate man for it? It must be valuable. Or important.'

'He told me he couldn't read it himself, but it apparently contains spells, some of which are powerful.' I hesitated. 'They include healing spells. That's why I wanted to take photos. To see if any of those spells might help you regain your mobility. If you can read them, that is.'

Aunt Ruth's eyebrows went up, but she kept her voice level. 'I probably can. I'm well versed in witchy language. But I can't cast any powerful healing spells without my magic mirror. Without it, I'm reduced to casting simple domestic spells or the equivalent.'

I let this sink in for a minute while my stomach twisted with guilt. 'You didn't need me to come over and help you around the house, did you?'

'No, but with your mother gone, I needed to get you over here so I could teach you about magic, now that you're coming into your menopausal witchy awakening. I couldn't leave it any longer.'

That was ambiguous. 'You couldn't leave it any longer because I needed to learn soon... or because you thought you wouldn't be around to teach me later on?'

She looked away. 'That's a discussion for another time. It's moot now, anyway. I can't teach you any of the advanced stuff until you've mastered the basics, and we need to get hold of that witch's spell book too.'

My head spun. 'You've lost me, Aunt Ruth. You said you couldn't use the spell book without the magic mirror.' *Which I broke.* I internally cringed with shame.

'Ah, but we need to have the spell book so we have something to trade with the warlock for getting the magic mirror repaired.'

Now I got it. I absolutely had to find the spell book for Aunt Ruth's sake. 'But the spell book belongs to Chirtlewood House. I can't give it away. I'd be fired. What about copying it?'

'Yes, that's the plan. I didn't mean we'd give away the original. We only need to borrow it for a while.'

'Okay.' Something in Aunt Ruth's expression rang alarm bells in my head. 'Making a copy is difficult? Is that what you're not telling me?'

'It's problematic. We can't just pop down to the print shop to have it photocopied. That will only produce blank pages. There'll be strong witchy protection in place, for sure.'

'So, we need powerful magic to copy the spell book?'

Aunt Ruth nodded. 'That's the only way. And, at the moment, I can't do it myself.'

Fuuuuck.

'We'll have to let the warlock do it,' she continued.

Now it made sense. He would fix Aunt Ruth's magic mirror in return for making a copy of the spell book to keep for himself. Then, with her magic mirror repaired, Aunt Ruth could copy it too and see if the healing spells within could help her walk again.

I breathed a sigh of relief. We had a plan. Find the spell book, find the warlock, get the magic mirror fixed, Aunt Ruth heals herself. Those are the ducks to put in a row. Several complicated—if not impossible—ducks, but I'd line them up somehow.

Aunt Ruth changed the subject. 'How did your date with Raven go?'

I shook my head, exasperated with the memory of it. 'It went well, up to a point, anyway. He... sort of... disappeared on me. I haven't seen him since. It was weird. Is there... uh, is there something special about Raven?'

'Ah, I wondered if this might come up.' Aunt Ruth nodded vigorously. 'All I'm going to say is: talk to him about it and keep an open mind.'

Well, that helped... not.

I MADE BRIE, APPLE and ham sandwiches for lunch. Aunt Ruth and I ate them in the living room. Afterwards, I phoned a company I'd looked up to build a wheelchair ramp up to the house and arranged for them to do it the next morning. Once I knew Aunt Ruth didn't need me for anything, I drove to Richmond upon Thames.

Elvis—I'd call him Elvis because he hadn't said his real name—must have left Chirtlewood House on the morning of Ronald's murder before we'd closed the entrance. He'd only been there a few minutes in all. Why so short a visit? I intended to find him and ask.

He'd told me he was staying at a boutique hotel in Richmond. Of course, he may have been lying, but it was the only lead I had. The stress and upset of the morning were still all too real, and I couldn't even remember if I'd told the constable or the inspector about Elvis.

After I parked the car, I walked along the Thames into the heart of Richmond. It was a beautiful village with eclectic shops, a variety of restaurants and cafés and lovely views of the river. Somewhere, there would be a boutique hotel. To me, 'boutique' meant fancy and expensive, the sort of place I could never afford and wouldn't belong in even if I could afford it.

Google Maps listed a few hotels. I soon discovered they were all classified as boutique. Richmond upon Thames was an affluent place, and it accommodated affluent visitors.

At the first hotel, I struck gold when I asked the receptionist, 'Do you have anyone staying here who was dressed this morning like Elvis Presley, the rock star?'

The receptionist grinned. 'Sure, we do. We've got twenty of them. The Elvis lookalike convention is on this afternoon.'

I groaned inwardly. I might have to wait around to find the right one.

'It starts in half an hour if you want to watch. Upstairs.'

'Thank you.' I took the stairs instead of the elevator. Every little bit of exercise helps, I told myself. Every long journey starts with a single step, as the saying goes. Or a thousand steps. It seemed like a thousand, anyway.

Several Elvises (or should that be Elvii?) mingled outside a large double meeting room on the second floor. I stopped to catch my breath at the top of the stairs before venturing into the throng of rock and roll impersonators.

'You're the woman from Chirtlewood House, aren't you?'

I spun. My Elvis had found me himself.

'I recognised you,' he said. 'Did you come looking for me?' He raised one eyebrow and smirked. 'Or are you interested in the convention?'

'I didn't know there was a convention,' I said, unsure of how to introduce the subject. I couldn't simply come out and ask him if he'd killed Ronald and stolen the witch's spell book. He might push me down the stairs. Besides, the whole idea sounded far-fetched. But someone had murdered Ronald. Maybe Elvis had seen something.

'Why are you here, then?' Puzzlement creased Elvis's face.

'There was an... incident at Chirtlewood a few minutes after we spoke there. On the upper floor in the library. We gathered all the visitors together afterwards, and you weren't there. I wondered why. The house had only just opened. You couldn't have seen much of it before you left.'

'Oh, that. Unfortunately, I got a phone call, and I had to return here urgently. My friend, who's also an Elvis lookalike, needed help with his costume. I didn't have time to go back to the manor.'

That sounded credible. As an history teacher, I'd developed a good sense of when pupils were lying from years of listening to excuses why they hadn't completed their homework. Elvis appeared to be telling me the truth.

'I understand. Thanks, uh, Elvis. I don't suppose you saw anything or anyone suspicious? Someone in a hurry? Someone trying to conceal a bulky book?'

'No, sorry, I can't help you. What was the incident?'

I hesitated. Should I tell him? It would be in the afternoon newspaper, anyway, so I went ahead. 'Someone murdered a researcher in the library and stole some materials.'

Elvis's shock was genuine. 'That's terrible.'

'Look, can I give you my phone number? If you think of anything, you can call me. I'm kind of investigating this myself privately.'

'No problem.' He entered it into his phone.

I went downstairs and out into Richmond, where I spent a few minutes sitting on the riverbank, watching bird life on the river.

What should I do next.? And is Raven out there somewhere?

IN THE MID-AFTERNOON, I returned home. Aunt Ruth was in the dining room, talking to Raven about something at the desk where his books and study notes lay. At least he was home now and hadn't ended up as roadkill or a hawk's lunch.

I didn't want to disturb them, but they called me over.

Raven seemed contrite. 'I'm truly sorry, Heather. I guess I should tell you about my condition—'

I pulled over a chair. 'I think you'd better. I definitely want to hear this.'

'I'll leave you two to it.' Aunt Ruth rolled out of the room.

'Ruth knows all this,' Raven said. 'She insisted I tell you. I didn't want to at first because I didn't even know if you intended to stay in England or return to New Zealand. But you seem to be staying, and we're... attracted to each other... aren't we?'

'I thought so, but now I'm not so sure. Whenever we have a little time together, you vanish without warning. I didn't know what was going on. Is it that you aren't interested?'

He shook his head vehemently. 'It's not that. I have an affliction. It's from an ex-girlfriend.'

Oh right. Now he would tell me he's got an STD, and that's why he doesn't want to—

Raven continued. 'She was a witch, and when we broke up, she didn't take it well. She laid a curse on me.'

'A curse?' Not an STD, then. 'Is that why you change into an actual raven?'

He nodded, eyes downcast. 'Yeah. She thought that was a hilarious idea. The curse is that whenever I become excited, or aroused, or even experience joy at any level, I turn into a raven, like my name.'

'It could have been worse.'

'Yeah, I know. Anyway, I can't control it. Sometimes it takes a day until I shift back to human form.'

This horrified me. Sympathy for Raven filled my heart. What a terrible thing to endure. 'So... you couldn't prevent yourself changing when you were out with me because you were enjoying yourself? That's what you're saying?'

'Pretty much.'

'That must be a downer when it comes to relationships.'

'Completely.' Raven's expression was strained.

Questions whirred in my mind. 'How long has this been going on?'

He exhaled a long, held-in breath. 'Longer than I'd care to say. Your aunt has been helping me research ways to lift curses. Nothing's worked so far.'

'Your ex-girlfriend must have really wanted to get back at you for something. You weren't cheating on her, were you?'

'No, I wasn't cheating on her.'

'And you have no control over changing form at all?'

'I'm working on it. Sometimes, but not always, I can shift into raven form if I want to. However, I have no control over the curse aspect that forces the change when I am happy or excited. Nor can I change back at will. Sometimes it happens without a lot of warning.'

'That could be embarrassing. I feel sorry for you, Raven. But look on the bright side.'

'I don't need pity, Heather. You think there's a bright side to this? Tell me.'

'At least you're not a chicken-shifter.'

'Haha.' He didn't seem amused.

'Is there anything I can do to help?'

'I don't think so. Your aunt might be able to do something if we can find the right spell to lift the curse. That's what I've been looking for in these books'—he gestured to the volumes on the desk—'for years.'

'Years! Shit!'

Raven nodded sadly. 'My ex-girlfriend wanted me to suffer.'

'You haven't tried to talk to her and ask her to remove the curse?'

He raised his hands in the air, exasperated. 'I would, but I don't even know where she is!'

At least my ex wasn't as vengeful as Raven's. 'I suppose lifting a curse is high-level witchy magic?'

'Yes, it is. That's why I need your aunt to do it once we've found a suitable spell.'

Realisation hit me. 'But she can't do that without the mirror, can she?'

'What mirror? The one you broke?'

'It's where Aunt Ruth stores energy for powerful magic.'

A shadow passed over Raven's face. 'Shit.' He sighed. 'Anyway, we haven't found the right spell, so the mirror isn't the problem at the moment.'

Did this change anything? No. It just gave me more reason to find the stolen witch's spell book so we could afford to get the magic mirror fixed.

'And where does that leave us?' I asked. 'Regarding dating, I mean? Are you always going to take flight?'

'I should get it under control soon enough, once...'

'Once you become used to being with me.'

'Yeah,' he admitted. 'It's not a very romantic notion, I know, but it is what it is.'

'And what about if we want to have sex?'

Raven froze, his expression unreadable for a moment before a flash of light made me close my eyes. When the spots before my eyes cleared and I opened them, Raven was gone—at least, he was gone in human form. A black bird sat on the back of the chair, glaring at me. It launched itself into the air and out of a nearby open window. It disappeared into the distance.

Aunt Ruth rolled in. Maybe I'd made a noise, or she'd seen the bright flash of light. 'What on earth did you say to him, Heather?'

'I'm sure it was nothing he didn't want to hear, Aunt Ruth.'

Aunt Ruth peered past the chair. 'Cantankerous cauldrons! He's gone and pooped on the desk.'

Chapter 21

AFTER CLEANING UP THE mess, I asked Aunt Ruth if she wanted a hot drink. 'Maybe you could teach me how to make it with magic?' I suggested.

'We need to find the plastic picnic set to practise with first. It's in the attic somewhere.'

'Okay. I'll look for it some other time. I want to get back to Chirtlewood this afternoon.'

'But you said the police closed the place.'

'It's closed to the public. They might let me in, though, because I work there. I want to... talk to a few people there.'

Aunt Ruth narrowed her eyes. 'A few people? You don't mean the police, do you?'

'No. Okay, they're sort of not people who I want to talk to.'

'You mean you want to talk to the ghosts there?'

'You know about them?'

'Only the ghost stories that go around. The place is four hundred years old, and this is England. It's bound to have ghosts.'

'What makes them earthbound, Aunt Ruth? For so long? Surely, if there was something they had to do before they moved on, they'd have done it by now, or it's too late. Everyone they knew when they were alive has been dead for centuries.'

Aunt Ruth shook her head. 'It's impossible to say. Maybe they never did what they needed to do and simply forgot how to move on. Maybe there's a window of time before that option is closed to them. I wouldn't worry about it, Heather. There's nothing you can do about helping them with that. Even if there was, it's not your problem. It's their afterlife journey.'

She was right. I shouldn't interfere by trying to 'help' them. If they wanted help, they'd ask.

'I'll ask them if they saw who killed the researcher. That's if I can find any of them.'

'How many of them are there?'

'I've talked with two, and I've seen another one who was maybe a bit shy.'

'A shy ghost. I see. And if you learn anything, what will you do? Pass it on to the police? You think they'll believe you if you say the witnesses are ghosts?'

I frowned. 'You're right. I can't tell the police, but if the ghosts can tell me something, it might lead me to the murderer.'

Aunt Ruth gasped. 'And why do you want that information?'

'To recover the stolen spell book, of course.'

Aunt Ruth reached out and grabbed my arm. 'It's too dangerous, Heather. Leave it to the police. That's their job.'

I wasn't going to give way on this. 'I'll take care of myself. Don't worry.'

'Please reconsider. I'm worried about you.'

'I'll be fine.' I tried to sound confident.

'You could ask Raven to help you. I'm sure he'd be willing to do that.'

And he'd fly off at the first sign of excitement. 'I'll think about it.'

'You won't let me talk you out of this?' Aunt Ruth implored.

I shook my head. I had to do something. Sitting on my hands wasn't an option. If I solved the mystery and recovered the stolen book, I'd be delighted. What a start to my new life that would be. I had to try.

SHORTLY AFTERWARDS, I said goodbye to Aunt Ruth and drove to Chirtlewood.

The ambulance was gone. The police cars were still there, and so was the crime scene tape.

I asked the officer guarding the area if I could enter, and she phoned the inspector.

Inspector Pentecost came down the steps and approached. 'You've returned to the scene of the crime, then? Heather Nicholls, isn't it?'

'That's right.' What did she mean about returning to the scene of the crime?

'How can I help you? Did you forget to tell me something?'

Should I tell her about Elvis? No, that would be a waste of police time. I'd already checked him out myself. 'I'd like to come inside, if that's all right. There is tidying and other chores to do. I can stay downstairs, out of the way.'

The inspector regarded me with a curious gaze. 'We've finished downstairs. You can come in, but don't go upstairs or on the stairs at all. We're still working on those areas.'

'Found anything helpful?' My curiosity never stayed down for long.

'I can't discuss that at the present time, Ms Nicholls. Once we have examined everything relevant, we might share some information with you and your colleagues to see if it jogs your memory. I'm sure you understand.'

'Of course.'

She lifted the crime scene tape, and I ducked underneath it. Once inside, I went to the little office we all shared. There were a few things to tidy up, as we'd left in unusual circumstances that morning. But that wasn't why I was here.

I spent a few minutes doing the chores, then sat at the table where we'd had the pastries. When I was certain the inspector wasn't coming back, I whispered, 'My Lady. Are you here, somewhere?'

No answer. Naturally. Why would the countess of Chirtle hang around a pokey office when there is the rest of this marvellous house to roam in?

I made my way to the drawing room. It was full of the afternoon light. Dust motes swirled in the air disturbed by my entrance.

The furniture was roped off so visitors couldn't sit on it. I walked on the designated pathway around to the bay windows that looked out onto the expansive lawn and gardens.

Movement caught my eye. A dog. No owner was in sight.

Was it Scruffles? I couldn't tell from where I stood. Maybe I needed to get my eyes checked again. I'd put that off for ages. Eventually, I'd have to have glasses.

'My Lady? Can you hear me? May I talk with you?' I said to the empty room.

Doubt filled my mind. Why would the countess be listening? Even if she was, would she come because I called?

But she did.

She appeared nearby, reclining on a chaise lounge. Her hair was tied up in a giant red bundle, contrasting with her white facial makeup. 'Heather. Thee hast called. Fortunately, I had naught to do this day. For what purpose didst thee call me hither?'

'Thank you for coming, My Lady. There's something I want to ask.'

'Well, then.' She tossed her head nonchalantly. 'Inquire of me what thee desire.'

'There was an incident this morning. A gentleman was killed in the library.'

'Oh, that. Maisey hath told me of the tragedy. Most dreadful. What a calamity. Poor gent, he hadst not a chance.'

'Do you know anything about it? I mean, did anyone see what happened, or see anyone leaving the house in a hurry, or—'

'Nay, the earl and I wast in my bedchamber, engaged in passionate activities.'

'Ah.' The thought of the elderly earl and his younger wife having ghostly sex passed through my mind and made an imprint that might be forever ingrained in my memory. 'So, you wouldn't have heard anything either, My Lady?'

'Alas, our attentions wast occupied elsewhere. The earl wast most eager.'

'Is that so?'

'Forsooth, being deceased hath its advantages. One nay longer needs to dread the onset of discomfort during energetic nuptial activities.'

My face warmed. Couldn't she change the subject? 'You said Maisey told you about the murder. Who's Maisey?'

'Poor girl. She wast the daughter of one of our serfs and succumbed of the spotted ague. I believe the gentry of the present day name it "measles", do they not? She resides in the manor with us. Her family's hovel wast destroyed long ago for a road or something.'

'Oh, I've seen her. She was watching when the police interviewed everyone in the entrance hall.'

'Aye, I remember now. Maisey recounted the tale to the earl and me earlier.'

'But she didn't see who killed Mr Morris, My Lady?'

'Nay. None of us did.'

So, this was a dead end. 'Thank you, My Lady.'

The countess huffed an exaggerated breath and waved her fan. 'Verily, I beseech thee, Heather, to discontinue using this "My Lady" honorific when addressing me. I understand 'tis an imposition for thee to utter it, and I am, by no means, unaware that society hath changed immensely since my time. Times wast, in my youth, far more stringent in regards to matters of amorous rite, wage and general etiquette. 'Tis clear to me that, of late, thee and thy compatriots hither and yon hast adopted the use of first names in conversation, which wast quite unbecoming in my day. I do not see it as such nowadays amongst you millennials.'

'I'm not a millennial, My L—, I mean, Charlotte. Shall I call you Charlotte?'

'Charlotte is acceptable. Banger, then. Thou art a banger. I wilt confess I am at a loss with regards to what 'tis thee bang.'

'You mean "Boomer". But it's Gen X for me. It's a narrow window of people born around the same few years.'

'Gen X! Ah, a term of which I hast heard, in all its futuristic splendour.' She clapped her fan closed with a snap. 'Hast thee visited the stars, or does that still remain an aspiration?'

That caught me by surprise. 'No, and it's not something I plan to do either. How do you know all these modern-day terms, Charlotte?'

'Paying heed to the guests. 'Tis true that oft times their rant does seem quite nonsensical. Still, I am able to extract portions of the nearby dialect.'

I nodded. 'We've gotten off track. I'd hoped you or the earl, or Maisey, might have seen who killed Ronald Morris and could describe them to me.'

'Forgive me, my dear. Mayhap thee ought to seek out Ronnie himself.'

My eyes widened. 'Ronnie? You mean, I can get in touch with him somehow?'

'Verily, aye. He wast present in the dining hall when I saw him last. Pray, allow us to investigate if it be true he is still thither.'

I was flabbergasted at the possibility that I might talk to Mr Morris's ghost directly, or even that his ghost might be hanging around.

'Time is of the essence. For he wast already in a state of fading.'

'What do you mean by "fading"?'

The countess replied grimly, 'He is passing into the ether. I know not of his fate, but I am aware that once they begin to dissipate, they art soon gone and nevermore art they seen.'

'All right, let's go.'

I scurried out of the drawing room into the downstairs passage and turned into the dining room. The countess was already there. She must have taken a ghostly shortcut.

Ronald sat in a chair at the vast oak table, scribbling with an invisible pen on invisible notes. The chair back was evident through his translucent torso.

'Mr Morris?' I gasped, still struggling to take in this other-worldly situation.

He looked up. A distinctive lump stood out on the side of his head.

'Heather, isn't it?' He smiled, his mood a real contrast to anything I might have expected. Why wasn't he upset at being murdered?

Maybe all earthly cares and stresses dissolved after death.

'I'm so sorry, Mr Morris. What happened?'

He shook his head, sadness now on his face. 'Some bugger hit me with something heavy when I was in the library.'

'I know that much. They hit you with a candlestick. Did you see who it was? Can you describe them?' He was fading fast now, and desperation clawed at my throat.

'They came from behind me. I didn't hear them. I was busy taking notes from the witch's spell book.'

He was only an outline now. 'But did you see who hit you?'

'It was over so quickly. I didn't even have time to react. It was— Wait, what's this? There's a light here. A bright, warm light.'

'He is about to depart,' the countess whispered. 'Tarry not!'

I couldn't detect a light, but I understood the urgency. 'Mr Morris. Quickly! Who did you see?'

He opened his mouth and seemed about to speak, but no words came forth. The other side of the room was visible through the back of his throat. Then he found his voice, faint and barely audible.

'It was... it was...' He struggled, his arms and legs wisping away.

I groaned. It's too late. Why is it in movies when someone is about to say who shot or poisoned or stabbed or hit them, they always say 'it was...' and then die? Why did no one ever say the name of the murderer first? It was the most important piece of information.

Ronald would disappear without telling me the name. Like in those damned movies.

Only his head and the top half of his torso remained hovering above the dining room chair. His smile widened. Perhaps the light was a happy one, or it illuminated somewhere he wanted to be.

With a herculean effort, he breathed out his last few ghostly words. 'It was from behind me. I didn't see them.'

He vanished.

'Shit!' What a let-down. I wanted to help Ronald, but I didn't know how.

'Is everything all right, Heather? I heard voices.'

I spun. Inspector Pentecost stood in the doorway.

I glanced at Charlotte, who walked around the table to the windows, and turned back to face the inspector.

She followed my gaze. 'Who were you speaking to? There's no one here.'

Charlotte obviously wasn't revealing her presence to the inspector. 'Oh, I was on my phone.'

'You sounded upset.'

'It's been a disturbing day, Inspector.'

'Of course. So... when you say you were talking on your phone, you don't mean this one you left in the office?' She held up my phone. 'I noticed it in the office when I went to look for you.'

I reddened. Heat flushed my face. *Shit. How do I get out of this predicament?*

I took a deep breath. 'Sometimes, I talk to myself, Inspector. Especially in times of stress. You know how it is.'

'No, I don't.' She strode forward and put the phone on the dining table.

'Thanks,' I muttered.

Her gaze hardened. 'No problem. I thought I'd tell you in person, seeing as you are here. I'll phone your colleagues shortly. You can reopen Chirtlewood tomorrow as long as you completely seal the library off—door shut, locked if possible, and roped off. We don't want anyone going in yet as we might want to have another look at things.'

'That's great. Thank you, Inspector.'

She turned and left the room without responding. I wiped my forehead to remove the sheen of sweat that had accumulated there. No doubt the inspector had noticed it. What was she thinking? That I was a little crazy, maybe? Hopefully, she'd think I was merely having a hot flash.

That would be preferable to her thinking I was lying, hiding something or guilty. Or all three.

Charlotte was still there, peering out through the windows.

I joined her. 'My brief career as an amateur investigator isn't going well.'

The countess inclined her head. ''Tis early days. Perchance thee shalt require assistance.'

'I have someone I can ask, but he's a little unreliable.'

The countess grinned, audibly cracking her caked-on white makeup. 'I'll help. I shalt call upon yon earl and his faithful companion, Scruffles, as well as young Maisey.'

MY PHONE RANG SHORTLY after midnight, waking me from a fretful sleep.

I sat bolt upright and looked at the display. Rose. I scrambled to join the video chat. 'Rose. What's the matter?'

'Nothing's the matter, Mum. I'm only calling to see how you are. I'm between lectures.'

'It's very late here. Midnight.' The witching hour.

'Oh, sorry! I've muddled up the time zone conversion. I thought it was ten o'clock. I'll call back later.'

'No, wait. I'm awake now. Let's talk.'

'Okay, great. How are things going?'

'You wouldn't believe it.' I told her about the murdered researcher and how I'd started my own private investigation and tracked down Elvis.

Rose punctuated my story with sharp intakes of breath and gasps of horror. 'That's terrible, Mum! Are you safe to continue working there?'

'I'm sure I am. I love working at Chirtlewood House.' *Besides, I need a job, and I'm intrigued by the ghosts. I wouldn't leave, even if it was dangerous.*

I didn't mention the ghosts to Rose. One day, I would have to, because she might inherit the witch skills from me.

'You've gone quiet, Mum. I sense there's something you're not telling me.'

My daughter was far too astute. 'I'll talk to you about it face-to-face when I see you next. It's... something I learned from Aunt Ruth.'

'Okay.' Rose's tone suggested that it wasn't okay. 'Weren't you going on a date the last time I spoke to you? How'd that go?'

'About as well as eating a package of soggy sandwiches. I have no complaint about the food, though. The date itself didn't work out. We're going to try again soon.'

'Try again? You're trying to date? Well, I suppose you are out of practise.' She sniggered. 'The dating scene has changed a bit since last century, Mum.'

'I gathered that,' I said dryly.

'I have a confession to make. Don't get mad. I told Dad where you are.'

'You what? I specifically asked you not to do that.'

'Yeah, well, he kept insisting. He said he needed your address to forward on some papers about the house for signing.'

'No, my lawyer will email them. He tricked you.'

'Yeah, I realised that afterwards. Sorry, Mum, I wasn't thinking. But at least he won't come knocking on your door, will he? You're on the other side of the world.'

He'd better not.

'I need to get back to sleep, Rose. I've got work in the morning, and it's late.'

'Okay. Sorry about calling after midnight. Speak soon.' She disconnected.

I put the phone down and fell asleep almost immediately.

Chapter 22

A SOMBRE MOOD HUNG in the office the next morning when we ate the pastries Melissa had brought in. We drank a toast of tea to Ronald Morris. Lydia shed a few tears again.

We all missed him. Even me, who had only known him briefly.

After Lydia said it was time to get the house ready for visitors, she pulled me aside once Penny and Melissa had left the office.

'I know you can see our ghosts,' she said. 'So, you're a witch, Heather. How advanced are you?'

She'd caught me by surprise. 'Um... I'm a beginner. I didn't even know anything about witchy things until recently. I was told the abilities don't appear in my family before the mid-forties.'

Lydia laid a hand on my shoulder. Her expression serious, she asked, 'Do you have a mentor?'

'Yes. Do you mind me asking... how do you know about witches, Lydia? Are you—'

'Yes, I am. I'm quite new at this myself. I have a few simple spells and supernatural senses. I first saw our ghostly occupants about a year ago.'

A thrill of joy raced through me. Lydia was a witch too!

'Maybe we can learn together! If it works like that, and if you want to, I mean.'

She smiled. 'That would be great. Have you started on the correspondence course yet?'

'Not yet. My first lessons haven't arrived, but I've signed up.'

'It's so nice to find another witch. There aren't many of us around. Only a few descendants of the old witch families remain.'

I had a sudden thought. 'Do Penny and Melissa know?' I whispered.

'No. And we shouldn't tell them either. You've heard of the Salem witch trials, haven't you?'

I nodded. 'I know they had similar horrors here, too. Burning witches at the stake and drowning them. But that was centuries ago. It's not like that now.'

'No, but memories run long and pain runs deep. Witches keep to themselves for safety.'

'Makes sense.'

'Penny and Melissa might suspect that I can see the ghosts,' Lydia said, 'but neither of them has ever said anything. In this village, and in this house and others like it nearby, supernatural things occur. Bumps on the stairs. Doors slamming when no one is nearby. Sometimes, a ghostly figure appears to visitors. I'm sure they accept the paranormal exists. And the library contains many books on those subjects.'

Melissa called out from the other side of the door. 'We're opening the entrance! It's time. What are you two up to in there?'

'I was giving Heather a bit more training,' Lydia called back. 'We'll be there in a tick.'

I wanted to talk to Lydia more about this, but we needed to get on with managing Chirtlewood for visitors.

Penny and I went upstairs, leaving the others downstairs. The library was closed off, as the police had instructed. Penny took up a position on the landing near the top of the grand staircase. I moved from room to room, checking that nothing was out of place and keeping tourists in sight. The first of them were already coming upstairs, a young couple with Canadian accents. I watched as they entered the countess's bedchamber.

I followed them inside and answered their detailed questions about the countess and her life. Charlotte made that easier by pacing around behind them—without alerting them to her presence—and telling me most of the answers.

'Oh, you're so knowledgeable,' the young woman said afterwards. I grinned. I'd learned almost as much as them, like the countess had died at age forty-seven by breaking her neck after tripping on her dress at the top of the stairs, cutting short her career of manipulating people for political influence.

Once they had gone, Charlotte drifted over to me. 'I hast assembled the party,' she said. 'Shalt we commence the hunt for the villainous knave? Pray tell me, to what direction shouldst our inquiry lead us?'

I had no plan beyond the idea of forming a plan. How did private investigators get started on a case? They had leads. I didn't have any leads apart from Elvis, and I no longer considered him a suspect.

'Tarry nay longer!' The countess crossed her arms. Her ghostly foot tapped silently.

She clearly wasn't used to being kept waiting. My mind raced, searching for ideas. If I had no clues to track down the murderer, I could try to find the book. Maybe the killer had sold it, and if I could find it, I might solve the murder at the same time.

My priority was the book, anyway. I could leave the murder for the police to tackle.

'Are you able to leave Chirtlewood house and grounds?' I asked Charlotte. 'Or are you tied to this area only?'

'Chirtlewood and nearby is our earthbound centre, though we can venture to Richmond and Ham House and Hampton Court and Kingston and a few other nearby places. Pray tell, art we to journey forth on an adventure?'

'The murderer stole one of the library books. A witch's spell book. Finding it might help solve the mystery.' And help Aunt Ruth.

'Splendid! I know just the shop in Richmond. 'Tis the Apothecary's Potions and Scrolls. 'Tis said they buy and sell ancient occult tomes.'

'Really? Doesn't it attract attention from the public?'

'Most of the common folk pass by the store with nary a glance, for they perceive it to be nothing more than a trifling curiosity shop. Only witches know the sooth of its intent, that the inside is filled with potions and tools used by witches.'

'All right. Let's go there as soon as I finish here for the day.'

'Heather, as I already hast said, I hast assembled the party. They await thee at the front steps.'

'Near the entrance? They're not frightening the tourists, are they?'

'Who can say what they may do? The time drags, and 'tis yet too long in tarrying. We wilt be off forthwith.' She swept off towards the grand staircase, tossing her long hair over her shoulder.

I followed as fast as I could, struggling to keep up.

Charlotte breezed past Penny, who shivered.

'Where are you going in such a rush, Heather? Is something wrong?'

'No, not at all. I, um, remembered something I have to do. I'll be back soon.' I descended the stairs after Charlotte, who had already drifted to the landing halfway down.

'Don't leave me alone up here!' Penny called. A pang of guilt stabbed me in the chest. Penny would be nervous about being alone so close to the room in which someone had murdered Ronald only yesterday.

'Wait!' I shout-whispered to the countess as she strode to the front door.

Should I ask Lydia if I could take an hour or two off for an appointment or something to explain my sudden absence? She wasn't anywhere in sight, and Charlotte wasn't waiting. I continued past Melissa, who was busy selling a ticket to a new visitor, and outside, then down the steps to the gravel pathway.

A small group of ghosts hung around under a tree to the side of the path leading to the house, apparently invisible to the visitors nearby. I breathed a sigh of relief.

Charlotte and Thomas, the earl, stood together. The earl appeared decades older than the countess, though in life they had an age gap of only four years. Unfortunately, in death, it appeared their ghostly forms bore the age and condition in which they'd died. The countess appeared strong and fit, whereas the earl was a slightly hunched figure with a walking stick who might struggle with anything more taxing than a garden stroll.

The dog, Scruffles, dashed about playfully near the earl's feet. Beyond them, the young girl, Maisey, scratched at the spots on her face. She'd probably done that for centuries. They would never disappear.

'Allow us to be off!' Charlotte said, hands on hips. 'I shalt guide the way to the Apothecary's Potions and Scrolls.'

I wasn't so sure this was practical. I didn't want to be non-inclusive, but I was leaving work without authorisation, and I didn't want to be gone too long. 'My Lord,' I said, addressing the earl directly, 'are you able to manage the journey on foot?'

'Zounds, nay,' he harrumphed. 'I hast a wheelchair contraption. Lady Chirtle can push.' He snapped his fingers, and a ghostly ancient wheelchair appeared before him. It consisted of little more than a tatty leather seat and a basic wooden frame comprising arms, handles and wheels. The earl settled gently into it. Charlotte took up a position behind it.

'I guess that'll work,' I muttered.

We set off, Maisey leading, the countess and the earl at the rear, and me between them with Scruffles running back and forth around everyone's legs, in a bizarre procession to Richmond village. The countess chatted incessantly, requiring me to respond, which drew odd glances from people we passed by, who could only see me talking and gesticulating to myself. Behind me, the earl complained about everything from the weather to the state of the river to the outrageous dresses young women wore nowadays to the raven who appeared to be flitting alongside the river, keeping pace with us.

Was that Raven himself? There was no way of knowing.

Charlotte turned off the riverfront after we reached the village and ducked into a narrow side street. She turned into another one that ran parallel to the river behind the main riverside shops. The few buildings here appeared to be industrial, and the few retail ones had outlaid little on signage, marketing and even paint.

She came to a halt outside a two-storey building, an old villa that had been converted into a shop. 'Verily, we hast arrived.'

I opened the door and went in. A chime rang. My ghost companions came through the window next to the door, traversing through the glass as if it wasn't there. I hadn't known passing through walls was really a thing for ghosts, but it was. Nothing much surprised me about these guys now.

A man of about sixty with silver-grey hair under a pointy black hat spied Charlotte and approached us. 'Welcome back, Charlotte. I was expecting you.' He glanced at me. 'Who are you?'

I introduced myself and explained how I knew Charlotte and her companions. The man, who introduced himself as Herbert, must also be a witch—a male one.

'You're interested in finding an old book?' he asked.

'Yes.' How did he know? Lucky guess? 'I understand you buy second-hand books. I'm looking for one that may have been brought in here sometime since yesterday morning.'

'What's the title? I bought a few books yesterday.'

'I don't know the title, but I would recognise the book if I saw it. It was old, leather-bound and had a silver-etched title. It's said to be—'

'A witch's spell book,' Herbert finished for me. 'Wow. I'd definitely be interested in that if someone offered it to me, but nothing of that description has come my way for ages.'

I sighed. It was just my luck that this lead also went nowhere. 'Are there any other stores like yours in Richmond or nearby where I could ask about it?'

'No. This is the only reputable specialist shop of its kind in the greater London and Surrey area. If you leave me your contact details, I'll call you if someone comes in with a witch's spell book of that description.'

'All right. Thanks.' I scribbled my name and phone number on a notepad on the counter.

'No problem. So, you're at the beginning of your witchy studies?'

Damn, Herbert has uncanny intuition. 'Yes. I'm still waiting for the first lesson of the correspondence course to arrive.'

Herbert clapped his hands with glee. 'Oh, it's exciting to meet a witch at the start of their learning.'

Scruffles pawed at my leg. I reached down to pat him, but my hand went right through. Charlotte and Maisey were browsing through the shop. The earl watched on from his wheelchair, looking bored.

Herbert beamed. 'I expect your mentor will want to bring you here to buy a few basic items. Every witch needs and should have their own workbooks, equipment and vital ingredients for spells. I can save you a trip by recommending a selection right now, if you like?'

'I should wait until my aunt is ready to help me with that. She's my mentor.'

'Naturally, if that's what you want to do, but I can offer you a ten per cent discount for your purchases today only. It's my standard offer for new customers.'

I tried, but I couldn't say 'no'. Herbert grabbed a basket and my arm and led me into the depths of the shop. What were the basic items? A cauldron and a selection of newts, toads and various herbs? I had no idea.

It turned out that I was right about the herbs, and thankfully wrong about the newts and toads, which I did not wish to take home, dead or alive. While Charlotte and Maisey perused jewellery and other accessories, Herbert put item after item into my shopping basket: incense, herbs, oils, powdered minerals, small crystals, books on basic household spells, workbooks for the correspondence course, and other stuff I didn't even recognise.

'Do I need a cauldron too?' I asked. The basket was becoming heavy, and I didn't want a cast-iron cooking pot added to the pile.

'Oh, no. You can use an air fryer. They're much less messy.'

'I don't have one.' That was too modern a device for Aunt Ruth.

Herbert had already grabbed a box from a nearby shelf and tucked it under his arm. 'That'll do for now to get you started.' He led the way to the payment desk.

'I'll need more than this?'

'Yes. It's not cheap starting out. Let me add this up and apply your discount.' He tapped at a calculator for a minute before he told me the total price.

I swooned. 'I can't afford that.'

'That's not uncommon, and I understand. I'll extend you credit. I know you're working at Chirtlewood. You can pay off the balance over a few weeks.'

'Thanks.' I think.

We set off, with the countess once again pushing the earl's wheelchair. It seemed to require no effort on her behalf.

My shopping bags were heavy. Too heavy to carry all the way back to my car at Chirtlewood, especially with my lack of fitness. By the time we'd reached the riverside, I was panting and had to put them down. I couldn't afford a taxi, but I had little choice.

A taxi stand was close by. I took my time loading my purchases into the trunk so the ghosts could settle themselves on the back seat. Five minutes later, we were back at Chirtlewood. I transferred my purchases to my car and hurried inside.

Lydia met me in the entrance hall. 'Where have you been?' she asked. 'We're short-staffed without you here too. Penny was too nervous to be upstairs on her own, so Melissa joined her, and I've had to monitor the entire ground floor by myself.'

'Sorry. I had a lead on my investigation into Ronald's murder, and I needed to follow it up straightaway.'

'It looked to me like you were out shopping. I saw you put loaded shopping bags into your car.'

'Well... that was from the shop that I went to for the lead. You can ask—' I hesitated. Lydia might not have seen the ghosts with me. They'd vanished once the taxi turned into the car park. I didn't want to blame my leaving work on them. It had been my choice.

'Ask who?' Lydia crossed her arms. A hint of irritation had crept into her voice.

'No one. Never mind. I'm sorry.'

'Remember, we've got to work as a team, Heather. If you need to leave work for something, that's fine, but give me as much warning as possible, please, so we can try to work something out. All right?'

'Sure.'

'Okay. Take over the entrance hall and ticketing. I'm going to make a cup of tea after being run off my feet for the past hour.'

She headed towards the office, leaving me cringing with guilt at having let the team down.

Chapter 23

I WAS ON MY LUNCH BREAK in the office munching on a ham and Swiss cheese sandwich when Lydia entered the room with Inspector Pentecost and a constable. They regarded me with grim expressions.

'What?' I almost choked on a mouthful of food.

The inspector spoke first. 'Heather Nicholls, I'd like you to come to the station with us for a brief chat.'

I slammed my sandwich down on the plate. 'Are you arresting me?'

'No. I want to ask you a few questions, that's all, and it's best to do that at the station.'

On her turf, where she would have the psychological advantage. Well, I wouldn't let that trouble me. The rest of her words were lost as my mind raged with confusion and anger. I got to my feet, the chair scraping loudly on the floor as I pushed it back. 'You can't be serious. Am I a suspect?'

Inspector Pentecost didn't answer. She inclined her head towards the constable, who stepped closer while I protested my innocence.

Lydia eyed me sadly, shaking her head, muttering, 'I don't believe this.'

The inspector spun on her heels and walked out.

I gave up remonstrating and followed. It was best to get it over with. Penny and Melissa watched from the landing on the stairs, gasping. They must have thought I was being arrested. At the bottom of the staircase, Maisey stood motionless, her head inclined as if in curiosity or confusion.

Outside, cloudy skies released their rain. It pattered on the police car as the constable drove us to the police station in Kingston upon Thames. I was escorted into a small and cramped interview room with a desk and two chairs in the centre. The walls were a faded, institutional green. I was left there for ages with nothing to do except contemplate what the hell was going on.

Eventually, the inspector came into the room and offered me a plastic cup of water, which I accepted. She sat opposite me and opened a manila folder and stared at its contents for a couple of minutes.

My skin crawled. What was she looking at? Was she about to accuse me of murder? They had to have found something suspicious that pointed to me, but what?

'Ms Nicholls,' she began. 'I want you to tell me again everything you remember about what happened up to the time you entered the library and found Mr Morris's body.'

I explained it all again, almost word for word as I'd done before. My memory was clear. But this time, I included my meeting with Elvis a few minutes earlier, and how he'd already left the house when we gathered up the visitors after discovering Ronald's body.

'Elvis. Is that so?' The inspector's voice dripped with sarcasm.

'There was a convention on at a hotel in Richmond. You can check. He got a call and had to return there in a hurry. That's why he wasn't in the house when we rounded up the visitors.'

'So, you're telling me I need to find all these Elvises, or Elvii, and interview them?'

I shook my head. 'You could, but it would be a waste of your time. I'm sure Elvis isn't the killer.'

Inspector Pentecost's eyes narrowed almost imperceptibly. 'Your meddling might be interfering with the case.'

'I'm not meddling. I'm only asking questions.'

'So, you're investigating this crime yourself, are you?'

Fortunately, I stopped my big mouth from saying I was investigating it with some ghost friends. Instead, I nodded.

'All right. Putting this Elvis character aside, I've a few things to talk to you about.'

'Okay.' Beads of sweat formed on the back of my neck. I smothered a shiver.

'You were upstairs talking to Mr Morris shortly before his death. You've told me that, and a colleague of yours has confirmed it.'

Melissa. 'That's right.'

'You were very interested in the academic volume Mr Morris was studying. It is quite valuable, isn't it?'

'Yes, I believe so.'

'You didn't mention this book in your statement.'

That's what this was about. 'You're right. I forgot. When I gave my statement, I was concentrating on Mr Morris and on where I and everyone else was at the time the visitor screamed.'

The inspector stood and sauntered around to the front of the desk. She leaned back against it and looked right down at me. I tried not to squirm under her accusing gaze. 'That's rather convenient, forgetting to mention the theft of a priceless academic volume that you were very interested in yourself.'

'It's nothing but a misunderstanding.' My feet twitched. The lines on my forehead creased. Darts of worry raced through me—anxiety that the inspector might accuse me of theft, if not murder.

'That is as may be... but the facts are that you were overheard saying you wanted that book for yourself. You are a new member of staff at Chirtlewood. Your interest in that researcher and that book were noticed.'

'I was friendly to Ronald like everyone else. That's all. I *never* said I wanted the book for myself. That's not true at all. Your theory is crazy, Inspector. Absolute nonsense.' How dare she! Accusing me because I was kind to one of our regular visitors. The audacity of it!

Inspector Pentecost crossed her arms. 'I have to consider all angles. Your behaviour was suspicious, and you had opportunity and motive. Do you have anything to say about that?'

I didn't, because I was speechless. The best I could manage was a strangled protest of denial.

She set her jaw. 'Very well.'

'Are you arresting me? Do I need a lawyer?'

The inspector straightened. 'Look, I'm not arresting you. I merely wanted a chat. You're free to go, but I don't want you to leave the Surrey area. Is that clear?'

'Yes.' I stood, relief flooding through me. I'd done nothing to deserve this appalling treatment. 'Are you going to call my colleagues in for questioning like this?'

'I may or may not. Constable McDonald will give you a ride back to Chirtlewood.'

I left the room, fuming. What would the others think of this? Would they regard me with suspicion? Would I even keep my job?

At the door, I glanced back. Inspector Pentecost stood, arms akimbo, watching me intently.

BACK AT CHIRTLEWOOD, I went to the office to finish my sandwich and found it had dried out and was unappetising. I gave up on it, threw it into the bin and returned to my role of overseeing visitors.

I crossed the entrance hall. Lydia, at the ticket counter, called me. Frowning, I went over to her.

'What was that all about?' she whispered. 'With the police?'

I shrugged exaggeratedly. 'I honestly don't know. The inspector was treating me like... like I was a suspect.'

'I suppose we all are until the police find the murderer.'

'Yes, but she didn't take anyone else in for questioning. Only me.'

'Don't let it get you down, Heather. She's only being thorough. What did she ask you?'

'She wanted clarification over my statement. I'd forgotten to mention the stolen book. That was all.'

An expression of horror came over Lydia's face. 'One of our precious volumes was stolen?'

'Yes. The one poor Ronald was studying.'

'How horrible!'

What was she referring to as being horrible? The book being stolen, or Ronald being killed for the book? Perhaps both. 'I hope the police catch the killer soon,' I said. So they would leave me alone.

'I'll put up a sign offering a reward for the safe return of the stolen book,' Lydia said. 'You never know. We might get it returned that way.'

No, we won't. It's too valuable.

New visitors entered the house, and Lydia turned to help them with tickets. I wandered to the great hall and found it busy. Three couples were checking out the portraits, coat of arms, suits of armour, weaponry and furniture in the room. I forgot about my encounter with the inspector and fell into a routine of answering the tourists' questions, pleased for the distraction.

Chapter 24

THE AFTERNOON PASSED by, and by the end, my feet ached and I needed to rest. But my fitness was improving every day. Especially from having to go up and down that bloody staircase. Before long, I'd be back to my old self and I wouldn't get so worn out.

I said goodbye to my workmates and headed for the car. I was about to turn the key when my phone rang.

'Hey, Heather. How are you? Had a great day?' It was Elvis.

'Not really, Elvis. It's been pretty stressful, to tell the truth.' I didn't know his real name, so I had to call him Elvis. It didn't sound strange, though. Who knows, maybe he was such a fan he'd changed his name to Elvis, anyway. 'Why are you calling? Did you remember something important?'

'No, it's not that. I wanted to offer you my help.'

'Your help? With what?'

'With your investigation. How's it going? Getting anywhere?'

'I've gone down a few dead ends, that's all.'

'Look, I've got a few days free. I can help you. How about you let me take you to dinner, and we can talk about getting together as a team?'

'I don't know about that, Elvis.'

'What have you got to lose? It's just for a few days. You said you were new in town and didn't know anyone.'

Did I say that? I couldn't remember.

He continued. 'I'm close by. Let's meet up and discuss it.'

'Where are you, exactly, and where are you suggesting we go?'

'I'm here in the car park at Chirtlewood.'

I froze. He must have watched me walk to the car and get in before calling. That was creepy.

'We'll go somewhere local and make a plan,' he continued. 'As I said, I've got a few days free. If we talk about it, we might come up with a few leads. Maybe I'll even remember something important after all.'

That was possible, and I didn't want to pass up the chance of uncovering any new leads, especially as I'd gotten nowhere so far. Despite my unease, I agreed. 'All right, let's do that.'

'Great! I'm in the hire car to your left. Come and join me.'

When I got into the car, I barely recognised Elvis because he wasn't wearing the elaborate get-up he'd been wearing yesterday. Now he was dressed in casual black trousers, a collared checked shirt and a dark blue sweater.

He grinned at me. 'I'm glad I convinced you. This could be fun.' He backed out of the park and accelerated, scattering gravel. I grabbed the door handle for safety. Elvis continued grinning. 'I know a good place for dinner in Richmond.'

To my astonishment, he parked near the Italian restaurant Raven had taken me to on our date. Surely, Le Amore can't be the only reasonable eatery in the area. 'Isn't this a bit upmarket? This is quite expensive for me. We're going to chat about the investigation. Maybe a pub meal would be better?'

'Upmarket suits me,' he said. 'Besides, we're here now.'

My unease remained, though I couldn't pinpoint why. Elvis seemed like a nice enough man, and he'd offered to help. Why did I have a spinning sensation in my stomach and a tension headache coming on?

A waiter showed us to a table. Elvis ordered wine and a meal for both of us, which I wasn't expecting and didn't appreciate.

'I can order for myself, you know.' He'd not bothered to ask what I wanted to eat and presumed he knew best.

'Sorry. Old habit.' He gestured with his hand as if sweeping away the subject.

I regretted taking him up on his offer, but I wanted to find out if he remembered seeing or hearing anything that might help me find Ronald's killer and locate the stolen spell book, so I said no more about his rudeness. In the back of my mind, my daughter's voice echoed, admonishing me for not saying 'no' to joining him for dinner.

Elvis launched into a monologue about how he saw himself as a bit of an amateur detective, having learned everything there was to know about investigation through watching detective shows and reading crime novels. I hardly got a word in before the meals arrived, and then, while we were eating, he propounded his theory about how someone must have sneaked in unseen to commit the crime, then sneaked out again.

'That's not possible,' I said. 'One of us would have seen them.'

'It's the only logical explanation, unless it was someone in the house itself.'

I hadn't fully accepted it before now, but someone in Chirtlewood House at the time must have murdered Ronald and stolen the witch's spell book. It was the only plausible explanation.

But who?

We finished our dinner. Elvis offered to fill up my wine glass, but I declined. He refilled it anyway, his eyes gleaming at me.

I didn't drink it. He was on his third glass and shouldn't be driving. This whole meeting had been a complete waste of my time. Elvis hadn't any new information. All I'd learned was that he had a high opinion of himself.

'Thanks for the meal and the conversation. I'll get a taxi back to Chirtlewood to retrieve my car. I'll pay for my meal on the way out.' Though I could scarcely afford it, and I hadn't chosen to come here. Why hadn't I insisted we go somewhere cheaper?

I stood.

Elvis motioned for me to sit. I did so, in case he was about to reveal something useful after all.

'There's no need for you to pay. I'll cover it.' He sculled the last of his wine and put the glass down unsteadily. 'It's still early. How about we go back to my hotel for a while?'

Warning lights flashed in my brain. That's what this was about. 'To your hotel?'

'To my room, of course. You said you wanted to get together.' He reached under the table and tried to touch my leg, but I moved it swiftly to the side.

'That's not what I agreed to at all. We were going to discuss the investigation into what happened at Chirtlewood.'

'Yes, but we can have a little fun as well, can't we?' There was an lustful gleam in his eye.

I got up and headed towards the exit. A waiter came up to meet up demurely.

'He's paying,' I said, jerking my thumb over my shoulder.

I pushed open the door. Behind me, the cash register rang. Elvis told someone to get a move on. I hurried outside.

Where the hell was a taxi when I needed one?

They'd be in central Kingston. I'd walk there. It was only a few minutes.

I'd barely taken a few steps when someone grabbed my arm and spun me around.

Elvis glared at me. 'Don't leave,' he said in a low voice.

I stared at him incredulously. 'This is not going to happen.'

He resisted my efforts to break his grip and leaned closer. 'I bought you an expensive dinner. You owe me.'

I took a step back. 'No, you tricked me. I'm not interested in going to your hotel room.' I tried to tug my arm away from him, but he clung on, his grip tightening.

A figure emerged from the darkness to stand beside me in a moment. 'What's going on here?'

It was Raven. With a streetlight directly on the other side of him, he stood in silhouette, but his voice—and the menace in it—was unmistakable. He stood determined, his jaw set.

'This isn't your business. Fuck off,' Elvis snarled.

Raven grabbed his fingers and bent them backwards.

Elvis howled in pain and took his hand off me. I stepped forward and shoved him. He stumbled back, trying to keep from falling.

'You tricked me,' I repeated, shaking my fist at him. 'You said you wanted to help with the investigation, but all you wanted to do was ply me with drink and get me into bed.'

'Don't come near her again,' Raven said, his voice measured but authoritative, 'or I'll do worse than bend your fingers.'

Elvis turned and scampered towards his car. I glared after him.

'Thanks, Raven.' Then something occurred to me. 'What brought you here? You weren't following me, were you?'

'No, I wasn't. I came to apologise to the staff for disappearing the other night when I was here with you. I suppose you had to pay for the meals.'

'Don't worry about that.'

'I'll treat you next time.' Raven gestured to Elvis's hire car as he sped away and contemplated me ruefully. 'Were you two on a date?'

'No, he told me he had information for the investigation and wanted to help, but he was lying. He brought me here under false pretences.'

'I see. You know, I could help you if you want.'

'Thanks, Raven. I might take you up on that. Let's talk about it tomorrow.'

'Give me a minute to speak to the manager inside. We can get a taxi home.'

'I'd like to get my car. It's at Chirtlewood.'

'That works too.'

He went inside. I stood in the light from the doorway, waiting for him, staring out at the reflections on the River Thames. It was wide and mysterious and surely held a lot of buried secrets.

Raven came out. 'I've prepaid enough to cover another meal here, in case I take flight again.'

I chuckled. 'Is that likely?'

He shrugged.

On the spur of the moment, I leaned forward and kissed him on the lips. He wasn't expecting it. Then I felt his arms around me, pulling me closer, as he kissed me back.

And then nothing.

I'd closed my eyes. I opened them to find a hovering bird squawking at me.

'Oh, Raven, I'm so sorry. We have to find a way around this.'

He squawked again and flew off, disappearing into the night. When I could no longer see him, I turned and strolled into central Kingston to catch a taxi back to Chirtlewood House.

TERRY PHONED ME LATER that night, or rather, in the early hours of the next morning.

'Do you know what time it is here?' I snapped. 'You deliberately called me at this unreasonable hour.'

'It's your fault that you're in the UK rather than at home, so don't blame me,' he said. 'Anyway, it's important. The lawyer emailed to say the buyers are going to go ahead with the house purchase. They only need to sort out their finance.'

'You didn't need to phone me about that in the middle of the night, Terry. I'll read the email in the morning.'

A muffled sniggering came over the phone line. 'I wanted to be the one to tell you. This is your last chance to come back home, Heather. I forgive you for leaving me. Come home, we'll cancel the house sale, and get back to our lives.'

'You forgive me?' I was flabbergasted. No longer half asleep now, I got out of bed and walked up and down the bedroom to dissipate some energy. 'How dare you say you forgive me? You were the one having the affair. It was you who did nothing around the house while I worked my guts out. Good riddance to you, I say.'

'Now hang on, love, we can talk this out—'

'You've got to be fucking joking, Terry.' *I said 'fuck' again. Wow.*

'I'm serious. I want to talk to you face to face, save our marriage—'

'There's nothing to talk about unless it's about our daughter. I'm in a much better place now without you. I only want to sell the house, divide the assets, take my half and go my own way.'

'I understand you're angry, but try to see it from my point of view. You'd had a hysterectomy, and you were off sex for a bit. I merely filled the void with a colleague.'

'You filled her void, yes. And I wasn't "off sex", as you put it. I was recovering from major surgery. The surgeon explained that to you.'

'Yeah, I wasn't really listening at the time,' he admitted.

'You what?'

'You heard. Sorry. Don't hang up. I've something to tell you. I'm coming over.'

'No, you're not. You're too lazy and too stingy to get a plane ticket.'

'No, really. I'll show my undying love for you by coming to the UK, and I'll bring you home with me.'

He made it sound like a certainty, but I was sceptical that he'd ever get on a plane. 'When are you planning to do this?'

'I've got a ticket booked for tomorrow.'

'What? You can't have.'

'I do. I'll send you a photo. Wait a sec.'

My phone beeped. A photo of a ticket bearing his name popped into view.

'That's stupid, Terry. I'm not going back with you. You're wasting your money.'

'We'll see about that.'

'I'm hanging up.'

I disconnected and threw my phone onto the bed. It bounced off it and landed on the carpeted floor on the other side.

I sat, too angry to go back to sleep now.

Chapter 25

NEXT MORNING, RACHEL phoned me before I left for work. 'Looks like your house sale might go through. The buyers are waiting for the final word from their bank for the finance, but they're confident.'

'Thanks, Rach. Terry phoned and woke me in the middle of the night to tell me about it.'

'How inconsiderate of him.'

'Sure was. And he said he's flying over here.'

'Shit. You don't have to see him if you don't want to, Heather. Remember what we talked about.'

'Okay, thanks. How are you doing?'

'I'm good,' she said. 'As usual, super busy with work. I miss you and our catch-ups. How long are you staying in the UK?'

'I don't know yet. I've organised daily care for Aunt Ruth and some work on the house. She's in a good state of mind, considering what happened to her, but I want to stay longer to make sure she's okay. Weeks, maybe months.'

'Okay. Well, I might come for a flying visit in a few weeks if I can squeeze enough space into my work calendar.'

I chuckled. 'That'd be great, Rach.'

AT CHIRTLEWOOD, THE police allowed us to reopen the library.

I stood at the doorway, looking in. It gave me the chills that someone I knew, even slightly, had been murdered in there two days before.

Or maybe the room itself was chillier than before.

'Have you talked to Charlotte or any of the others about Ronald?' I asked Lydia after she came upstairs to swap places with Penny, who had been patrolling with me.

Lydia nodded. 'They didn't see or hear anything. Charlotte gave a quite vivid account of what she and the earl were doing at the time, though.'

'I got the abridged version, thankfully. She took me to the Apothecary's Potions and Scrolls yesterday. The man there told me that no one had offered to sell him a witch's spell book. I left my number in case someone turned up with it.'

'Hold on. Charlotte went with you?'

'Yes, she showed me the way. The earl and Maisey came too.'

'That's amazing! They've never done that with me.'

What should I say to that? Did Lydia think I was boasting that I had a better relationship with the Chirtlewood ghosts than she did, even though I'd only been there a few days? She might feel upset or slighted by that.

Instead, she smiled. 'I think Charlotte must really like and trust you.'

A warmth spread through me. Spontaneously, I gave Lydia a hug, which she reciprocated.

'Wow. What was that for? I'm not complaining, mind you.'

I separated. 'For being you. I like and trust you too. I'm sure we're going to be good friends, Lydia.'

'Me too, Heather.'

IN THE MID-AFTERNOON, I summoned enough courage to enter the library rather than experience the chill and foreboding from the doorway. It seemed to lift as I circled the room, as if I were dispelling residual evil vibes by my presence. Was this another manifestation of my witchiness? I'd have to ask Aunt Ruth about it. Or maybe Lydia could tell me.

For a while, I stood in front of the shelf where the volume Ronald had been studying belonged. A few dust motes had gathered in the space. I couldn't bring myself to grab the duster and remove them. With the spell book stolen, it seemed appropriate that the space be marked with dust.

I eyed the shelf space thoughtfully. How had the killer taken the witch's spell book from the house? It was a large volume. Someone would have to slip it into a backpack or under a coat to hide it—it would be too obvious stuffed under a sweater. But I couldn't remember anyone wearing a coat that day. It was summer, after all. Neither could I recall any visitors with a backpack. Usually, we ask visitors to leave their bags behind the ticket counter so they don't accidentally knock over or damage some valuable piece of art when they turn around.

I had an epiphany. Maybe the witch's spell book had not left the house at first. That meant it was either still here, or someone came back for it later when things had settled down a little and no one would notice them taking it away.

None of the visitors that morning had returned, though. I was sure of that. The only people here after the police let us back into the house were Lydia, Penny, Melissa and me. Surely, it wasn't any of my colleagues?

So, maybe the spell book was still in the house, and the murderer would return for it at a later date. They must have hidden it somewhere on the same floor as the library. The killer would have climbed over a rope cordoning off the display area of a room and found a hiding place behind furniture or in a cupboard or dresser drawer.

I needed to search for it. This had to be the answer to the missing book. It remained in the house, hidden somewhere on this floor, and I'd search for it until I found it.

Lydia was talking to some visitors in the earl's bedroom. She might be a while, because they kept asking her questions and she was a fount of knowledge. She wouldn't disturb me.

I headed for the countess's bedchamber.

No one else was in there. A chill breeze swept over me when I entered, similar to air conditioning when I entered the airport building after walking across the tarmac in Singapore. Only this wasn't air conditioning—Chirtlewood House didn't have that. It was chilly ghost air.

Charlotte might be here, or she might have left not long ago.

The mirror bore no image of her. Maybe she was elsewhere in the house or in the grounds or even in Richmond.

I started poking around, opening the dresser drawers one by one. Most were empty. One held supplies, including lightbulbs for the fake gas lamps, which seemed incongruous with the rest of the room.

After searching the dresser, I crossed the room to the basin that originally would have contained cold water for the countess to wash her hands. The seventeenth-century en suite.

It was empty.

I cast around, searching for other potential hiding places. The armchair. A quick search on, behind and under that revealed nothing but a little dust, and I sneezed.

Soon, there was nowhere remaining to search but the bed. I reached up to the canopy at the top and ran my hand around the edge of the entire bed. Nothing there but more dust. I sneezed again, and my eyes started running. Couldn't Chirtlewood House afford proper cleaners? Must it all be left to us house guides when we're already overstretched?

I knelt and lifted the valance to peek under the bed. It was too dark to see clearly, so I used the flashlight on my phone. I groaned when it illuminated various small debris items, including chocolate wrappers and discarded entry tickets that had somehow ended up under there, but no hidden book. Worst of all was a used condom. Some visitors must have been having whoopie in the countess's bedchamber when all the staff were busy elsewhere. And there was something else, or rather, there wasn't—

'What are you doing?'

I turned and stood. Melissa stood there with a questioning expression.

'Checking to see if we need to vacuum under here,' I said.

'We haven't had time, being short-staffed and all.' She shrugged. 'You know that.'

'I'm not judging. I might stay late to dust and vacuum the room one evening, or come early one morning.'

'Nice idea, but I hope you're not thinking of cleaning the whole manor house by yourself. You don't have to do it alone. We'll set up a roster to share all those chores we don't have time to do normally. If we all pitch in with overtime, it'll get done.'

'All right. Thanks, Melissa.'

'You're welcome.' She left the room and headed towards the stairs.

I waited until I heard her footsteps on the stairs before getting down again to check that I hadn't been imagining things.

I crawled towards the head of the bed and shined my phone flashlight on the floor between the used condom and a discarded bus ticket.

Yes, I was right. A dustless square was evident where something had sat for a while. The killer had concealed the witch's spell book there and removed it later. I was sure of it.

On my feet again, I pocketed my phone and did my best to dust off my clothing, but I still looked like I'd had the contents of a vacuum cleaner blasted at me. It wouldn't make a good impression on the tourists. I went to the bathroom to tidy myself up.

Did Penny and Melissa know the murderer had stolen a book from the library? I hadn't told them myself, and I'd forgotten to mention it to the police in the first interview, so they wouldn't have overheard. Either Lydia had told them or they didn't know. We hadn't had time to discuss it.

Charlotte materialised in front of me, and I jumped. 'What, pray tell, wast thee searching for beneath my bed, Heather?'

'Oh, Charlotte. You startled me. I was looking for the stolen witch's spell book.'

The countess nodded. 'Ah, I see. Thee hast yet to locate it, then?'

I shook my head. 'Or the murderer. The police don't seem to be making any progress either. Or, if they have, they haven't told us about it.'

'Let's wend investigating again. Thee, me and the others. 'Twast excitement last time.'

'But where will we go? I haven't any new leads.'

'None at all?' The countess sounded disappointed.

'Wait.' A thought occurred to me, but I didn't like it much. 'I've got an idea.'

'Splendid. Permit me to call upon the others to make haste.'

'It'll have to be after work for this, Charlotte.'

'I cannot abide any delay, Heather.'

I shook my head. 'For this idea of mine, we have to wait for the right time.'

The countess's mouth firmed into a line. 'Very well, then,' she murmured. 'Until we meet again. Fare thee well.'

Chapter 26

THE REST OF THE DAY went without incident. The ghosts' heightened anticipation made me jittery. As Chirtlewood's closing time drew closer, they flitted around the entrance hall and up and down the stairs with nervous energy. Scruffles barked at most of the visitors, who were alarmed when they couldn't see a dog nearby. Charlotte herself appeared before a young couple making fun of the earl's portrait, gave them a deathly glare and sent them skittering down the stairs and out of the house. Even Maisey paced about the entrance hall instead of hiding in the shadows like she usually did.

'What are those ghosts up to today?' Lydia whispered to me in a quiet moment. 'They're all hyped up over something.'

'I've offered to take them for a drive later,' I said.

Lydia smiled wryly. 'Good luck with that.'

We both returned to helping visitors. The afternoon was a busy one.

At five o'clock, we closed the house and tidied up before leaving. I'd warned Charlotte to have everyone ready and waiting in the car park, and I made sure I was the first to leave.

But when I reached the car park, I found myself alone. Where were the ghosts?

The earl poked his head through one of the back seat windows. 'We wast awaiting thine arrival. Tarry not!'

Of course, they'd entered the car by passing through the doors. They didn't need to wait for me to unlock it.

I got in. Charlotte sat in the passenger seat. Maisey sat in the back with the earl.

'Nice horseless coach thee hast hither,' the earl said.

'Wherefore art we lingering?' Charlotte said. 'Pray, allow us be off. To whither art we journeying, I wonder?'

'We're going to follow someone,' I said. 'Penny or Melissa. Whoever comes out first.'

'What the devil for?' the earl demanded.

Here it comes. What I was about to do was crappy but necessary. 'The killer hid the witch's spell book in the house after the murder and removed it later. None of the visitors there at the time have returned. So...'

'That only leaves the staff,' Charlotte concluded. 'That is thy notion.'

Maisey spoke, enunciating her words carefully in a singsong voice. 'Lydia, Penny, Melissa, Heather.' It was the first time she'd spoken in my presence.

'I'm excluding myself,' I pointed out. 'Obviously.'

'Thee may be attempting to deceive us,' the earl said. He might be old, but his mind was still sharp, as was his acerbic wit.

'Why would I do that?' Exasperated, I turned right around in my seat to face him. 'Why would I ask you—let you—help me investigate the crime if I was the murderer and thief myself?'

'Thy cunning red herring,' he replied.

'Red herring? What do you know about red herrings?'

'He reads detective books,' Maisey sang.

'Look, Thomas—'

He scowled at me.

'I mean, My Lord, if you are going to accuse me, you can damn well get out of the car now.'

'I assure thee I shan't!'

'Penny is coming,' Charlotte said.

I'd almost missed her because I'd been arguing with the earl. She got into her car and sped off. I reversed out of my park and tailed her as closely as I dared, so she wouldn't notice me following.

'Wherefore do we pursue Penny?' the countess asked. 'Do thou forsooth suspect that lady for the murder of that gent and the taking of the precious tome?'

'I think a staff member may have stolen the book. I might be wrong, but I'm sure they hid the book in the house and removed it later. If Penny took it, she may even have it in her car right now. If we follow her, we might see her with the book when she gets out.'

''Tis a fanciful notion, is it not?'

'Yes, but what else do we have to go on? I can't imagine Penny, Melissa or Lydia doing this, but one of them must have taken the spell book.' Ahead of us, Penny made a late turn, almost catching me unawares. I followed.

''Tis not right for ye to assume the lady be the killer,' Maisey sang. 'Murder, murder, dig another grave. Hie, hie, to catch the knave.'

'If it be true the lady is the one who hath done these nefarious acts, shalt we then lop off her head?' Charlotte asked.

'Nay!' boomed the earl to his wife. 'That is the occupation of the constables! Though 'twouldst be a meet spectacle to see that lady head mounted on a stake at the gates, for 'twouldst present a fair dissuasion to other malfeasants.'

'We're not chopping off any heads,' I said firmly. 'And neither are the police.'

'Thee people hast become far too merciful of late,' the earl grumbled. 'And too soft. In my day, thither wast nay footpaths for the peasants. They hadst to jump clear if a carriage came past.'

'Ridiculous,' I muttered.

'What wast that?'

'Never mind. Keep an eye on Penny's chariot for me, will you, everyone?'

After a while, Penny came to a stop outside a greasy café. We pulled in a short distance further on. She gave no sign of having noticed me following her.

Maisey peered out the back window. 'Penny got out of her horseless coach and stepped inside.'

I turned in time to see her enter the café. She didn't have a book with her. Maybe it was still in her car.

We sat for a few minutes. Charlotte tapped her fingers silently on the door handle. Maisey twirled her hair. The earl twirled his moustache. I slouched in the driver's seat, getting bored.

'Art we to do nothing but tarry hither?' Charlotte demanded.

I sat up. I'd had an idea. 'You can do something while we wait. Can you sneak down to Penny's car and have a look inside? Including in the trunk? See if the stolen spell book is there?'

'I shalt take up this task,' Maisey said, and jumped through the car door and ran down the footpath to Penny's car.

'Verily, Maisey may be quite the shrinking violet,' Charlotte said, 'but nay one can deny her spirit for journey and exploration.'

I didn't reply. Guilt and shame crept over me for spying on my colleague by proxy. All I was going on was intuition and random chance. I could rely on the former, but the latter was a cruel mistress. For all I knew, Penny was one hundred per cent innocent, and I was poking into her personal life without her knowledge or approval. What did that make me? Nothing good.

'Pray, do not feel discouraged,' Charlotte said, as if reading my mind. 'For 'tis thee who sought to investigate, and investigate we shalt.'

'Yeah, right.' She was correct, but it didn't ease my conscience.

Maisey came running back and dived through the rear window into the car. Once my heart palpitations had settled—for I still wasn't used to the ghosts passing through solid objects—and Maisey had turned the right way up and sat down, I asked her if she'd found the stolen book.

'What wouldst it be like?' she asked.

'It's large and bound with leather. Did you see anything like that?'

'Naught as such.'

Okay. So, either Penny didn't steal the spell book, or she'd already taken it somewhere else. Maybe yesterday. So, I couldn't rule her out, anyway. I'd gotten nowhere with this excursion.

'Thither I tread and saw strange wares of leather, masks I hadnae ever seen afore, to be worn at rich folks' galas, and shoes of a kind with high heels! And thither wast something else—a whip!'

'A whip? Are you sure?' I blurted out my question before I could stop myself. I did not need to know this about Penny.

'Aye. 'Twast forsooth a whip. Black as night, like the garments.'

Oh crap. Quiet, steady, proper Penny. Sure, her disposition was sometimes a little sour. But I would never have guessed she was a closet dominatrix!

I shivered. I'd pried and learned something I couldn't unlearn.

'Is thither a ball or some such nonce of which we shouldst be aware?' the countess asked.

'I don't think Penny would go to a ball,' I said, rueing my actions. 'I think we're out of luck here. Let's go back.'

'Most certes not; we hast come this far and wilt not relent,' Charlotte said. 'We wilt press onwards and follow that lady home and observe if it be true this incantatory volume is present.'

'Let's not do that.' Given what was in her car, who knew what we'd discover at her house?

'Allow us take a ballot on the matter,' the earl declared. 'Whoever's in favour, declare it with an "aye!"'

"Ayes!" resounded all around the car. I frowned at being outnumbered. I could refuse to drive, but I'd asked for their help, so I couldn't deny them now. Or could I?

'Penny got back in to her horseless coach,' Maisey said urgently.

'Follow that lady.' Charlotte glowered at me.

I started the car and pulled out after Penny. Being summer, it was still light. I tried to keep another car between us to reduce the chance of her spotting me tailing her. It seemed to work, at least until we entered the suburb of New Malden and turned off the main road.

'What under the heavens art thou doing?' Charlotte asked as I dropped further behind.

'Trying not to be too obvious,' I said. 'Look, she's turned into that driveway. We'll stop here.'

'I'm fading,' Maisey wailed. She appeared about to cry.

'Fading? What do you mean?' A shot of alarm went through me. Had I done something to my ghostly passengers unwittingly?

'Thou art quite far from the scene of thy demise,' Charlotte said. ''Tis nay surprise thee find yourself waning, as wilt yon earl and I anon. Ere we reach Chirtlewood, thee shalt be restored to thy previous state.'

'I can't see me spots any more,' Maisey said. 'Am I dying? Again?'

'Nay, thee might not but set thine anxieties to ease. Thou shalt hast an hour or two ere thy form is dematerialised.'

'Disappear?' I asked. 'As in completely vanish and not come back?' I didn't want the death of one of the ghosts on my conscience. Or would that be an undeath? Maybe a re-death? I shook my head, confused.

'I hast beheld such a sight,' Charlotte said. 'Yet I know not what transpired after.'

'Let's go back, then,' I said, restarting the car.

'We ought to first investigate the bower of Penny for the tome of incantation. See if it be true the lady hast borne it off.'

'Ooh, can I come too?' Maisey bounced up and down in her seat, her fading issue forgotten for now.

'Naturally.' Charlotte smiled. 'We shalt all accompany. That shalt be more expeditious.'

'Fie upon that!' the earl said. 'I shalt remain hither. I hast nay wish to tramp about some servant's lodgings, hunting for a volume.'

'Thou art ever so cantankerous, my beloved,' the countess said. 'The remainder of us shalt wend forth, aye? We hast the entire hovel to look through, do we not?'

Maisey exited the car and pelted down the street. The houses beyond her were visible through her torso. It made my skin crawl. Charlotte went after her.

'She's not actually going to disappear forever, is she?' I asked the earl as I turned the car off.

'Not unless she dillydallies.'

I was still concerned, but Maisey wasn't the type to dawdle.

Ten minutes later, they returned to the car and slipped inside. I started it and did a U-turn before heading back towards Kingston and onwards to Chirtlewood, eager to get them home as quickly as possible.

'Don't tell me everything you found there, only if you found anything that appeared to be a witch's spell book,' I said.

'I noticed naught of the sort,' Charlotte said.

Maisey stayed silent. I glanced in the mirror, worried she had evaporated, but she appeared more solid. Her spots were even starting to rematerialise. It was the first time I'd been relieved at the sight of measles spots.

'Maisey? Did you see a large, leather-bound book anywhere?'

'Nay. I did look hard, too.'

'I bet you did.' How could they search an entire house in ten minutes? They didn't have to open anything, did they? All they had to do was stick their head through a cupboard door or into a drawer.

'But ye shouldst hast seen the lady's basement!' Maisey said. ''Twast a chamber made for torture!'

I absolutely did not want to hear that. Penny had a secretive kinky side to her nature and possibly a lucrative side hustle that went along with it.

'Maisey, I said not to tell me what you found unless it was the spell book.'

'Ye hast said nay to know all that I hast found, so I dinnae be telling ye that. But I swear, if ye just took a peek inside her wardrobe, ye'd see it all.'

'That's enough, Maisey.' Unbidden thoughts ran through my mind. I'd never unsee them, and they were almost enough to drive me off the road. *Concentrate on my driving! I'm more fragile than the ghosts.*

We arrived at Chirtlewood. The ghosts thanked me for the outing—apart from the earl, who said I'd wasted his time. Scruffles barked at the earl as he hobbled towards the front entrance, and a broad smile creased the earl's face.

When they had gone inside, I went home, the events of the evening preying on my mind. I couldn't rule out Penny as a suspect—she may have taken the book from the house yesterday. Other than her, there were only Melissa and Lydia. Surely, Lydia wouldn't have done such a thing, but she was a witch, and it was a witch's spell book that was stolen…

My thoughts were leading me to a place I didn't want to go. Lydia was the colleague I was closest to, the person who had helped me the most in my new job. Surely, she wasn't a murderer and a thief, but if it wasn't her or Penny, it must be Melissa, and she wasn't a witch, so why would she want a witch's spell book?

Or was I off track?

Maybe.

MY PHONE RANG AND WOKE me the next morning. Sunlight peeked from around the edges of the blinds, so it wasn't the middle of the night. As I grabbed the phone, I checked the time. It was 6 am.

I groaned, partly from being woken up, but mostly because the caller was Terry. 'Hello?'

'Good morning, love of my life.'

'Leave it, Terry. Why are you calling?'

'Two things. I guess you haven't seen the email yet.'

My body and mind were warring between wanting to go back to sleep and wanting to be alert. I sat up to tilt the odds towards alertness. 'What email? I haven't checked my emails for a day. I've been busy.'

'Doing what?'

'Never you mind. What email?'

'From the estate agent. The house sale has fallen through. The buyers couldn't get finance after all.' He didn't sound upset about it.

'We'll wait for another offer, then.'

'Don't you see, Heather? It's a sign that it's not meant to sell. It's a sign that we're supposed to be back together. In our home.'

'No, Terry. It's only a sign that the buyers couldn't get finance. What was the other thing?'

'Oh, that. I'm at the airport.'

My stomach crawled. 'Which airport?'

'Heathrow. Hey, it's enormous. I'm in a line waiting to pass through Immigration. There must be hundreds of people here.'

Good. That will delay him. 'Go home, Terry. I don't want to see you.'

He ignored that. 'I'll find a place to stay and then I'll come over to your aunt's house and fetch you. We'll go home as soon as we can book return flights.'

'That's not going to happen.' I did a mini fist-pump. *I said 'no'. Yay, me.*

'Look, just tell me your aunt's address, and we can talk it over.'

A smile spread across my face. *Thanks, Rose.* She might have told Terry I was in the UK, but she hadn't told him exactly where I was.

And neither would I. Eventually, he'd lose patience or run out of money and go home by himself.

'Heather? What's your address?'

'I'm in Birmingham.'

'Birmingham? I could have sworn Rose said you were in London or nearby.'

'Maybe she got mixed up.'

'All right. I'll call you when I get there. This queue is moving at last.' He rang off.

I chuckled to myself. The bastard had given me the run-around for years. Time for him to get a dose of his own medicine.

Chapter 27

AUNT RUTH MET ME IN the kitchen while I was preparing breakfast.

'Do you want me to get you some toast and marmalade?' I asked.

'Thanks, dear, that'd be lovely. And a cup of tea, if you don't mind.'

'No problem.' I still preferred to make the drinks myself rather than have Aunt Ruth make them with magic. Especially if I was in the kitchen at the time. I didn't want to be hit by flying saucers.

'Come into the living room when you're ready. I've got something to tell you.' There was a grave tone to her voice that made me stop what I was doing.

'What's wrong?' I asked.

She rolled off. 'Let's have our breakfast, and I'll tell you afterwards.'

I took in our toast and tea on a tray and set it out on the dining room table. 'What's this about, Aunt Ruth?'

'It's a couple of things. Let's talk about the easiest one first.'

'Okay.' She was worrying me now. I wish she'd just tell me, instead of saying that she will tell me. The suspense was awful.

'Raven has been gone all night again. That's unusual for him. He is normally here, studying his books. The last couple of times he's come back saying he was out with you and turned into bird form.'

'Yes, Aunt Ruth, but you know this already. We've talked about it before.'

'The problem, Heather, is that if he turns into a raven whenever he spends some time with you, he and I will never have time to work out how to lift the curse that afflicts him.'

'It's not my fault he keeps turning into a bird.'

'No, but we have to minimise that somehow. If it keeps happening, and I hope it doesn't, maybe you should consider living somewhere else until this whole thing is sorted out.'

'Live somewhere else? I came over here to help you after your accident. And you want to teach me witchcraft.' I couldn't believe this. I'd abandoned my old life—though it was mostly crap, I'd still abandoned it—and flown halfway around the world to help my aunt, and now she wanted me to leave.

'It would only be for a while, until we can get Raven's curse lifted, and only if he keeps changing form. He needs to continue with his research while I can help him. If you moved out temporarily, you could still start the witchy correspondence course, and you could phone me whenever you want advice.'

I put my cup of tea down. My toast lay on its plate, getting cold. 'He's been working on removing the curse for years. You might never succeed.'

'We're close, I'm sure. But we'll never get there if you keep trying to jump his bones.'

I gagged. 'I'm doing nothing of the sort.' I was, but I was damned if I would admit it to my aunt at the moment.

She inclined her head in a noncommittal gesture, which I took to mean that she didn't believe me and that this part of the discussion was over for now.

'What's the other thing?' I asked.

Aunt Ruth pushed her plate and cup aside. She leaned forward on the table. 'I have a problem. I've only got a certain amount of time to live.'

I drew my breath in sharply, my head reeling with this thunderstrike. 'You're terminally ill? What is it? What has the doctor said, exactly? What treatment options are there?'

She contemplated her fingernails. 'A doctor can't help. Well, maybe a witchdoctor could, but I don't know any of those guys.'

'I don't understand.' My head was now pounding in time with my heart.

'I'm not going to give you all the details,' she said. 'It won't help. I have a few weeks left. Then...' She left her sentence hanging and gazed at me.

'Weeks? Shit. Oh shit. Wait. What's wrong exactly?'

She sat back in her chair. 'All I can say is that I've got until early September. The third of September, to be precise. Then... no more me.'

I struggled to get my head around this. 'You know the exact day of your death? For real?' And it was only three months away!

'Yes. You see why I want to get you started on your witchy learning.'

'Forget the learning. What about you? There must be something I can do or someone I can call for help or advice. Isn't there?'

'My situation is unique, and it's a consequence of a terrible decision I made a long time ago. I don't want you to get involved.'

'I am involved. I'm your niece, and I live here with you. Oh, Aunt Ruth, now I'm really afraid for you.'

'There's nothing you can do, Heather. The only thing I want you to do is concentrate on learning whatever witchy things you can, once your correspondence course arrives, and ask me about everything you want to know before September. Oh, and don't worry about your future. I'm leaving you this house and everything I have.'

I sat in stunned silence, trying to take all this in.

Aunt Ruth rolled towards the hall. 'You'll be late for work, dear. You'd best get ready.'

I went after her, but she'd shut herself in her room. I waited outside, debating whether to knock or not.

If she'd wanted to continue the discussion, she would have. There was no point waiting. I'd have to corner her later and get the details out of her somehow.

I GRABBED MY BAG AND the car keys and headed out to work. Dark clouds swirled, blocking the sun. A storm could be on the way. My head ached. I opened the windows to see if fresh air would help, but it wasn't fresh—it was full of exhaust fumes. I swore, shut the window again and drove on to Chirtlewood.

A police car sat parked by the entrance. I drove around the back and parked, trying to be positive. Maybe they had good news. Maybe they'd found the murderer, and it wasn't any of my colleagues after all.

I went inside through the back entrance and turned into the office. Lydia, Melissa and Penny sat at the table, silent. The atmosphere was foreboding. Inspector Pentecost stood, her legs apart, her arms folded. Her eyes bored into mine.

'Hello,' I said. My voice squeaked a little.

'Good morning, Ms Nicholls. I need to talk to you about something.'

'You do?' I glanced at the others. None of them returned my gaze.

'Your colleagues know about this. In fact, I'm here because one of them made a call to the police last night about being followed home.' She glanced at Penny.

I swallowed involuntarily.

The inspector continued. 'Fortunately, Ms Bishop got the number plate. When the constable on duty looked it up, they found it was registered to a person who lives at the address you gave me, Ms Nicholls.'

I remained tight-lipped. What could I say that wouldn't make me sound like a stalker?

'But of course, it was you driving the car, wasn't it, Ms Nicholls? You've been driving it to work, including today.'

'Yes, it was me.' There wasn't any point in denying it.

'You did what? Drive here today or follow your colleague home last night? Or both?'

'Both,' I admitted weakly.

'And that included stopping for twenty minutes while she grabbed a bite to eat before you continued to follow her. I think Ms Bishop and your other colleagues want an explanation for this behaviour, and I'm here to make sure you give them one.'

'All right. I'll explain.'

'This has better be good, Heather,' Penny said. 'It gave me the chills when I noticed someone tailing me. I thought—I thought the murderer might be coming after me as their next victim, like in one of those serial killer books.'

Oh, the drama, Penny. Play it up. 'I didn't mean to give you a fright. It's about the stolen spell book.'

'What about it?' Lydia asked, looking up for the first time.

'I discovered where it had been hidden in the house after the murder. The dust was clearly disturbed. The spell book wasn't taken from the house until later.'

'Are you still trying to do my job?' Inspector Pentecost asked.

'As far as I know, you didn't search the house for a book missing from the library.'

'No one told us it was missing until you remembered to mention it the next day,' she shot back. 'Besides, we're investigating a murder. The theft of a book doesn't concern me.'

'What missing book?' Penny asked. 'And what's it got to do with me?'

'An old witch's spell book was stolen. The one that Ronald—Mr Morris—was studying.'

'So what?' Melissa said. 'Why did you follow Penny home? That's just creepy.'

My face reddened. Yes, they thought I was a stalker. Or worse. 'As I said, the book was hidden in the house and moved later. It can only be one of us who moved it.'

'And you thought it was me.' Penny's voice was ice cold. 'How dare you?'

I shook my head. 'I thought nothing except I had a crazy idea that if I followed one of you, then I might find the stolen spell book.'

'You might.' Penny's tone had ice on it. 'Well, you were right about one thing. It was a crazy idea, and it gave me a scare, Heather.'

I squirmed a little but tried not to show it. 'I'm sorry. It was wrong of me to do it.'

'You're damn right.' Penny's nostrils flared.

Lydia stood. 'I'll consider this incident as you being overzealous, Heather, and I'll overlook it. We'll put it behind us.' She glanced at Penny, who took her time to nod in agreement. 'We work as a team here, and that means trusting each other. I understand your desire to solve the mystery and find the stolen book—we all like a little mystery, but usually that's in a book or on television. So, forget your investigation and focus on what you were hired to do—be part of our team managing this house. If you can't do that, you can't work here. Consider that a warning.'

Inspector Pentecost added, 'Leave the detective work to the police. That's our job.'

I'd really screwed up. My intuition, and logic itself, told me one of my colleagues must have stolen the witch's spell book. Almost certainly, that meant one of us was Ronald's killer, and it wasn't me. I didn't want to drop this, but if I wanted to keep my job and regain the trust of my colleagues, I had to. Or at least pretend to do so.

'I apologise. I'll abandon the Sherlock Holmes activity.' And now I was a liar too.

'I don't think I'm required here any longer,' the inspector said. 'I need to get back to the investigation.' She strode towards the door, but paused right beside me and turned to whisper in my ear. 'Which you have interrupted. If there's another incident like this, I might charge you with wasting police time.'

I shivered at her breath on my face as much as her words.

The inspector left.

Lydia spoke up. 'There are no pastries this morning because Penny was too upset to remember to buy them, so let's just get the house ready to open for visitors.'

She walked past me without another word. Penny was next, brushing past me with her head raised. Melissa came last, and pointedly stopped by me and said, 'Perhaps you'd better quit, Heather. You're not fitting in with the team here.'

NOTHING I'D PLANNED had turned out well.

I paced up and down in the ballroom, avoiding the others. Visitors came and went, but somehow, they knew not to approach me. I must have been putting out misery vibes.

In a few quiet minutes between visitors, the countess appeared in front of me. I walked right through her before I'd even realised she was there. It was only the chill that brought me out of my melancholic reverie.

'Thee violated me,' she said.

'I'm really sorry, Charlotte. I wasn't watching where I was going.'

'Hmph. It matters not.' She inclined her head and looked at me questioningly. 'Pray tell, what ails thee? Thy countenance is most forlorn.'

'Last night's adventures have got me into trouble. The other house guides are angry and upset with me.'

'Didst thee inform them of thy suspicions that one of them is the villainous thief and murderer?'

I sighed, stopped pacing and turned to face Charlotte. 'I did. I said a lot of stuff I shouldn't have because I couldn't keep my big mouth closed.'

'Verily, these recent decades hast seen an upheaval of speech. Nay longer do people say what is most pleasing to the ear, but rather, each individual does express their mind and heart.'

'It's called honesty, and this morning, it didn't do me any good.'

Charlotte pursed her lips. 'So, wilt we follow someone else home this evenfall?'

'No. I'll lose my job. I love this job... but I can't continue to work here if I think one of my colleagues is responsible for...' I stopped short of saying it. I couldn't even contemplate it without a sickening sensation forming in my stomach.

'Verily, this seems a conundrum that hath a political tang,' the countess said. 'When I lived, I wouldst rapturously ponder such matters. Thus, if thee do persist with thine inquest, thee stand to be summarily cashiered. However, if thee do not pursue it, thee shalt resign from thy post in vexation of not knowing the sooth of the circumstances. Is it so?'

'Pretty much.' I sighed. 'Maybe it's the best thing. I thought I was making friends with my colleagues, and now they don't trust me, and I am suspicious of them.'

'Alas! It certes wast the jolliest amusement we hadst for ages. I daresay, possibly even a hundred years.'

Oh gods. Now I was responsible for ruining the best fun a household of ghosts have had in a century. 'I'm glad you enjoyed the outings. Unfortunately, we weren't successful, and I might have been completely wrong about the whole thing. Probably was.'

'Thee shalt never discover the sooth unless thee persist in thine inquiry, wilt thee?'

I didn't want to argue the point with her. I couldn't; she was right. 'It's no longer an option for me,' I said weakly. 'I don't want to lose this job. I have to earn enough to care for my aunt.'

Aunt Ruth. All she'd told me that morning came rushing back. I'd put it out of my mind, buried in my own troubles, but Aunt Ruth was dying. Or going to die. On the third of September, apparently. And she wouldn't tell me how she knew that or what, if anything, she could do about it.

Now guilt crept through me as I realised how selfish I'd been, thinking of myself instead of how I might help Aunt Ruth.

Instead of being a help to her, I'd fucked things up entirely. I'd broken Aunt Ruth's magic mirror, so she couldn't do advanced magic any more. Her hot boarder, Raven, is so enamoured with me he can't concentrate on his study to find a way to lift his curse, and he shifts into raven form when I get too close. Aunt Ruth is so upset that she'll run out of time to help him she suggested I might have to move out.

I groaned. I was ruining my relationship with my aunt, who kindly offered me a place to live after my marriage disintegrated. I'd torpedoed my budding friendships with my colleagues by spying on one of them and losing their trust. Melissa even told me I should leave, and I couldn't think of any good reason why I shouldn't.

I wanted to investigate the murder myself and find the stolen witch's spell book to help my aunt. All I'd done was lose everything important to me in my new life. I'd wrecked it.

Mired in my negative thoughts, I'd totally forgotten about the countess. I dragged my consciousness out of the depths of despair.

She'd gone.

Now even the ghosts were deserting me!

The rest of the afternoon passed without serious incident. However, none of my colleagues bid me good night when I left. I drove home in a total funk.

Chapter 28

AT HOME, I MADE A CUP of white hot chocolate and sat in my room, sipping it, not even wanting to seek the company of my aunt. Misery was once again consuming me, and I couldn't find the effort to lift myself out of it.

My phone rang several times before it brought me back to reality. A new, bleak reality I'd created for myself.

I pulled it from my bag. 'Hello?'

'Ms Heather Nicholls?'

'Yes, that's me.'

'Excellent. This is the airline here. We have good news for you. Your luggage turned up eventually. We've had it redirected from Anchorage, Alaska, and it will arrive in London Heathrow tomorrow morning. You may come and pick it up at the lost luggage desk in Terminal Four after nine o'clock.'

I was stunned.

'Ms Nicholls?'

'Th—thank you,' I stammered, barely able to believe what I'd heard. 'I'll pick it up after I finish work tomorrow, in the early evening.'

'That will be fine. Good day.' The airline representative rang off.

I shook my head. I'd already bought all the stuff I needed to replace what I'd lost. Now I'd have extra. Twice as much stuff and nowhere to live, if Aunt Ruth forced me out.

Whatever next?

My phone rang again. Damned airline. Now they'll tell me they sent my bags to London in Canada instead of London in the UK.

But it wasn't the airline this time. It was Terry.

'I'm here in Birmingham,' he said. The optimism in his voice shone through. He truly believed he was going to meet me and take me back to New Zealand with him. My conscience almost twinged about disappointing him.

Almost.

'Birmingham? What are you doing in Birmingham, Terry?'

There was a pause before he answered. 'You told me you're in Birmingham.'

'No, I said Bermondsey.'

'Where the hell's that?'

'East London.'

'Bloody hell, Heather.'

'I've already told you I'm not going back with you, Terry.' Even as I said it, I questioned myself. Perhaps I should go back. I'd screwed up my new life here in England, and I had no idea how to undo the mess I'd gotten myself into.

'All right, I'm exhausted after a long flight and the train to Birmingham. I'm going to stay here overnight and come back to London tomorrow morning. I'll book flights home for tomorrow night. I've forgiven you for leaving me. We can go home together. Call it a new start. Your school has said they'll take you back. We can go back to how everything was before.'

'You think so?'

Terry might have heard my response, but he didn't pick up on my tone. 'I know so. I'm nothing without you, Heather. You're the love of my life. Hold tight. I'm coming to get you and take you home.'

He rang off. Or ran out of credit.

I put my phone away in disbelief.

When I finished my tea, I lay back on the bed, thinking things through. Why shouldn't I give up and go back to what I knew? It might be a mundane existence, but at least it was familiar.

There are worse things than that.

But Aunt Ruth? I promised to help her. She'd said she had three months to live.

I closed my eyes. The idea of her dying was too painful to contemplate right now.

Aunt Ruth said there was nothing I could do to help her. And all she seemed to want to do was to help Raven, and I was interfering with that.

I had made a connection with Raven too. Did I want to give up on that so soon?

I could work on the correspondence course in New Zealand. It's by correspondence, after all. Email goes everywhere. And Aunt Ruth would only be a phone call away. While she is still alive, anyway. Though even then, she might hang around as a ghost.

I must have fallen asleep. When I woke, it was dark. Hunger pangs clawed at my stomach. I'd skipped dinner. Better go downstairs and find something to eat. Even two-minute noodles would do. Or toast. Can't go wrong with toast and a white hot chocolate.

Downstairs, I made hot buttered toast and a hot drink and took them into the dining room. The light was on there, but the room was empty. Maybe Aunt Ruth or Raven had been in there recently. Aunt Ruth never turned off the lights when she went to bed. Something about avoiding lightbulb explosions, she'd said.

I ate my toast. Melted butter ran down my chin. I'd literally slathered it on. Buttered toast was a comfort food, and extra butter meant extra comfort.

'Heather?'

I looked up as I wiped my chin with my sleeve, twinging with embarrassment at my messy eating. It was Raven. 'You're back.'

'Yeah, I got back just now.'

'What happens to your clothes when you shift into bird form?' I blurted. I'd wanted to know that for a while.

He chuckled as he came in and sat next to me. 'They change with me. Luckily, my ex-girlfriend allowed me that dignity.'

'Or she didn't think about it.' Angry ex-partners were liable to do mean things. Myself included.

'Maybe. I'm starved. All I've had to eat since last night was a few insects. I think I've still got some wings stuck in my teeth.'

I put my toast down. 'Yuck.'

'Yeah. You can see why I'm desperate to get rid of this curse.'

'I can.' I peered more closely at him. 'You seem a bit frazzled.'

'Yeah, I was lucky to get away from a hawk. There's a few in Richmond Park, and they sometimes venture out over Kingston. One of them spotted me, but I escaped. They're quick, but they're not smart.'

'Shit. It's difficult for you, isn't it?'

'Yes.'

'You look tired too. Do you want me to make you something to eat?'

'No, thanks. I'll get something myself in a few minutes. I wanted to see how you were after that incident. I hope you got home safely.'

I smiled. 'Thanks for intervening.'

'No problem. Say... when I came into the room, you seemed quite miserable. What's going on? Want to talk about it?'

Raven's eyes shone with a deep concern. He genuinely cared. A warm glow swept through me.

'Aunt Ruth told me some bad news.' I didn't want to be too specific. Did Raven know, or not? It wasn't my place to tell him.

He lowered his head. 'I wondered when she might mention the third of September.'

'What is it about that date specifically? How can she be certain of it?'

'I don't know. She hasn't told me that. I'm sure it's complicated.'

'I bet.' So, Raven didn't know either or would not tell me. 'My job isn't going well. I may have to leave.'

He looked up sharply. 'I thought you loved that job.'

'I do, but I've upset my colleagues.'

Puzzlement spread over Raven's features. 'That doesn't sound like you.'

'I said I suspected one of them stole the missing spell book, and by implication, is a murderer.'

He sat back, shaking his head. 'Okay, I can understand why they're upset, but why did you make such an accusation in the first place?'

I took a deep breath, then I started talking fast, so fast I became breathless trying to explain it. My suspicions. Searching for the missing spell book. Finding how it had been hidden first and removed later. My logical conclusion that only one of my colleagues could have done it.

Raven listened intently until I'd finished. I waited for him to tell me I was being ridiculous, that I'd ruined my relationship with my colleagues over nothing, that I was downright flipping crazy.

His expression conveyed that he wasn't thinking any of those things. 'I believe you. From what you've said...' He frowned. 'One of your colleagues must be the perpetrator.'

'You think so?'

'I do.'

'Listen to us. We sound like detectives.' But Inspector Pentecost told me to leave everything up to her team.

'Maybe you should share your suspicions with the police.'

I shook my head. 'The inspector already knows what I think. She gave me a stern telling-off for stalking Penny.'

Raven rubbed at his chin as he considered his reply. 'So, what are you going to do?'

'There's nothing I can do. I'll be fired or get into trouble with the police if I try to investigate further. I've already upset my colleagues. I can't do anything. They already want me to leave, and I don't want to stay if it's possible that one of them committed that terrible crime.'

'So, you're giving up.'

'What else can I do, Raven? I'm out of options.'

'Do you always give up so easily?'

'What? No. I don't give up like that. Never. Whatever I have to get done, I do it.'

Raven shuffled closer to me on the couch and took my hand in his. 'You said, "whatever I have to get done". What do you mean by that?'

'I mean, that if I have something I have to do, then I do it. That's what I do.'

'And by something you have to do, you mean...' His eyes widened, inviting me to complete the sentence.

I was stumped. What did I mean?

'Heather, I think you mean that when someone tells you what to do, you get it done. Isn't that right?'

'Um. Yes, I guess.' My voice had gone up an octave. My breathing increased. Nervous tension gripped my neck.

'Why is that, do you think?' Raven's voice was soft. His gaze held mine for a few moments until I looked away.

'I—I don't know. I suppose I don't want to disappoint people.'

'So... you do stuff for other people because they want you to do it. That's when you don't give up, but when it's something for you, you do give up. Is that right?'

I didn't answer. One of my eyes was itchy. I wiped at it.

Raven continued. 'I understand this, Heather. Maybe you fell into a pattern in your life in which you did everything for everyone else. Your husband. Your work. Your child. Whoever else. You forgot to do things for you.'

Now I covered my eyes with my free hand. They were moist.

Raven squeezed my other hand. 'If you're constantly trying to prove your worth to someone, you have already forgotten your value.'

He released my hand, got up and left me on my own.

Chapter 29

WHEN I WOKE THE NEXT morning, I was still undecided about what to do. I made myself breakfast and went into the dining room to think about it all while I crunched my toast and drank my tea.

Raven's kind words the previous night were just that—kind—but he didn't know what things were like for me.

I'd always regarded my value as a person by the roles I performed. History teacher. Mother. Wife. Didn't everyone do that? Wasn't that what made someone worthwhile as a person?

With Rose having left home, my hard work at school being unappreciated and my husband cheating on me, my old life had imploded. But it was still my life, and it was fixable. I still had a role as a mother, the school wanted me back, and Terry loved me—or said he did. I could forgive his indiscretions, couldn't I?

Raven was a free spirit and didn't see things the way I did. Here, in the UK, I wasn't valued either. I'd ruined everything.

I put my head in my hands.

A minute later, the phone rang. Terry.

'I've booked the tickets,' he said. 'The flight leaves at ten tonight. We have to be there at about seven. My train from Birmingham won't leave me much time, so I'll meet you at the airport. Heathrow Terminal Four. All right, Heather?'

'Good morning, Terry.'

'Morning,' he said belatedly. 'Did you hear me? You'll meet me at the airport?'

I hesitated. My next few words might dictate the entire rest of my life. What did I want to do?

'Please come home, Heather. You'll see I've changed. I'm nothing without you.' Terry was pleading now.

'I know,' I whispered.

'So, you'll come home with me? You will meet me at the airport, won't you?'

I looked around the dining room, where my tea and the rest of my toast sat cold and unappetising. What would my life be like if I stayed? Uncertain. I'd lose my job or have to quit. I'd have to avoid Raven and move out of Aunt Ruth's house to a crappy bedsit somewhere. That's all I could afford as I conserved my pitiful savings while searching for another job and waiting for my share of the divorce money, which could be months away.

Or I could go back to my old life. It was familiar, and its familiarity made it comfortable, even if it was mundane and predictable. I'd carry on looking after my husband and being an underappreciated schoolteacher. I'd fade away into a dull, ordinary existence, but one I already knew well.

Perhaps fading away in a mundane existence was better than crashing and burning here, where I'd ruined everything that I'd touched, like a King Midas in reverse.

'Heather?' Terry prompted. 'I need an answer.'

'I'm thinking.'

'Please think faster. I'm running out of credit.'

I choked up, but I got the words out. 'I'll be there.'

Our call was cut off after that, but I was sure he heard me.

I sat with my head in my hands, upset and confused. I'd hoped for so much when I left him and came to England, but it wasn't working out. It was a shambolic wreck, a—what's the word Rachel uses to describe some of her legal cases?—a clusterfuck.

Raven's words from last night circled in my head, like seagulls above discarded soggy chips. I'd dismissed them as being irrelevant—after all, he didn't know what it was like to be needed by someone as much as Terry needed me. I had an obligation to my husband. Yes, he'd cheated on me, and I blamed him for that... but was it that simple?

I wasn't sure. All I knew was that Terry said he needed me.

I needed to be needed. That was how I'd always known I had value as a person. Was that what Raven was talking about last night? I wasn't concentrating. I'd been in a bit of a funk.

After disposing of the rest of my breakfast, I texted Lydia to report myself sick. I was sick in a way—sick of being me, sick of the mistakes I'd made. This was the easy way out. I didn't have to quit, and she wouldn't have to fire me. I'd simply vanish.

But what should I say to Aunt Ruth? Neither she nor Raven were up and about at this early hour. Should I wait until Aunt Ruth came out or wake her up?

No. I couldn't face talking to her. She'd blame herself, thinking that because she'd told me I might have to find somewhere else to live temporarily, I decided I couldn't stay in the country. But that was only a small part of it.

In the kitchen, I found paper and pen and wrote a note saying I was going back to New Zealand that night. This way, I'd avoid talking to her and avoid the awkwardness of the conversation and any ensuing arguments.

Neither would I have to talk to Raven. That would be painful. I truly liked him. I had the feeling that he would tell me I was giving up and running away.

Wasn't I? Yes. I may as well admit it to myself, even if I couldn't summon the courage to admit it to others.

I didn't want to take the time to pack my new stuff. Besides, I didn't have a suitcase to put it in. All I had to do was pick up my recovered suitcase at the airport, meet Terry and check it in for the flight home. I could text Raven later on and ask him to send me the witchy stuff I'd bought—if I still wanted it.

I let myself out of the house and walked to Kingston train station, where I caught a train into central London. During the half-hour trip, the train became packed, and I was squeezed into my window seat by people standing in the aisles looking down at me with vacant expressions. Of course, these strangers couldn't know I was running away from my problems again, but I still imagined they did.

Waterloo station was mayhem, with hundreds of commuters walking across the concourse in all directions, emerging from the platforms to hurry towards the exits or the underground. They weaved around each other with skilful ease, while I bumped into several people before I'd gone even a few metres.

To catch my breath, I bought a takeaway coffee and a pastry from a tiny concourse eatery. I ate it and sat leisurely until the whirlwind of activity around me had died down considerably.

Once it was quieter, I texted Rachel.

I'm not wanted here, and everything has gone to shit. I'm flying back to NZ tonight. See you soon.

Five minutes passed without a response. It was evening in New Zealand. Maybe Rachel had gone to bed.

I video called Rose. It wasn't too late for my daughter.

After exchanging pleasantries, I asked her if she knew her dad had flown to England to take me back with him.

Rose gasped. 'No. I had no idea. I'm amazed he would do that. He's never been beyond Australia before, has he? Is he with you now?'

'No, he's in Birmingham.'

'Why is he in Birmingham?'

'Never mind. I'm going to meet him later today. Tomorrow morning, your time.'

Rose's expression changed to one of surprise. 'Have you forgiven him for cheating on you?'

I gritted my teeth. 'No, of course not.'

'Then... why, Mum? Have you forgotten what we talked about? About you standing up for yourself?'

'It's not that simple, Rose—'

'Isn't it? Dad isn't good for you, Mum.'

'I know, but he says he's changed. He says he needs me.'

Rose stared at me with a stunned expression. 'That's not what life is about, Mum. We talked about this.'

'You talked about it. I listened.'

'You didn't listen well enough. Something must have happened. Tell me what's going on.'

I took a deep breath, then spilled it all. Everything. Even the ghosts, and how I'd fucked up everything. 'And that's why I have to leave,' I ended.

'What bullshit is that, Mum?'

'It's not bullshit. It's my life.'

'All you're doing is running away from your problems again.'

'Maybe.' I couldn't deny it. It was true.

'At least think about your options before getting on that plane.'

'I'm out of options, Rose. I'll call you when I get home.' I disconnected.

An uneasiness settled in me. I'd avoided arguments with Aunt Ruth and Raven, then invited one with Rose. Maybe I wasn't one hundred per cent sure of my intentions after all.

It was only ten o'clock, and I had the rest of the day to fill in before having to be at the airport. One of the airports. London had five scattered around; one of them was Heathrow, and that had five terminals itself. I wasn't burdened with luggage. What should I do?

Sightseeing. I could see something of London before leaving. One of the art galleries? No, that made me think of Raven. I'd do something else.

After a few minutes' deliberating, I caught the tube to Tower Bridge and lined up with other tourists to visit the Tower of London. I'd seen photos of it before, so it was eerily familiar even though I'd never been there. It was so *old*. A thousand years old. History was baked into its stone walls and cobblestones. And dungeons.

I marvelled at the ancient stone castle and grounds. *There must be ghosts here.*

The famous Tower ravens strutted around on the grass and appeared unafraid of the visitors.

I approached an official guide. 'Excuse me? Why don't the ravens fly away? What's keeping them here?'

'Ah, madam, you're asking about the rumour that if the ravens all left the Tower grounds, London would fall. Am I right?'

'Yes. I'm curious.'

'Yes, madam, at the Tower, we take that rumour extremely seriously. That's why we clip their wings to prevent them from leaving.'

So simple. So matter-of-fact. As I watched the crippled birds parading in the courtyard, I couldn't help think of Raven. What would he think of me now after our conversation last night?

I might never know.

A flood of guilty thoughts overcame me. I muffled a sob. Aunt Ruth and Raven had been kind to me, and how was I treating them? With disrespect, that's how. Running away without even saying goodbye, telling myself it was the best thing for everyone. Well, it wasn't. It was the easiest thing for me. It was wrong on many levels, yet I was going ahead with it.

A pain thumped in my head.

To distract myself, I joined a queue of people to pass by the Crown Jewels. It wasn't possible to stop moving—there were too many tourists for that. Security guards were everywhere.

'It's amazing these are displayed for the public,' I said to the woman in front of me.

'They're replicas,' she said. 'They'd never put the real ones in here.'

'Really? I'd never have guessed from the look of them.'

'No. And being fake doesn't stop us from queueing up to see them, does it?'

Fake. Just like the ravens in the courtyard outside.

And me. Wife. History teacher. House guide. Friend. Witch. All fake.

I had wanted to get away, but no matter how far I ran, I couldn't get away from myself.

It took only a few minutes to view the fake crown jewels, and then I was back in the courtyard. There, a young woman sat alone with her back to the stone wall of the tower. Everyone ignored her. She was richly dressed in a wide billowing brown dress that spread over her legs and the ground. Some tourists even stepped on it. A beaded bonnet covered her hair, and a pendant of gold hung from her neck. Her face was pale.

She caught sight of me staring at her and beckoned me. I had no doubt this was one of the Tower's ghosts. But whom? Anne Boleyn? Lady Jane Grey? Arbella Stuart? I'd seen their faces in an art book. But which one was it? I wracked my memory. *Damned post-op brain fog.*

I went over and sat next to the ghostly figure. She was only a teenager. 'Hello. How are you?'

She turned to face me, expressionless. 'I hast been a disembodied spirit for nigh an eternity.'

'I know.' That was obvious from her outfit. Close up, I recognised her from the history books. 'You're Lady Jane Grey. You're a fascinating historical figure.'

'Thee know of me?' A spark of curiosity showed itself in her face. 'Pray tell, how art thee aware of me? 'Tis an art reserved for those who practice witchcraft. Take heed, for if thee discloses thine abilities, thy life may be forfeit to a fiery demise.'

I shook my head. 'That doesn't happen now, thankfully. Are you lonely, or do you have company?' *What a stupid question. The Tower of London must be crammed with ghosts.*

'My dearest confidante and companion, Anne, and I art forever bound together within these walls and places nearby. We spend time together. We wast fated, for in the end, our heads wouldst both roll beneath the executioner's blade. Alas, nay matter one's rank or station in life, one cannot escape the reach of Death.'

'Yes. How terrible.'

'I wast but a tender age when the headsman's blade befell upon my neck. 'Twas not my wish to ever don the crown, yet I didst. Sixteen wast my piteous years when I ascended the throne. For nine days, I reigned, until my beloved husband and I wast arrested and entrapped within the Tower. For three months, we remained sequestered in the Tower until the day of my head's removal from my shoulders.'

I blanched at the thought. 'That's awful.'

She pointed at the green space before her, the infamous Tower Green. 'Aye, 'twas right *thither* that my life ended.'

'I'm so sorry to hear that, Lady Jane. What happened to you was evil and unfair.' I glanced around. 'Is your husband with you?'

'Alas, nay, I hast not beheld him since that fateful day. Oh, how I wish they hadst not made me Queen.' She put her head in her hands.

How could I comfort her? I couldn't put my arm around her shoulders, like I wanted to. She was a ghost. Incorporeal. Instead, I said, 'They made you Queen because of your father. He was the last man who could trace his bloodline back to King Henry the Eighth.'

'That naughty day.' She smiled weakly. 'Thankee for thy kind visit.'

'Don't blame yourself. Nothing of what happened to you was your fault.'

I bid her goodbye and left the tower with a mixture of wonder and disappointment at what I'd seen. I caught the District Line west and changed onto the Piccadilly Line to Heathrow.

It seemed to take ages. It was easy to pick out the travellers. Several people lugged suitcases onto the train and sat with them between their knees or stood with them in the doorways. Thankfully, my luggage was already at the airport, waiting for me, having travelled via Alaska.

After a while, we emerged above ground and raced through the outer suburbs, stopping every couple of minutes. The train remained busy, and by the time we pulled into Heathrow Terminal Four, it was crowded again.

It was only mid-afternoon. I had so much time, but no wish to do anything except get to the airport.

My phone had a signal again now that I wasn't deep underground in the tube tunnels. Terry hadn't called. He must still be on his way here.

After some searching, I found the lost luggage office and collected my long-lost cases. They were quite battered, for which the attendant apologised. It didn't matter. They only needed to survive one more journey before I would retire them from service for good. I grabbed a luggage trolley and piled them on it. Next time, I would travel with only *one* suitcase.

But there wouldn't be a next time, would there?

The airport had many eateries, and I sampled three of them for coffee and snacks and an early dinner while waiting for Terry to call. At seven o'clock, he did.

I swallowed my nerves and answered. 'Hello? Where are you?'

'In the terminal building. I'm waiting at the information desk. Where are you?'

'Nearby. I'll come and find you.' I disconnected.

And that was it. A ten-second discussion to determine the course of the rest of my life: a return to the same old, same old.

A prison sentence with no time off for good behaviour.

What would Aunt Ruth think of me? And Raven, after his 'giving up' talk yesterday?

Heat rushed through my face. I'd avoided speaking to them this morning. I'd run away. I *had* given up.

Was that who I was?

More importantly, was that who I wanted to be?

I got to my feet and leaned against the luggage trolley. Maybe I was overthinking everything. I'd failed. Time to go back to my old shitty life. *It's that simple, really.*

I fished in my pocket for the airport terminal map I'd picked up when I arrived. Whoever heard of an airport needing its own map? But this place certainly did.

As I pulled it out, a folded piece of paper came with it. I opened it. Someone had scrawled a message on it:

*Believe in yourself. You are braver than you think, more
talented than you know and capable of more than you
imagine. Go after your dreams and don't let anyone put you in
a box.*

Raven

My heart melted like whipped butter on French toast. I read the note over and over. People surged around me. I didn't move until someone almost fell over the trolley.

The phone rang, shaking me out of my introspective state of mind. Terry.

'Where the bloody hell are you? We have to check in.'

His anger flustered me. 'I'll be right there. Two minutes.'

I stuffed the note in my pocket and referred to the map. The information desk didn't look far on the map, but it took me ten minutes to walk there. The airport was like a small town.

'About time,' Terry grumbled. 'I'm glad you've come to your senses, Heather. Now let's get checked in and get out of this godforsaken place.'

'The airport?' I asked.

'The whole bloody country.'

I followed him as he headed for the check-in counter, not knowing even what airline he'd booked on. Turned out it was one of the better ones. It must have cost a packet.

'How did you pay for this, Terry?'

'I extended the mortgage by a bit.'

'A bit?'

'Enough for business class.'

'That's a lot more than a bit.'

He turned, snarling. 'I had to come and get you. If you'd not run off here, I wouldn't have had to do it. It's your fault I've had to spend our money on the flights.'

'Our money? We separated. The only asset we have in common is the house, and you can't extend the mortgage without asking me. You should have spent your own money on these airfares.'

'Let's not have a fight now, Heather. Just be grateful I came to get you before you got into too much difficulty over here by yourself.'

'Difficulty?'

'You know you need me by your side.'

'Actually, I managed damn well by myself.' I bit my lip. That was a lie. I'd screwed everything up, but I wasn't going to admit it to him.

We reached the counter. I dug in my purse for my passport. Terry handed over his own and the tickets. A minute later, he'd checked in our bags, we had our boarding passes, and we were heading for departures.

With each step, my mood worsened. I had a headache coming on, and my feet dragged as if my shoes were made of lead. Raven's words echoed in my mind like lottery balls bouncing around in their randomiser machine. Rose's assertion that Terry wasn't good for me and my life shouldn't be about his needs rang in my head. The messages competed for my attention.

The departure gate came into view. Terry grabbed my arm as if to prevent me from bolting. *Did he think I might?*

'This is going to be a big weight off my mind,' he grumbled, 'going back home and getting back to normal.'

Normal. Overworked in a shitty job. Unappreciated by my cheating husband.

Nothing to look forward to.

We reached the departures gate. Another few steps, and there would be no turning back. Ever. A mundane, ordinary, thankless life waited for me on the other side of that gate.

I pulled my arm free.

Terry turned, startled, his face reddening. 'What the bloody hell is it now?'

'I'm not going with you.'

'You're... what?'

People pushed past us. We were blocking part of the entrance to the departures area.

'I'm not going. Since you got here, all you've talked about is what you need. You haven't given a single thought to what I need or want. You haven't changed at all.'

He opened his mouth to speak, but nothing came out. He closed it again.

I continued. 'You might need me, Terry. Hell, I'm sure that you do. You need someone to cook and clean and look after you and pay the bills. But that person will not be me. That's not what I want my life to be anymore. I want more than that.'

Terry's eyes narrowed. 'What's this rubbish? Who've you been talking to? Your crazy aunt?'

'Never you mind. I don't want other people controlling me anymore. That's what you do. Control me.'

'I don't. I might tell you what to do, but I don't control you.'

'Listen to yourself. You don't even make sense.'

He grabbed at my arm, but I stepped back. 'If you want to fly, you have to give up what weighs you down.'

'What mumbo-jumbo is that nonsense? Did you make it up?'

'No. It's written on the sign behind you.' I pointed. 'The one saying, "Pack light or miss your flight." I simply repurposed it. You've weighed me down, Terry. You've held me back since the day we were married. Well, now I want to make something of myself on my own.'

'You're crazy. You'll come running back to me when you fail.'

I squeezed Raven's note in my pocket. 'I'm not going to fail. I'm going to succeed. I'm going to win.'

A surge of people bustled me from behind, trying to get past. I extricated myself with difficulty, squeezing against the flow. Terry tried to follow me, but the crowd swept him into the departures' area with them. He called out to me futilely before he vanished around the corner.

Terry would fly home without me. My luggage would go with him, but I didn't care. *It's only baggage. Part of my old life I don't need any longer*.

I turned and strode towards the tube station. I had a job to get back to, a stolen witch's spell book to find and a murderer to catch.

It might be difficult, but I was going to give it a damn good try.

Chapter 30

I REACHED KINGSTON train station at about eight o'clock. It was still busy with late-working commuters returning home. On the concourse, my phone rang. Rachel.

'Heather, what the fuck's going on? You texted to say you're about to fly home. Are you sure? Are you at the airport now?'

I'd forgotten the text I had sent her. *Brain fog*. 'I had a crisis of confidence for a while, but I'm staying.'

Rachel's sigh of relief was audible even with the people walking around me. 'What happened?'

I explained in detail, and as I did, a renewed certainty that I'd made the right choice struck me.

When I'd finished, Rachel said, 'I'm proud of you, girlfriend. I'm sure you're doing the right thing. I'd love to talk longer, but I've got to get ready for work.'

'Okay. Let's chat again soon.'

I caught a taxi from the train station because I was so tired after being out for over twelve hours and having such an emotionally charged and eventful day.

They must have seen or heard me coming, as both Aunt Ruth and Raven were waiting for me in the living room. Aunt Ruth clutched my note in one hand and gripped the arm of her wheelchair in the other. Her knuckles were white. Raven was unsmiling, but had a curious gleam in his eyes.

'What do you call this?' Aunt Ruth said.

The note I'd written or my return? 'I had a crisis of confidence,' I said, trying to cover all excuses. 'I'm sorry. Really sorry. I didn't want to walk out without saying goodbye, but I didn't know how to handle it this morning. It was like I was in a box and all the walls were closing in and they were going to crush me and I couldn't breathe anymore.'

Aunt Ruth dropped the note and wheeled over. She pulled me down for a hug. 'It's all right, dearie. I understand. Your note made me very sad, but it's my fault. I didn't understand the pressure and strain you were under. Of course, you've had an extremely hard time lately.'

I pulled out of the hug. 'You've had it much worse than me,' I said, misty-eyed. Her terrible injury. The hospital stay. The enigmatic third of September date Aunt Ruth said would be the date of her death.

Raven stepped forward and took my hands in his. 'I'm so glad you've come back.'

'Thanks. I'd hug you too but I don't want you to turn into a raven again.'

'Haha. That's a good idea for now.'

'I want to solve the mystery and find the stolen spell book to help Aunt Ruth.'

'Let me help you with that,' Raven said, grinning. 'We'll make a great team.'

'I'm sure we will. Thank you.'

'You're welcome.'

'Aunt Ruth, do you still want me to move out of here? Can I stay a little longer? I won't interfere with whatever you and Raven are doing.'

'Of course you can stay. I always meant for you to stay. I was only in one of my moods when I said I thought you should leave. Ignore that. And, look, something arrived in the post for you today.'

She wheeled over to the table and picked up a solid rectangular package, slid it onto her knees and came to where I'd sat on the sofa next to Raven. 'This must be your correspondence course for witchy learning.'

'Oh! Great.' I took the package and tore off the wrapping. It contained bundles of booklets, diagrams, maps, recipes and various other esoteric-looking materials. 'This is going to take me a while to get through. Is it the entire course?'

'Yes. Basic knowledge and spells, how to store magical power and so on. It covers a lot. There's also a test.'

'A test? To see if I pass the course?'

Aunt Ruth chuckled. 'Not that sort of test. It's evaluating what your witchy discipline might be. That indicates where you'll develop the most witchy talent. If you're lucky, you might do other stuff too, but probably only major spells in your primary discipline. And you already know you can see ghosts, like most other witches.'

'Wow. That sounds interesting. Can... can we do the test tonight? If you and Raven aren't busy, that is?'

'Sure. Why not? And you'll need to buy some witchy materials before you start the course itself.'

'I've got some already. I went to the Apothecary's Potions and Scrolls shop a couple of days ago.'

Aunt Ruth smiled. 'Excellent.'

Raven came back from the kitchen with a takeout menu. 'How about I order us some pizza?'

I beamed. Things were looking up. 'Sounds great.'

We ordered the pizzas and chatted for a while. I told Aunt Ruth and Raven about my encounter with my ex-husband and how stupid I'd been thinking that I should return to New Zealand with him. How I'd blinded myself to how things were with him before I'd left. And how I'd extricated myself from him at the airport.

'The funniest thing was that the airline finally found my lost luggage, and I retrieved it and checked it in for the flight.'

'What?' Raven said. 'You mean it's on its way back to New Zealand now? And you think that's funny?'

'I've already replaced everything I needed. And with my luck, my stuff won't get there, anyway. But I'll ask for it to be rerouted back here.'

The doorbell interrupted our laughter. Raven went to answer it and came back with the pizzas.

'Bags the ham and pineapple one,' I said.

'I don't know how you can eat pizza with pineapple on it,' Raven said. 'In Italy, that would be sacrilegious.'

'You're missing out,' I teased him, grabbing a box at random. It was the right one.

After eating, Raven said he had something to do and went out.

Aunt Ruth and I searched through the contents of the correspondence course until we found the witchy discipline test. I'd asked her what form the test took, but she kept me guessing. My best guess was multiple choice questions.

It wasn't that. A cardboard fold-up construction like a flimsy dolls' house opened up. A plastic bag full of miniature furniture came with it. Aunt Ruth seemed to enjoy watching my consternation as I followed the instructions and put all the little pieces where they were supposed to go.

'Now what?' I said when I'd finished.

'Hold that thing in one hand.' She gestured to the final piece, a thin rectangular piece of metal.

'That's a magical battery,' Aunt Ruth said. 'Minimal magical power storage. Only enough for the test.'

'Okay.' Clever. I'd have a little taster of real magic as well as finding out my discipline or whatever.

'Turn the page. Now the fun begins.'

I turned the page. Several numbered exercises followed.

'What's your discipline, Aunt Ruth?' I'd not asked her before.

'Telekinesis. I can move objects. That's how I can magically make tea. Bigger objects require more magical power. For anything major...'

'You need your magic mirror.' I groaned. That another screwup I had to fix sooner rather than later.

'How about you try the first exercise? It's about weather control.'

'I'm already good at that, Aunt Ruth. At my age, I can produce wind several times a day without even thinking about it.'

She hit me lightly across the arm. 'Farting doesn't count. This is actual wind, rain, even lightning for higher-powered witches. The exercise will be to produce that in miniature in a room in the cardboard house.'

'Okay.' I read the instructions. The exercise was simple. Battery in one hand for magical energy. Other hand outstretched. Look at a tiny chair in the dolls' house. Think of creating wind.

'The chair should topple over if you have this discipline,' Aunt Ruth said.

I concentrated. The chair flew back and embedded itself in the cardboard wall.

'Well, that looks conclusive,' Aunt Ruth said with a wry grin.

'Should I do the other tests?'

'Of course. There's still battery power.'

I tried them all. Most failed. Some were questionable positives. Overall, though, it looked like weather control was going to be my thing.

'Is that a good result?' I asked Aunt Ruth.

'There's no good or bad. It's how you use it. Some night soon, when you're part way through your course, we'll spend a couple of hours outside, and I'll show you how to draw magic from the surrounding elements. While you're inexperienced, you'll only control small amounts of magical energy. Later, as you gain experience, you'll have more at your disposal. Eventually, you'll need some place to store it—'

'Like a mirror,' I said, lowering my gaze.

'Some things work better than others. Mirrors are excellent. A pottery knick-knack isn't. You'll have to experiment to see what works for you, and then you'll bind yourself to it to ensure it can retain magic for months, rather than only hours.'

'There's quite a science to this, isn't there?'

'Rather too much, if you ask me.'

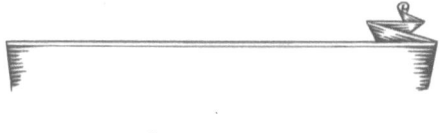

Chapter 31

THE NEXT MORNING WAS a little brighter, but the threat of a thunderstorm hovered perpetually nearby. Dark clouds swirled near the horizon.

I went to work bearing pastries and chocolates.

Lydia met me in the office. 'I see you came prepared,' she said, glancing at the tasty treats. 'I wasn't sure if you'd even come back at all.'

'I love this job, and I want to stay, if you can all forgive me.'

'Chocolates definitely help.'

Melissa also brought pastries, so we spread them out over the day, an idea of which I was thoroughly in favour.

Penny arrived last. 'Heather, I'm glad you came back,' she said. 'I may have over-reacted the other day. Everyone wants poor Ronald's murderer to be caught. The three of us had a long talk yesterday about what you did and concluded you had good intentions, even if what you did was inappropriate. Let's forget about it.'

I hugged her. 'Thanks, Penny. I'm sorry for scaring you.'

Our time prior to opening the house was back to normal, or so it seemed. We ate pastries and chocolates, shared gossip and anecdotes, and laughed a lot.

But I hadn't put aside my suspicions. I merely concealed them. In my mind, one of these women was a malicious criminal.

And I had a plan to figure out who it was.

IN MY LUNCH BREAK, I went outside for a gentle walk. I'd been on my feet all morning. They would ache by the time I'd finished work, but a stroll would help improve my fitness. The gardens were filled with topiaries in the shapes of griffins, unicorns and dragons. A maze of hedges with a sundial in the middle sounded like fun, but I avoided it in case I got lost and was late back from my break.

Inspector Pentecost phoned me while I strolled through the gardens.

'Ms Nicholls, do you remember me telling you not to leave the Surrey area until I conclude my investigation?'

'I remember now, but I'd actually forgotten. Why are you calling? I'm still here.'

'Yes, well, your name popped up on a screen when you checked in last night to fly to New Zealand. We had officers waiting to apprehend you in the departures area, but you must have changed your mind. Wisely, I would say.'

'I was seeing my ex-husband off. He wanted me to go with him, but I wouldn't. He checked me in.'

The inspector was silent for a while. 'That sounds complicated.'

'It is.'

'All right. Thanks for clearing that up, and let me be clear—don't leave the area.'

'I won't. I promise.'

She hung up without saying goodbye. I strolled around a corner and stopped. Maisey sat on the ground in my path. She looked up at me with a melancholic expression.

'Are you okay, Maisey?' I asked. She didn't look it.

'Miserable. T'wouldst be a sorrowful affair if it be true we do not venture forth anon. I'd most heartily like to wend out.'

'I hope we can go soon.' I scrutinised her. 'What's making you sad, other than that?'

She sighed and stared at the ground. 'Simply musing on my miserable life. T'weren't proper, poor me. I wast born into wretched servitude and toiled from the age of six. From sun up to sun down, t'wast. Until the spotted fever took me at twelve.'

'Measles, it's called now.' Unfortunate girl. What a miserable existence. 'I'm so sorry, Maisey, that happened to you. Your life was sadly too short.' A thought occurred to me. 'Is that why you haven't moved on? You wanted to experience more?'

'I suppose so. 'Tis a whole new world now. Ye hast healing potions that work like spells of the ancient druids.' She stood and strode towards the house without looking back.

I HAD A PLAN. IT WASN'T much of a plan, and I didn't know if it would work, but it was all I had, and I eagerly waited for the day at Chirtlewood to end before I could put it into action.

Melissa gave me a long sideways glance when she left Chirtlewood. Maybe she wondered what I was up to. All day, I'd been restless, hopping from foot to foot, pacing up and down the passageway upstairs and popping in and out of the library. If nothing else, I was getting fitter.

I drove into Kingston and went to the Apothecary's Potions and Scrolls shop before it closed.

Herbert approached me. 'Heather. How are you getting on with your witchy studies?'

'I received the correspondence course yesterday, but I've already started.'

'Wonderful.' Herbert brought his hands together in a quiet celebration. 'So, you want to talk to me about that stolen witch's spell book, do you?'

'I do. Are we alone?' I asked.

'Yes. No one's brought in anything of the description you gave me.'

'Okay. I thought I'd check, anyway. Could you do me a huge favour? It might have turned up somewhere else, but I don't know who to ask.'

'You'd like me to call around a few places?'

How does he always know what I'm about to say? 'That would be great.'

'There's no need to call around. We have the Witchnet for that.'

Of course. I'd forgotten about that. So, too, it seemed, had Aunt Ruth. Or maybe she was distracted by other issues—like her impending death. The date she'd declared would be her last was only three months away.

'Can you show me the Witchnet, please, Herbert?'

'No problem. It's about time to close up the shop, anyway. Then you and I can go to the office at the back.'

He locked the door and led the way to a small but comfortable office with weird knick-knacks hanging on the walls. Maybe no one wanted to buy them, and Herbert didn't want them taking up room in the shop, yet couldn't bear to dispose of them.

Herbert pulled up a chair for me and sat at another behind the desk. I peered at his computer as he searched for old witchy books for sale.

To my astonishment, there were pages and pages of them. 'I had no idea there'd be so many.'

'There's a thriving second-hand market. Some of the oldest books, or those containing powerful magic, go for massive amounts.'

'So I see.' My eyes watered at some of the prices being asked.

He turned the keyboard and mouse over to me. 'Scroll through and see if you can find the book you're looking for.'

I started searching. Why hadn't I thought of this earlier? Why hadn't I asked for help earlier? It was another foible—or flaw—of mine that I needed to change. People are often willing to help when they are asked—I was—as long as they're not being taken advantage of.

'Any luck?' Herbert asked. 'Can I get you a cup of tea while you're searching?'

'Oh, yes, please.'

I scrolled to the end. Nothing. I sat back.

'No good?' Herbert put the tea down next to the laptop. I took a sip. It was white, no sugar, exactly how I liked it. More mind reading?

'It's not here, but I expected that. The thief may be holding on to it until things settle down before selling it.'

'Or they want it for themselves,' Herbert suggested.

'Is there a shop you know of with a reputation of being... dodgy?'

'Dodgy? Dishonest, you mean?'

'Yes. The kind of place that would buy stolen books like that witch's spell book without asking any questions about where they came from.'

'Why do you want to know that?'

'Because that's the most likely place the thief would go.'

'And it's the least likely place from which you'll get any assistance.'

Shit. Herbert was right. My entire plan relied on figuring out where the book might end up and intervening before it gets there.

'And don't look at me. I'm not going to pretend I'm in the market for stolen books, so don't suggest it.'

'Of course not. Thanks. This has been useful. If nothing else, it tells me the murderer most likely still has the stolen book.'

'I hope you're right, Heather, but they might already have moved it on. It could be anywhere in the world by now.'

I groaned. This idea was useless. I'd gotten nowhere.

'Sorry I can't be of more help. Or encouragement.' Herbert placed a supportive hand on my shoulder.

'That's fine. You've been helpful. Thank you.' I turned to go, but an idea occurred to me, and I turned back. 'Does the Witchnet have personal ads?'

'Yes, it does. They are used for a lot of things, though mainly for dating. But you're not thinking of hooking up with someone, are you?'

Had he batted an eyelash at me when he asked that? 'No, I meant I could put in a personal ad to tempt the thief.'

'What a great idea! Here, let me show you how to do it.'

Herbert tapped at the keyboard for a few seconds and navigated to a part of the website where I could enter an ad. Now all I had to do was think of how to word it. It had to be something tempting enough to draw the murderer out of hiding, but not obviously a trap.

After a minute, I wrote:

Powerful warlock in town for a few days seeks rare or important witchy materials, particularly spell books. Top prices paid. Contact < > here:

This was the hard part. I couldn't give my phone number—all my colleagues knew that. Raven? Aunt Ruth? Could I pull them into this?

'You're hesitating,' Herbert said. 'Ask a friend to help you with this. I can't get my establishment involved. It'd ruin my reputation.'

'I know someone.' Raven had offered to help. I phoned him and explained the outline of my plan, hoping he wouldn't ask for details, because I hadn't thought that far yet.

'Sure. I can pretend to be a powerful warlock,' he said. 'That might be fun.'

'It could be dangerous.'

'Then you'll definitely want me around.'

I got off the call. Herbert grinned at me. 'It sounds like it's falling into place. I have another suggestion, though. Put an ad on the *Antiques and Collectibles* website too. Only witches and warlocks use the Witchnet, but anyone might see it on the other site.' He leaned close, brushing me. 'I'll show you the website.'

Five minutes later, I'd loaded an ad that might work for non-witches:

Book collector in town for a few days seeks old, unusual books about witchcraft practices. Top prices paid. Contact < > here:

Herbert smiled. 'Looks good. I think you've got everything covered.'

'Yes. Now, please—'

'Relax. My lips are sealed.'

'Thank you, Herbert.'

'No problem. Please remember to buy your witchy supplies from here.'

I laughed. 'I promise.'

I completed the contact details at the end of the ad, bid Herbert good evening and drove home. The personal ad was now live, and now all I had to do was wait for the book thief to take the bait.

Chapter 32

THE NEXT MORNING, RAVEN announced that he'd received a text offering 'a rare witch's spell book for sale from a private collection'. The seller had asked for an exorbitant price, as expected.

'That's got to be it,' I said. 'Meet with the seller, and we'll catch them red-handed with the stolen book. I'll call Inspector Pentecost too.'

Raven shook his head. 'She told you to leave the investigation to her, right? Imagine if this person is a genuine seller with a witch's spell book of their own, and not the murderer and thief you're after.'

That wouldn't have a positive outcome. 'Okay, we'll do it on our own.'

'All right. I'll arrange a meeting for eight tonight in Richmond somewhere.' He tapped out the message.

We waited on the edge of our seats for a reply. It came within a minute. 'Agreed.'

I grinned. 'We've tempted them into our trap. All we have to do is make sure we catch them. Maybe we can record the meeting on our phones.'

'I'd already thought of that,' he said. 'Then we'll have some evidence for Inspector Pentecost.'

THE DAY INCHED ALONG. I was on edge the entire time, studying my colleagues discreetly to see if one of them was acting differently. Maybe excited by the prospect of making a lot of money by selling a valuable spell book, for instance? But if one of them was my target, they were as cool as a penguin in the winter. No one acted suspiciously at all.

Except me, it seemed. In the middle of the afternoon, when I stepped into the countess's bedchamber on a routine patrol for visitors, she stared at me out of the mirror.

Startled by her unexpected appearance, I took a pace back, and she stepped out of the mirror to stand in front of me. 'Pray tell, Heather, what mischievousness is afoot? Thou art as jittery as a hare on a hunting day.'

'Hi, Charlotte.' I lowered my voice. 'I'm going to find the stolen book and solve the murder at the same time. Tonight.'

'Ooh, is it so?' She looked keen. 'I'm coming with thee.'

I guessed she would say that. Probably all the other ghosts would come along too. They could be helpful. But would Raven be aware of them? Would he freak out if he was?

There was only one way to be sure. And I hoped he wouldn't mind the spectral company.

'Thanks, Charlotte. I'll pick you up at about seven thirty.'

'Splendid. We shalt apprehend the scoundrel. Art thou quite sure about not lopping off their head?'

'That's out of the question.'

She sighed. An icy breeze wafted over my face, and I shuddered.

'My most humble apology,' she said.

'It's perfectly fine. I understand you're disappointed.'

'Wilt we place the culprit in the pillory, then? That mercy seems too lenient.'

I shook my head. 'Once the police have them, they'll go to court and a judge will determine how long they will spend in prison.'

Charlotte nodded her approval. 'Chirtlewood is too modern for the purpose, but the Tower's dungeons art said to be still of such remarkable quality.'

'Mm hmm. We'll see.'

Footsteps sounded in the hall. Charlotte vanished like a light being switched off.

Moments later, Melissa entered the room with a family of tourists in tow. She looked around, and seeing no one else there, asked, 'Who were you talking to?'

'I was practising my talk for visitors, making sure I remember everything.'

Melissa smiled. 'Good idea. These nice people from Canada would love to hear it all.'

AFTER WORK, I PHONED Inspector Pentecost and asked her if she had made any progress on the investigation into Ronald's murder. She wasn't pleased to hear from me.

'I can't discuss an ongoing investigation with you, Ms Nicholls.'

'So, you don't have any suspects?'

'There are plenty of suspects, and you're one of them. Beyond that, I can't say anything except that we are working on multiple lines of inquiry.'

'But those are not leading anywhere, are they?'

'I won't rest until I apprehend the murderer, Ms Nicholls. Don't worry about that. Justice will be served in due course.'

I thanked her and rang off. She had nothing. The investigation was stalled.

Solving the mystery was up to me.

Chapter 33

I ATE A QUICK DINNER of lamb chops and chips and talked with Raven about how to handle the meeting with the murderer/thief. We came up with a plan of sorts. Raven would wait in a highly visible spot, his phone audio recording, while I kept out of sight so as not to alert the target about the entrapment. Once they turned up, I would start video recording and approach them both. By then, we should have enough evidence to turn over to Inspector Pentecost.

At seven fifteen, we left the house. I had to collect Charlotte and the others. I stopped in my tracks on the driveway. What could I tell Raven? Did he even know about the existence of ghosts?

Perhaps I shouldn't go to pick them up. It might complicate things. But how could I avoid it after promising Charlotte? I'd be ghosting the ghosts. She mightn't forgive me.

No, I had to stick with the agreement and take them along.

Raven opened the car door and turned to see why I was dawdling. 'Is something wrong?'

'No. I remembered I need to go to Chirtlewood first, that's all.'

'Whatever for?'

'Um... to pick up a few things.' Now I was calling them 'things'. Lucky they were not here to hear that.

'Okay, sure. Let's go.'

We got into the car, and I drove off. The evening traffic had died down. The Thames was peaceful. Early evening sunlight reflected off it as dazzling flashes between the shadows cast by dark clouds whizzing overhead.

'Um... do you have an opinion on ghosts?' I blurted out.

Raven turned to face me, his forehead creasing in puzzlement. 'An opinion on them? What do you mean? Are you asking if I'm scared of ghosts? No, of course not.'

'Right.' *Wrong question. Try again.* 'Do you think ghosts exist, Raven?'

He chortled. 'Of course. I can't see or hear them myself, but I've known of their existence for a long time. I'm sure you've heard the stories of Chirtlewood being haunted. Have you seen any of the ghostly residents, by any chance?'

I took my gaze off the road to glance at him and grin. 'I sure have. In fact, they want to come with us tonight.'

'Oh, so they are the reason we're making this detour. Well, this will be a first for me, I think, sharing a car with a bunch of ghosts. How many are there?'

'Three, probably. And a dog.'

'A ghost dog?'

'Yes, truly. You might even hear him bark. Some people do.'

I pulled up right in front of the entrance to Chirtlewood and didn't bother switching off the engine. Charlotte, the earl, Maisey and Scruffles were waiting on the house steps. They smiled and cheered and approached the car.

'Are they here?' Raven asked.

'Yes, they're coming.' Maisey and Scruffles had bounded over and were already inside. Charlotte took one look at Raven sitting in the front passenger seat and frowned before getting into the back.

There was a problem. There wasn't room for everyone.

After a short while, Raven asked, 'What's going on?'

'Just waiting for the last one.'

The earl was still hobbling over. He was almost there, his cane tapping silently on the cobblestones.

Raven raised his eyebrow. 'Will you introduce them to me? Or is that a ridiculous question, seeing as I can't interact with them?'

'They can see and hear you. I can pass messages if you want to talk. I'll introduce you to everyone on the way.'

The earl was trying to squeeze in, but there wasn't much room. Scruffles leaped up onto Charlotte's lap. Finally, the earl slid in, sandwiching his wife between himself and Maisey.

Raven shivered. 'It's freezing. Did you open a window?'

'That's the ghost chill. The temperature drops with ghosts around.'

'Noticeably.'

'I'll put the heater on,' I said and drove off. As we continued, I explained who our ghostly companions were, and Raven introduced himself. It all seemed a bit eerie.

We reached Richmond a few minutes later, still well before eight o'clock, and I parked a street away from the agreed meeting point. It was still light, not even twilight yet, being early summer.

Raven appeared jittery. That could be from the ghost chill. It made me shiver, too, even with the heater on full blast.

'To what mysterious place art we bound?' the earl demanded. 'I shouldst not wish to squander my valuable hours once more.'

'We're going to keep out of sight in the shadows,' I said.

'We?' Raven looked puzzled. 'Just you. I'm going to wait outside the pub, as agreed.'

'The ghosts and I,' I clarified.

'Oh, of course.'

We got out of the car. We all set off towards the White Hart pub, the earl propelling himself in his ghostly wheelchair. When the pub came into view, I stopped in the shade under a tree, pulled my phone from my bag and concealed myself as best as possible. 'I'll wait here. I hope she shows herself.'

Raven gave me a reassuring smile. 'I'm confident she will. Her texts showed she was eager to conduct the trade. She's expecting to make a lot of money.' He strode on until he was standing outside the pub, first glancing inside, then scouting around the street for anyone approaching.

There wasn't anyone else, apart from Maisey, Charlotte and Scruffles, who had all gone with him. The earl had remained with me.

'Might not but we tarry in this place?' the earl demanded. ''Tis certain the revelry wilt be unfolding yonder. And thither is an alehouse. Pray, allow us procure ourselves a libation!' He wheeled himself off towards the White Hart.

How could the earl get a drink? He was incorporeal. He couldn't drink beer or wine or... Oh. Maybe he could drink spirits. Surely not. I admonished myself for coming up with a rotten pun, which I promised myself not to share with Raven, but the earl was intent on a drink somehow.

Raven stood near the entrance to the White Hart, oblivious to the surrounding ghosts.

Charlotte and Maisey went inside. Why were they doing that? Maisey wasn't old enough in one regard, but she'd died a long time ago, so I supposed the age limit didn't count.

Scruffles barked as the earl approached.

Raven's gaze swept the area. Maybe he could hear the barking ghostly dog.

He brought his phone out of his pocket and stared at it. Is he sending a message, or did he receive one? It was impossible to tell at this distance.

Raven shoved the phone in his pocket and hurried back to me. My heart rate shot up. All the ghosts had entered the pub now.

'The meeting point has changed,' Raven said. 'We should have anticipated this might happen.'

'Where is it now?' And what was I going to do about our ghostly companions?

'Outside Wimbledon theatre at eight fifteen. Come on. Let's get back to the car.'

'Do you think she's been watching us?'

'No. You're out of view from the pub, and if she saw us arrive together from somewhere else, she would have realised this is a trap and wouldn't have phoned me to arrange a new meeting place. We're still good, but we need to get moving.'

'The ghosts are in the pub, though. I need to round them up.'

Raven rolled his eyes. 'There isn't time for that, Heather. It'll take too long to get them all back to the car. We barely have enough time to get to Wimbledon as it is. We need to go now. We'll have to come back for your ghost friends... if they can't get home by themselves, that is.'

'Okay.' How would the ghosts feel about being left behind? There was no way I could ask them. But it was their own fault for wandering off into the pub.

We scurried back to the car and drove off. Raven directed us to Wimbledon. It wasn't far, and I easily found the theatre on the high street. With each passing minute, I lost confidence that our plan would work.

I parked within view of the theatre. Raven sauntered over. I guess he was trying to look casual rather than panicked, which we both were. This mission had gone south. We'd surely been rumbled.

It was quiet outside the theatre. If there was a performance on, it must have already started. Eight fifteen came and went. Then eight thirty. Raven paced up and down on the footpath. I tapped my fingers on the steering wheel, glancing both ways along the street.

Eight forty-five. No one had approached Raven.

Our target had outsmarted us.

Raven came back to the car ten minutes later wearing a downcast expression. It was time to give up. I did a U-turn and headed back the same way.

As we approached Kingston, I said, 'Let's go back to the White Hart. Pick up the Chirtlewood ghosts and give them a lift back.'

'I never expected to be part of a ghost taxi service.' Raven chuckled.

We passed through Kingston and on towards Richmond. Darkness was setting in now.

I pulled up on yellow lines outside the pub and leaped out of the car. 'I know I shouldn't park here, but I'll be as quick as I can.'

I raced inside. But Raven didn't wait in the car. He followed me.

'It's quiet in here for a Wednesday night,' Raven said.

It wasn't. The noise was damned atrocious. The earl sat alone in a booth, singing a bawdy navy shanty at the top of his voice, evidently drunk. Half-empty ghostly tankards sat in front of him.

'Why have you got your hands over your ears?'

'What's that?'

Raven pointed to my hands.

'Oh. The earl is singing. Badly.'

Over at the bar, an old bartender wiped the bar with a cloth. Something about him appeared odd. He moved slightly into better light, revealing that he wore a coarse linen tunic with a leather apron over the top. *A ghost bartender*. He glanced up and smiled at me toothlessly.

Charlotte sat by the window, sipping at a glass of wine. Ghost wine? Was that even a thing? Maisey was playing with Scruffles on the floor beside her. The few patrons in the pub were all on the other side of the room. Perhaps they sensed something out of the ordinary, like the chilliness.

Another bartender—not the apparition—called out to us. 'Would you like something to drink?'

'We might as well have something now we're here,' Raven said.

We approached the bar and ordered. I hurried to find a table as far from the earl as possible, though it made little difference. His tuneless voice grated throughout the whole inn.

Raven brought the drinks over.

'It's been an exciting date,' I joked.

'Thankfully, there wasn't enough excitement to cause my involuntary shift.' He grinned.

'The night is still young.'

We sipped our drinks.

'They should put some music on for atmosphere,' Raven said.

No, please don't. The earl was still hard at it. Actual music might encourage him to sing louder.

'We'll need to come up with another plan if we're going to solve the mystery and find that damned book,' I said.

'Let's think about that tomorrow, once tonight's disappointment is less fresh.'

'Oh. I didn't lock the car. I thought you were going to wait in it.'

'Don't worry. It should be safe in this area.'

'Maybe, but I'd prefer to lock it. Be back in a minute.' I stood and went outside.

Shit.

Three youths were inside. One of them appeared to be trying to start it somehow.

'Hey! Get out of there!' I marched over, waving at them to get out of Aunt Ruth's car.

The one in the passenger seat looked at me and stuck his middle finger up before turning back to the driver. 'Let's fucking go!' he shouted.

The car screeched away. They'd left the handbrake on. A girl in the back seat gawped through the rear window and laughed.

I ran back into the White Hart. 'Some bloody kids are stealing the car!'

Raven was on his feet in a shot, but he wasn't faster than Maisey, who took off straight through the wall and onto the street. Scruffles bounded after her. I raced outside on Raven's heels.

The car was still in sight. It stopped and started. The gears crunched, and I grimaced. Hopefully, the handbrake was off now, otherwise they would damage the car. *Damn those thieves.*

The driver swerved and side-swiped a parked car. I groaned. Now it *was* damaged.

Maisey and Scruffles ran down the street, trying to catch up as the car bunny-hopped. Clearly, the delinquent driver didn't have a licence, and if he'd stolen cars before, they must have been automatics. He wasn't used to a manual transmission.

Raven was on the phone to the police, already reporting the theft. He hung up.

Maisey gave up running. Scruffles kept going, but there was no way he would catch up. The car was picking up speed now.

Raven grabbed me and kissed me passionately on the lips.

A warm, shivery tingle wound its way through my whole body. I pulled him tight and deepened the kiss.

Wait, what?

He was gone. I'd been pressing myself so closely up against him that I lost my balance and nearly toppled forward. I looked up.

A raven streaked low through the air in pursuit of the car.

Raven, after the thieves. With luck, he would see where they abandon the car. There was nothing I could do about it myself. Maisey returned, huffing and puffing. How is it that ghosts could get out of breath? I'd have to ask sometime. In contrast, Scruffles bounded back, full of energy.

We went back inside the White Hart. The singing continued, albeit even more out of tune than before.

'What transpired?' Charlotte asked, alarmed. 'Didst thee apprehend the robbers?'

'No. They're gone.'

'Ah, 'tis true, in my days of yore, those who purloined horses wouldst pay a hefty price. Whipping and even hanging wast oft used to deter felons.'

Draconian. 'They were only kids.'

'Aye, and yet they still took thy carriage.'

The singing stopped. I looked over at the booth, where a dull thud sounded as the earl's head hit the tabletop. He'd passed out.

'We'd better go,' I said. Should I call a taxi, or walk? What would the taxi driver think about stopping outside Chirtlewood for a minute or two while the ghosts got out?

I pulled out my phone to call a taxi, but as I did, a familiar figure emerged from the corridor that led to the toilets, carrying a bulky tote bag that contained something large and rectangular.

Chapter 34

SHE HADN'T SEEN ME yet. Instead of phoning for a taxi, I punched the 'record' button on my phone, slipped it into my pocket and stepped forward.

'Melissa.'

She jumped. 'Oh, what a surprise. Fancy meeting you here.' She glanced around. 'Are you here with someone?'

Charlotte and Maisey watched from their seats, grim expressions on their faces. They'd realised what this was. I knew Melissa couldn't see them.

'I'm alone. What about you? Were you here to meet someone?'

Melissa clutched the tote bag to her side, but there was way of hiding it. 'I—I only popped in for a drink.'

'On your own?'

'Sure. Like you did.' She jutted her jaw out. 'See you tomorrow at work.' She made to move past me.

I stepped in front of her, blocking her path. 'Hold on a minute, Melissa. I'm curious. It looks like you've got an enormous book in your bag. May I see it?' I smiled pleasantly. 'I used to be an history teacher, and I absolutely love books.'

'You won't like this one. I need to go now.' She tried to get past me again. I wouldn't let her.

We were in a standoff. Melissa clearly would not show me what she had in her bag. I stared at the lump. It appeared to be about the same size and shape as the stolen spell book, but that didn't mean it was that book. She might have an excellent reason for not wanting me to see it. Maybe it was a record book for Alcoholics Anonymous meetings, or a gambling journal. She might even be in business with Penny, and it was their accounts. Even if it was none of those things, she didn't have to show me. It wasn't my business what she had in her bag.

The edges of her lips turned up slyly. Melissa surely realised I couldn't do anything without causing a scene. All she'd need to do is report this to Lydia, and I would be fired. I'd already been warned, and she knew it.

'Would you please move out of the way, Heather?' she asked, false sweetness in her tone.

'No. Not until I see if you've got the stolen witch's spell book in your bag.'

There. Now I'd done it. I'd refused to do what she asked me. There was no turning back.

Melissa lifted her head. 'You could lose your job for harassing a colleague, Heather, you know that?'

'I do, but I want to see if that's the stolen spell book in your bag, and you're not leaving here until you've shown me.'

'Get out of the fucking way, Heather.'

'No. I won't.'

It all made sense. Melissa overheard Ronald telling me how the spell book was extremely valuable. She was on the same floor at the time of his murder. She was one of the few people who could have hidden the book and retrieved it later. Even if she wasn't a witch herself, she must have known she could sell it for a lot of money.

One thing I'd learned about Melissa was that she coveted wealth. She desired expensive clothes and accessories, even if she bought them second-hand at the thrift store. She'd seen the witch's spell book as a fast route to riches.

Melissa pressed forward, shoving me aside with one shoulder. I stumbled back but remained on my feet. She escaped through the door onto the street.

I dashed after her. I couldn't let her get away. My car had gone, Raven had flown off, and I couldn't chase Melissa down the street. I wouldn't get fifty metres.

It was raining now.

She'd stopped by an old blue Volvo and was searching her bag. *She must be looking for the keys! That's her car. I can't let her get away!*

If only those kids had stolen her car instead of mine.

I hastened over to Melissa. With one quick movement, I lunged forward and snatched the tote bag from her. She let out a cry of surprise and tried to pull it back. But I held on tightly, refusing to let go.

'Give it to me!' she demanded, glaring at me with fury in her eyes. She dropped her car keys. I kicked them under the vehicle.

'No way,' I shot back. 'You're not going anywhere.'

Lightning crackled in the sky, swiftly followed by a loud peal of thunder.

Melissa glowered at me, but I stood my ground, refusing to let her win. We struggled, our bodies colliding as we fought for control over the tote bag. Finally, I got a firm grip on it and tugged as hard as I could.

The bag ripped open, and the book tumbled to the pavement.

It was the stolen spell book.

I grabbed it. 'Care to explain this, Melissa?' I stuffed it under my coat, pressed against my body, trying to protect it from the rain.

Her startled expression faded when she saw I had the spell book in my possession, and she put her hands on her hips defiantly. 'I found it, and I'm going to turn it in for the reward.'

'Liar. You killed Ronald Morris and stole it after you overheard him say how valuable it was.'

Her eyes drilled into me with hatred. 'You can't prove anything.'

'Inspector Pentecost will be interested to hear my theory, though. Surely, you'll have left behind physical evidence, like fingerprints or DNA. When I tell the police I found you with this stolen book, they'll arrest you and find that evidence.'

'It's your word against mine, Heather. I'll say I found you with the book.'

'But it will be your DNA and fingerprints on the candlestick you hit Ronald with, won't it?' I hoped my phone was still recording this. Would she confess if I pressed her?

Melissa scowled. Her expression changed. 'I didn't mean to kill him. I only wanted to knock him out so he wouldn't see me take the spell book. When he'd said how valuable it was, I had to have it.'

'Why was that?'

'I've worked at Chirtlewood for years. We're not paid much. Look at how the earl and countess lived. What luxury they had. And there are people today who are even richer. Vastly wealthy. Why shouldn't I have some of that? It's just one book from the library, but what I could sell it for would pay for a decent retirement for me.'

'What about Ronald's retirement?' I said grimly. 'You cut that short.'

'I told you that was an accident.'

'You hit him with a heavy metal candlestick. It was lethal.'

'I know. I had to. He saw me snatching the book.' She didn't sound contrite.

'So, he did see you, and it wasn't an accident, was it?' The rain continued to pound down, and I pulled the tote bag containing the book closer to my chest to protect it. 'Why didn't you simply take the book after hours when no one was around?'

'Ronnie was going to ask Lydia if he could borrow the book to take home for a few weeks. I couldn't take the chance she would allow that. I had to get it first. It was too valuable to let it slip away.'

'He died because of your greed, Melissa.'

She tilted her head, not bothering to deny the accusation. 'We can split the proceeds, Heather. How about it?'

'Not a chance. You'll pay for what you did.'

The ghosts, apart from the earl, had come out of the White Hart to watch our confrontation.

'Lop off her head!' the countess suggested.

Maisey glared at Melissa. Beside her, Scruffles barked.

A police car arrived and two police officers got out. 'Is there a Heather Nicholls here?' one of them asked.

'That's me,' I said.

'We found your car. Unfortunately, it's a write-off. It crashed into a wall in Teddington. Witnesses saw some youths push it into the canal.'

Great. That was all I needed right now. The insurance should cover it, though.

'We'll need a statement from you.'

'Of course.'

Melissa was edging away surreptitiously. I grabbed her arm. 'Officers, please call Inspector Pentecost. This is the person responsible for the murder of Ronald Morris.'

Chapter 35

THE POLICE OFFICERS detained Melissa and handcuffed her when I played them the audio recording I had of our conversation. She cried, but she didn't plead innocence. I didn't feel sorry for her. She'd brought this on herself.

We all took cover under the front awning of the White Hart. I pulled my coat further around me. The witch's spell book was tucked inside, protected from the rain. One of the constables remarked that the evening was becoming chilly because the wind was picking up. But it was because of the ghosts who crowded around us.

'This jaunt certes eclipses the others,' Maisey said. ''Tis a shame the earl didst not see all of the merriment and miching mallecho.'

'We shalt tell him about it when he wakes up,' the countess said.

How would I get them home? Raven had gone and probably wouldn't come back tonight. The car was wrecked. I'd need a taxi.

The inspector arrived in an Audi after we'd been kicking our heels outside in the cold for twenty minutes. She wore an evening dress and fancy make-up and had clearly been on a night out. When she saw me, her eyes narrowed. 'Ms Nicholls, if you're wasting police time again, I'll arrest you for interfering with my investigation.'

'I've solved it,' I said, indicating the police officers standing with Melissa, who was handcuffed and appeared completely deflated. 'I recorded a conversation with my colleague in which she confessed to the crime.'

Inspector Pentecost's gaze pinned me with narrowed eyes. 'Is that so? Let me hear this conversation.'

She listened while I played it, then nodded. 'I see.' She glanced at me with grudging respect. 'Your ad hoc investigation appears to have achieved something. But I'll need to take your phone into evidence for a day or two.'

Of course. I gave it to her, but clung to my coat tighter, concealing the witch's spell book so the inspector wouldn't confiscate that too. She gave me a long stare, then pointed. 'Is that the stolen book?'

'Yes, it is.' I sighed.

'Hand it over, please. We'll need it.'

I passed the book over. 'I—that is, Chirtlewood—need this back soon. It's historic and valuable and belongs in our library.' *And I need to borrow it for a while so Aunt Ruth can find a way to heal herself.*

The inspector nodded. 'That should be possible. The book itself might not bear evidence, given the number of people who have handled it, but I want to have a closer look at it, just in case.'

Good luck with that. It's unreadable except for high-level witches. 'Please let me know as soon as we can collect it. It won't be more than a few days, will it?'

'I shouldn't think so. I'll call you.'

'Thanks. It's important.'

The inspector gestured at Melissa and then to the police officers waiting in the background. 'Put her in the car.' She turned back to me. 'You're free to go, Ms Nicholls.'

'Inspector, my car was stolen. Could you ask someone to give me a lift home, please?'

She gave a wan smile. 'I'll do it myself.'

I took my time getting into the car, pretending to tie my shoelaces and adjust my clothing, so Charlotte and Maisey had ample opportunity to fetch the inert, snoring earl from the White Hart and get him into the back. He laid across their laps in the back seat. Scruffles squeezed in beside them.

'Where do you need to go?' the inspector asked. 'I hope you're local.'

'Kingston. But would you mind driving to Chirtlewood first?'

'I can do that.' She smiled. 'You want to make sure the place is fine after what's happened in the past few days. That's commendable.'

'Something like that.'

She drove off, the Audi purring like a tiger. Inspectors must have a good salary. The insurance money for Aunt Ruth's car would hardly stretch to another small second-hand Renault.

'It's cold in here,' the inspector said. She fiddled with the heater while turning a corner one-handed.

'I hadn't noticed.' I'd wrapped my coat warmly around me, though. Four ghosts in the car resulted in a considerable degree of refrigeration.

At Chirtlewood, I got out of the car and strolled up the steps to the front entrance. I made a show of checking that the door was locked, and I peered in the side windows. Once the ghosts had all extricated themselves from the car, including the earl, who was now awake, I got back in.

'Thanks. I had to see it for myself to make sure everything was all right. I'm sure you understand.'

'It's not a problem. I admire your perseverance, Ms Nicholls. I'm the first to admit when I'm wrong. Without your efforts, I don't know when we would have cracked this case.'

I grinned. 'Thanks.'

'I'll be in touch to return the book to Chirtlewood, and I'll give Lydia Barksworth a call after I've dropped you off home to inform her what's happened. Now, whereabouts in Kingston do you need to go?'

As I explained, she put the Audi in gear and set off.

Chapter 36

THE NEXT MORNING WAS sunny and calm. The storm had passed by during the night. When I got to Chirtlewood, I saw that Penny had brought the pastries, and there was one spare. She didn't yet know about Melissa's arrest.

I explained what had happened. Lydia, who'd been briefed by Inspector Pentecost, listened glumly. She and Penny had been colleagues with Melissa for ages. It would take them some time to get used to this.

'I put an ad on the *Antiques and Collectibles* website offering to buy old books related to witchcraft. Someone replied, and my friend and I arranged to meet them.' I sighed with sadness. 'It was Melissa. She had the book on her and confessed to stealing it, but she said she didn't mean to kill Ronald.' Though she obviously did.

'Oh! Damnation!' Penny appeared horrified. 'I never thought...' Her voice trailed off. She looked down.

'Dreadful,' Lydia said, her head in her hands.

'The police arrested Melissa. I'm sorry to give you this news, Penny. And Lydia, I believe the inspector told you last night. I wish it weren't true.'

'She must have wanted to sell the book. Perhaps it was valuable.'

I nodded.

Penny hugged me. 'I'm sorry I got so angry at you. I understand why you did it now.'

'Me too.' Lydia joined us for a group hug.

Joy filled me. I would not lose my job. In time, I'd be great friends with these two.

'I'm glad we know who killed poor Ronald,' I said.

Lydia blanched. 'I can hardly believe it.'

'Me neither,' Penny added. 'But there it is. Whoever knew Melissa would be capable of something like that?'

'She certainly concealed her avarice from us,' Lydia said. 'But, in the end, it overcame her.'

We stood quietly for a few moments, as if it was all too much to take in. My mind wandered. I had other issues to deal with.

Penny broke the silence. 'Why don't you have the extra pastry, Heather? You deserve it.'

'Ha. I think I'd better not. I've got fitter since working here, and I like that a lot, but doubling up on the pastries won't help. I'll gain weight.'

'It won't eat itself. Who cares about body shape at our age? It's more important to be yourself. Right, Lydia?'

'It certainly is. Treat yourself, Heather.'

'Let's split it three ways,' I said, reaching for a knife.

Shortly afterwards, we set to work. I carried the 'Open for visitors' sign to the bottom of the front entrance steps, while Lydia set up the ticketing area. Penny went to check on other things. We had to work harder as there were only three of us now, and we had to cover what Melissa would have done.

She would never be back. I supposed Lydia would soon advertise for another house guide. Pamela at the job centre would have another headache trying to find someone to do it, a task that would be even more difficult now that a murder had been committed in the house.

I went upstairs and into the countess's bedchamber. She wasn't present, but I said, 'Morning, Charlotte,' in case she was listening. I'd been doing that for a few days, and sometimes she appeared for a chat.

Not today, though. Her room lay quiet.

I wandered around the first floor. A few visitors made their way up the stairs, and I introduced myself. A young couple asked me questions about the history of Chirtlewood and the people who lived in it.

This was where I was truly in my element. I beamed and pulled them aside to point out the intricate details carved into the lintel above the earl's bedchamber. I showed them inside, where they listened as I recounted stories of the earl's youthful adventures, the English civil war and how the house changed hands, and various political intrigues in play at the time.

'Wow, you know so much about it,' the young woman said. 'It's fascinating.'

I'd picked up a lot from Lydia, Penny and Melissa. I'd read up on the history too. And some of the information came from the earl and the countess themselves. They were all too happy to pass the time talking to me about their lives almost four hundred years before.

'We are all well trained here,' I said, 'and Chirtlewood has a tremendous amount of history.'

'You really make it come alive,' the young woman's partner said. 'I'd never known history could be so interesting.'

I beamed. This was what I'd always wanted—willing and interested listeners. When I thought about how this couple compared to the teenagers I'd taught in history class, they were diametrically opposite. Helping visitors to Chirtlewood learn and appreciate its history and its people was a thousand times more rewarding than trying to teach ungrateful teenagers to appreciate Roman emperors.

The couple moved on, and I took the opportunity to phone Aunt Ruth.

'Heather, dear, is everything all right?'

'Yes, Aunt Ruth, it couldn't be better. I wanted to check if Raven has come home yet.'

'Oh, yes. He was drenched in the Thames, the poor man. It seems he shifted back to human form when he was sitting on the edge of Kingston Bridge, and he toppled in.'

'Oh no! He's all right, though?'

She chuckled. 'He's fine.'

'I had an idea. We all deserve a treat. Maybe we can go out to dinner tonight, the three of us. There's a nice Italian restaurant by the riverside. It's special. Great views. And if Raven does shift to bird form accidentally, I'll have you there for company.' I giggled.

'What on earth might you say to the poor man over dinner to trigger his curse? Is it salacious?' A muffled snigger followed.

'I'll be perfectly behaved,' I said. *For now.* 'I know you need him in human form to research how to reverse his curse.'

'That's right.' There was a pause. 'I don't have much time left to help him,' Aunt Ruth continued in a lower voice.

I swallowed. 'I'm going to call the inspector later and see if I can get that witch's spell book back from her,' I said. 'Then I will contact the northern warlock about copying it and having your magic mirror fixed.'

'I know you will, Heather. You're the best niece there could be.'

'Thanks, Aunt Ruth.' I smiled sadly. Each passing day was a day closer to September the third. She hadn't told me why she thought she would die that day, but I would do anything I could to change it.

Fixing her magic mirror would be the start.

About the Author

Raven Raine is the pen name of a reclusive author in New Zealand who writes **Paranormal Women's Fiction**.

I live with my partner, two children and two cats. I write by a window with a beautiful cherry blossom tree spread out before me, a steaming cup of coffee on the desk within easy reach, and the grating sound of cat claws on the furniture in the room behind. Frequently, one of the cats will sit on the desk or keyboard while I try to write.

Read more at https://ravenraine.com.